A Diver in China Seas

Fred Urquhart

Also by Fred Urquhart

Novels
TIME WILL KNIT
THE FERRET WAS ABRAHAM'S DAUGHTER*
JEZEBEL'S DUST*
PALACE OF GREEN DAYS

Short Stories
I FELL FOR A SAILOR*
THE CLOUDS ARE BIG WITH MERCY*
SELECTED STORIES
THE LAST G.I. BRIDE WORE TARTAN*
THE YEAR OF THE SHORT CORN*
THE LAST SISTER
THE LAUNDRY GIRL AND THE POLE
THE DYING STALLION
THE PLOUGHING MATCH
PROUD LADY IN A CAGE
SEVEN GHOSTS IN SEARCH*
FULL SCORE (edited by Graeme Roberts)
A GOAL FOR MISS VALENTINO**

Edited Books
NO SCOTTISH TWILIGHT (with Maurice Lindsay)
W.S.C.: A CARTOON BIOGRAPHY
GREAT TRUE WAR ADVENTURES
MEN AT WAR
SCOTTISH SHORT STORIES
GREAT TRUE ESCAPE STORIES
THE CASSELL MISCELLANY, 1848-1958
MODERN SCOTTISH SHORT STORIES (with Giles Gordon)
THE BOOK OF HORSES

Other
SCOTLAND IN COLOUR (with Kenneth Scowen)
EVERYMAN'S DICTIONARY OF FICTIONAL CHARACTERS
(with William Freeman)

* Reprinted with new introductions in this series by Kennedy & Boyd
**First publication in THE FRED URQUHART COLLECTION.

A Diver in China Seas

Fred Urquhart

WITH AN INTRODUCTION BY
COLIN AFFLECK

Kennedy & Boyd
an imprint of
Zeticula Ltd
Unit 13
196 Rose Street
Edinburgh EH2 4AT
Scotland

http://www.kennedyandboyd.co.uk
admin@kennedyandboyd.co.uk

First published in 1980 in London by Quartet Books, with
ISBN 0 7043 2255 2.
Text Copyright © Estate of Fred Urquhart 2017
Introduction Copyright © Colin Affleck 2017

Front cover image Copyright © Zeticula 2017
Back cover photograph from Fred Urquhart's own collection
Copyright © Colin Affleck 2017

ISBN 978-1-84921-108-6

Acknowledgements

'Pilgrimages to the Old Manse' first appeared in *Scottish Short Stories 1974* (Collins/Scottish Arts Council); 'A Diver in China Seas' in *The Scottish Review* and *The Texas Quarterly* (U.S.A.); 'Camp Follower' in *Blackwood's Magazine;* 'Auld Mother Claus' in *The Scotsman;* 'Nostalgia for a Waltz Dream' in *The Saltire Review* and Denys Val Baker's anthology *The Dreams of Love*; 'Local Boy Makes Good' in *The Saltire Review;* 'A Gone Woman' in *The Scottish Review;* and 'Like Arrows in the Hands of a Giant' in John Pudney's *Pick of Today's Stories*. I am grateful to these editors and publications for having printed the stories in the first place.

To MARGARET and GILES GORDON

Contents

Introduction

Fred Urquhart's *A Diver in China Seas* is a most unfairly overlooked collection of short stories. Consider some of the reviews by distinguished critics that greeted it on its first publication in 1980:

> ... Mr Urquhart is a writer whose range is unequalled by anyone working in Scotland today. ... the themes and settings in this new collection could hardly be more various. I regard that as a virtue – it shows a large capacity which was always, till recently, regarded as one of the attributes of genius. ... There are two long stories here which are both masterpieces.
>
> Allan Massie in *The Scotsman*, 27 September 1980

> ... if there were a Scottish Fiction Prize it would have to go this year to Fred Urquhart who produced two collections of short stories ... *A Diver in China Seas* ... and *Proud Lady in a Cage* .. , which in their wit, vitality, versatility, and devotion to truth, proved yet again that he has no living master, save Sir Victor Pritchett, in the traditional short story.
>
> Allan Massie in *The Scotsman*, 27 December 1980

You open this, read the first paragraph of the first story ... and you immediately recognise mastery: here is a writer with the old classic touch ... Neither the great Bates of "The Kimono" nor even Coppard in his finest tales wrote better than this. ... This writer has that absolutely individual touch that is essential to the successful short-story writer, and the necessary worldliness, and the feeling for the right word, right phrase. Urquhart has, too, the modesty of the true writer; under it lurks humour, an immense menacing wisdom, an ineffable pity and kindness.

Martin Seymour-Smith
in the *Financial Times*, 23 August 1980

[It] is . . . filled with that bitter-sweet vitality and nostalgia for lost vitality which is Urquhart's hallmark. No-one else can bring dead dreams and old ways of living back to life like him . . . Urquhart manages better than anyone writing now to imbue his fun, his sharp coarse dialogue, with a haunting background gloom.

Douglas Gifford
in *Books in Scotland* 8 (Autumn/Winter 1980)

[These stories] testify to the abiding virtues of vigour, humour and narrative clarity. Like a man tickling trout he dips into the life-stream and comes up with something alive and kicking, and however short the story the hues can always change.

Christopher Wordsworth
in *The Guardian*, 21 August 1980

All of these comments are justified, and yet the book is all but forgotten. The little critical and academic attention that has been paid to Urquhart's stories – and it is shockingly little, considering his stature – has tended to focus (with a few exceptions, such as 'The Bike') on those dealing with rural life in North-East Scotland, centred on the small town of Auchencairn (based on Laurencekirk). These are, of course, brilliant, incisive and truthful depictions of a way of life that has now vanished. However, Urquhart's success with these seems to have led to his other stories being undervalued. For example, in his *History of Scottish Literature* Urquhart's erstwhile co-editor Maurice Lindsay praised his stories that 'reflect the earthy vigour of the farming-folk' (while erroneously describing him as a 'follower' of Lewis Grassic Gibbon). On the other hand, according to Lindsay, 'He is usually at his weakest in those urban stories in which he allows his portrayal of the pathetic and limited ambitions of the tawdry or the deprived to become doused with music-hall comicality . . .' [1] This is grossly unfair; many of Urquhart's stories deal with disadvantaged people and many of them contain humour, but most of them are fundamentally serious and bear no resemblance to the comedy of the music hall.

In his obituary of Urquhart, Giles Gordon, a friend and former agent of his subject (and one of the dedicatees of this book), also praised the earlier stories of country life, but wrote: 'The stories of his later, rather bitter and isolated years – correctly he felt unappreciated by the present Scottish literary establishment – owed more to the kailyard than he cared to acknowledge.' [2] If 'later' includes the present volume (the second last collection that Urquhart published, when he was 68), this is an extraordinary view to take of such work, in which Urquhart demonstrates the full strength of his skills in characterisation and dialogue and perhaps his greatest sophistication of style.[3] These stories are not at all 'kailyard,' which Gordon was using pejoratively to mean sentimental, kitsch, comfortable, 'respectable', and presenting an idealised image of Scottish characters.

None of these terms apply; Urquhart's stories are often poignant or moving, but they are never sentimental, even (or perhaps particularly) when he is dealing with children or old people. Although they can be nostalgic – the older Urquhart did not like the modern world – they never fail to point out that the past too had its horrors. They present an unvarnished, realistic view of Scottish life and character; among the topics that appear in this volume are sadism, class antagonism, the horrors of war, bigotry, alcoholism, and a lack of Christmas spirit. It is perhaps true to say that, whereas Urquhart's earlier work dealt with sex and other controversial matters in a way that was seen as advanced at the time, by the 1970s some younger writers were dealing with these issues in a more explicit way. Indeed, when this book was published in 1980 many readers might have seen it as old-fashioned, as indicated by the writers to whom the favourable reviewers compared him; by that time V. S. Pritchett, H. E. Bates and A. E. Coppard were far from fashionable. However, there are more important literary merits than the depiction of explicit sex scenes.

Urquhart's ability to create realistic characters through vivid dialogue has often been praised. This is not just a matter of choosing the right vocabulary; he also captures the rhythms of real speech. Another notable quality of his fiction, in this volume and elsewhere, is the way in which it is constructed to show how time passes, and how memory can bring different times together. This was an important feature of his first novel, *Time Will Knit* – as indicated by its title – and something he continued to develop.[4] An ironical view of life was also evident from the beginning; this is an important part of the humour that permeates his work. Perhaps the most important – if unfashionable – aspect of Urquhart's writing is his urge to tell stories and his ability to do so in an enjoyable way.

This book (like much of Urquhart's work) might have appealed to the growing feminist movement of the time, since it sees life from a predominantly feminine point of view. Of the ten stories, four have a female first person narrator; the other six are third person narratives with female main characters, except 'Local Boy Makes Good', where half of the central couple is a woman. Urquhart's sympathetic understanding of female characters in his work prompted Gillian Ferguson to suggest he deserved 'an honorary "womanhood."'[5]

'Pilgrimages to the Old Manse' is one of Urquhart's most subtle and complex pieces, revealing a great deal about social attitudes in Scotland through the experiences of a Scottish novelist from the landed gentry and an admiring reader from the working class. By opening with the narrator's 'second pilgrimage' Urquhart intrigues the reader from the start. What happened on the first one? In what sense are they pilgrimages? And who were Teenie Peebles and Agnes Inglis? Their stories then emerge through the details of the narrator's engagement with the works of Inglis and her two visits to the former home of her literary heroine, all cleverly intercut.

Agnes Inglis, it transpires, was a great novelist – "Scotland's Charlotte Bronte" – and a friend of Henry James. Urquhart's story itself has a Jamesian theme and ambiguity, revealing the secret of a great artist (or possibly revealing it – after all, can someone who mistakes a product of the respectable Edinburgh working class for a 'keelie' sprung 'from the Gallowgate in Glasgow' be regarded as a reliable informant?); and yet, at the same time, the rumbustious Scots dialogue of Teenie Peebles undermines the aloofness of aestheticism. With a bathetic effect Teenie describes her privilege of reading Agnes's manuscripts before anyone else as 'a bit of a trauchle,' and she thinks that Agnes should have done 'a bit dusting' instead of wasting time using her imagination. There are also James-related jokes, such as the failed attempt to get Teenie to type at Agnes's dictation, and the reader sometimes wonders how reliable the class-obsessed narrator is.

Urquhart plays another literary game here, dropping in references to his own life and literary friends. Like the narrator, he went to Broughton Secondary School and McDonald Road Library; he was probably thinking of himself when he has the narrator call herself '"a novelist of distinction", as they say, though what it really means is that your books don't sell and are read only by one in a million'; he too admired the historical fiction of his friend Naomi Mitchison; and the anecdote about Edwin

Muir (whom he knew) was told to Urquhart by his friend Mary Litchfield, who is here called Poppy because she was the model for the character Poppy Chiltern in Urquhart's story 'Once a Schoolmissy . . .' [6] This is a story partly about the difference between real life and literature, but it is itself a mixture of reality and fiction.

The story suggests that the most fundamental social constants are class, power and the relationship between them. The narrator has married a member of the upper classes and is now the sophisticated Lady Dalziel, but Teenie and her successor can spot her working-class origins at a glance, while recognising that her husband is the real thing. The servants know that respect is due to the upper classes in a formal sense, but power, as is demonstrated, can lie with the former; whether or not they write novels, they can cause damage to their employers' lives. Urquhart backs up this insight with the social signification of contrasting modes of speech. Lady Dalziel, having risen from the Edinburgh working class, uses Standard Scottish English; her upper-class husband uses what is evidently Received Pronunciation, with those embarrassing attempts at Scottish idioms favoured by the Scottish upper classes when addressing their Scottish social inferiors; the self-confident Teenie speaks unselfconscious Scots when alone with the narrator, but is much less broad in the presence of Sir Robert; the socially insecure Mary Selkirk speaks in a 'genteel' manner, before lapsing vituperatively into her native Scots; and Dawn, representative of the new generation (of the early 1970s) speaks a mixture of Scots and standard British youth slang.

The mysterious and exotic title of 'A Diver in China Seas' contrasts with its down-to-earth subject matter. Carrie, the narrator, is looking back in old age – and in the fear of death – at the people she has outlived. Urquhart memorably expresses this in the atmospheric first sentence: 'Now that I feel death's cauld hand crawling over me every night I keep turning my mind to the corpses I've seen in my day.' This morbid atmosphere is maintained throughout, although there is also a lot of humour; but that too can be fatal, since Jessie dies from laughing, or at least black, as when Nora tries on her mourning clothes – 'preening herself' – with her sister lying dead on the bed.

As Carrie describes her friendship with the two elderly sisters, a brief but vividly realistic picture of working-class life in pre-Second World War Edinburgh emerges, with such details as references to long-departed shops. Although Carrie does not explicitly admit it – her narration at this point seems disingenuous – it is clear that she went behind Nora's back to take up with the much older Mr Nasmyth, the former diver of the title, and married him for his 'good pickle siller'; but money does not count for much with 'death's cauld fingers plucking at' her, and the last paragraph has a chilling effect.

'Camp Follower' (one of the two 'masterpieces' identified by Allan Massie) is a brilliant piece of historical fiction, demonstrating the ground-level reality of the Peninsular War, in which Britain took part from 1808 to 1814, from the point of view of a poor young Scotswoman. As often in Urquhart's work, he begins *in media res*, [7] then returns, through Kirsty's memories, to her earlier life in Edinburgh, before explaining how she comes to be with an army marching through Spain.

Kirsty is one of the many underprivileged characters in Urquhart's work, people who, as the playwright Alexander Reid put it, 'have things done to them.' [8] More than once it is mentioned that, working in the baggage train or busy cooking, she has little if any idea of how the war is progressing, although the narrative is unobtrusively informed by Urquhart's reading about the history and background of the war, the vocabulary of the period (such as 'prog', meaning food or supplies), and the life and works of Goya. Kirsty's motivation for going with the army was her love for a soldier, but later her dependence on others leads her deeper into the horrors of the war.

The underlying theme is her discovery of her real identity. Love changes her; she had been a prostitute in Edinburgh, but refuses to return to that occupation. She becomes a model for Goya, who famously depicted the catastrophes of this war; the story is thus a companion piece to Urquhart's novella 'The Staig's Boy William' [9], in which the title character is painted by Stubbs. One difference is that Urquhart invented the Stubbs painting, whereas the Goya drawing mentioned on page 66 – 'For being of generous spirit' ('Por Liberal'), showing a young woman chained by the neck – is real and was part of the inspiration for the story, as shown by Urquhart's brief original notes. [10] In his pictures Goya turns Kirsty into things she isn't – a guerilla, a literate woman, a duchess – but he eventually reveals to her what she is.

Urquhart made some cuts to the story for its publication in *Blackwood's* (which thought so highly of it that it also issued it as a separate pamphlet), but he noted that he was 'not amused' by some of the further, anglicising changes made by 'Maga'. For example, Ferdinand VII became 'a sleekit wee man' instead of 'a sleekit wee bauchle,' 'deeved' became 'plagued,' 'brats' became 'children,' and so on. [11] He made sure that his full and robustly Scottish version appeared in this volume.

In 'Auld Mother Claus' an old working-class woman, Mrs Hyslop, takes a job playing Father Christmas in an Edinburgh store.[12] This may sound like a setting for a couthy tale, but Urquhart does not take a sentimental view of the children around Santa's sleigh or of the family Christmas. When Mrs Hyslop criticises a greedy child, he replies, 'Belt up, ye auld jessie. Ye talk like a jessie. Doesn't he, Ma? Are ye a jessie, Santy?' She has taken the job to avoid spending a week at Christmas with her family, who have moved into the middle class; there is a state of mutual hostility between her and her grandchildren, who are pretentious and posh and, she says, 'give me the pip.' Her grandson is very modern in his obsessive desire to become a successful sportsman and then a sports commentator on television. His absurd, pompous language contrasts with his grandmother's forthright Scots, contributing to the humour of the piece.

In its robust realism this story is far from a product of the kailyard; indeed, it was too remote from the idealisation of Christmas for *The Scots Magazine*, for which Urquhart wrote it, but which rejected it.[13]

'Nostalgia for a Waltz Dream' [14] is a reminder of the days before videocassettes, DVDs and television, when, although it was possible to follow an admired film around the picture houses of a city until it left, it might then never be seen again. Nance McQueen, plagued by the insolence of her rock 'n' roll-playing daughter (the story was written and is set in the late 1950s), remembers her own childhood in Edinburgh during the General Strike, when inter-generational relationships were quite different, although she does not seem to realise that her incomprehension of her daughter's musical obsession mirrors her father's of her cinematic one.

That the details of the poverty of the mid-nineteen-twenties are so convincing is not surprising, since they contain many autobiographical elements. For example, Urquhart's family lived for about 18 months in 1925 to 1927 in one or two rented rooms in Queen Street (facing Abercrombie Place, where Nance stays, across the private gardens; this was in the days when the New Town had gone out of fashion), and there he was terrified by Alsatian dogs on the stair. [15] Like the young Urquhart, Nance saves money from her tram fares so she can go to the cinema. But the autobiographical content goes further. Reminiscing in 1947 about this period, Urquhart wrote:

About that time I saw *The Waltz Dream*, a gay, light and frothy German film, starring Willy Fritsch, Mady Christians and Xenia Desni. I went into the cinema some time in the afternoon, probably about four o'clock. *The Waltz Dream* was just starting, and I sat entranced. Nothing I could write now could ever give an inkling of, or recapture, the emotions I felt then. I was completely carried away. I sat through another feature film and a lot of shorts and news-reels, and then I sat all through *The Waltz Dream* again. I expect I would have sat through it a third time. But the cinema was closing. It was about eleven o'clock when I got home, and my parents were just about frantic.

But I did not care; I had fallen terribly, desperately in love with Willy Fritsch. He was the true "Aryan" type, with blonde wavy hair, glistening eyes and magnificent teeth. I wonder what has become of him? He must be about fifty now. [16]

Urquhart has Nance watch the film and similarly become obsessed with Willy (spelt 'Willi' here) Fritsch. [17] Writing this story as fiction many years later, and transferring his experience to a woman remembering her feelings as a girl, Urquhart is able to show convincingly her adolescent fervour, a result of cinema's ability to take ordinary people temporarily away from reality.

In the very amusing 'Dusty Springtime', Elaine Linton (or Miss Nell), a well-known, middle-aged Scottish entertainer, is visiting Paris for the first time. She keeps breaking away from her description of this visit to tell us, in a conversational style, the eventful story of her life on the stage and off, before eventually explaining that she is in Paris to help her sensible grand-daughter to search for Miss Nell's alcoholic, sex-obsessed daughter. The attractively ebullient character of Miss Nell was suggested by Renée Houston, the Scottish actress and music hall star, whom Urquhart greatly admired, [18] and Miss Nell's radio panel show *Glamorous Grannies Who Put the World to Rights* is obviously based on the BBC's *The Petticoat Line*, in which Houston participated. [19]

Miss Nell always wanted to go to Paris in the spring, but she actually goes in July ('a gey dusty springtime'). It is later in the year than she wanted and also later in her life, but she shows that her heart is still 'young and gay', describing herself as 'not so dusty'.

Urquhart's notes show that the story is set in 1970, [20] so it is evident that the setting was inspired by his own visit in July 1970 to an old friend in Paris. Miss Nell 'adored Paris', and so did Urquhart. He wrote to his partner, Peter Wyndham Allen, 'Paris is wonderful. Everything I expected – and more.' [21] (This was Urquhart's first trip abroad; he was to make only one other, again to Paris, in the early 1990s.) The city as it was at that time is depicted in a lively way, including some incidents that Urquhart recorded in his journal, [22] illustrating how its idiosyncrasies struck someone who had never been there before.

'Like Arrows in the Hands of a Giant' is set in Auchencairn, the pseudonymous centre of the area of North-East Scotland where many of Urquhart's earlier rural stories take place, but it shows that perversity can be found in a small country town as much as in a city. The narrative voice sounds like that of a small-town gossip, unsympathetic to outsiders like Miss Alison and Miss Sarah: 'They were weird bodies who read a lot of books.'

This story resembles 'Pilgrimages to the Old Manse', in that it also deals with issues of class and power through the story of a girl from a Home and her relationship with the women who employ her as a servant and come to depend on her. However, this is a much harsher piece, which takes the power of a servant to an extreme. There is a warning in the first paragraph, where Jess's eyes are described as 'hard for all their milky-blueness.' Early on Miss Alison reacts to her lies by saying, 'What an imagination the girl's got!' Near the end Jess's malevolence prompts Mrs Beedie to say, 'But the trouble wi' her is that she hasn't got one ounce of imagination.' In fact, as Miss Alison discovers, Jess has too much imagination, but no empathy. Urquhart's portrait of her is a study of banal evil, structured in reflective patterns (such as her sending her baby to the Home she came from) that demonstrate her moral deterioration as her power grows, until the shocking and horribly ironic ending, which shows that there are more dangerous things than lies.

'A Gone Woman' is one of Urquhart's pictures of life in a Granton cottage like the one occupied by his grandparents (which also provided the main setting for *Time Will Knit*, and where he spent a lot of time as a child). The narrator looks back to her childhood holidays there with her grandparents, describing everything with the precise detail of an observant child and conveying the interest that she found in these surroundings.

The most striking thing about this story is its depiction of the lack of privacy for people living in such overcrowded conditions. Urquhart provides a lot of information relating to the lack of space in the cottage: about the sleeping arrangements, including the need for the grandparents to sleep in the kitchen (the only public room); the arrangements for washing, which again has to take place in the kitchen; the fact that the lodger has to keep his bicycle in his bedroom, there being no other space for it; and the way in which the need to take the key for the outside lavatory advertises the lodger's attendance there. Looking back at this, the narrator refers to people like the lodger who 'suffered in those times from lack of privacy and the subsequent loss of dignity that are so essential to human happiness.' But she immediately queries this view: 'Or did they suffer?' The implication is that working-class people were accustomed in the past to living like this. And then Urquhart has her ask herself another question: 'And do some people still?' This is a reminder that everyone has not attained the 'different environment' in which the narrator now lives, and which may have affected her point of view.

The cramped nature of the accommodation parallels the narrow outlook of the formidable grandmother, who disdains the lodger's girlfriend – the 'gone woman' –

because she has an illegitimate child. She disapproves of his relationship with her: 'Ye cannie touch pitch without gettin' defiled.' Despite such problems, the narrator's memories have a nostalgic glow, even a longing for the past, subtly emphasised by the repeated 'I didn't dream it' in the last paragraph.

The figure of Kenneth MacMahon in 'Local Boy Makes Good' could, as Urquhart put it, 'be called a twin-portrait as it is a mixture of the characteristics of my friends Robert Colquhoun and Robert MacBryde, the gifted Scottish artists known as "The Roberts"'. [23] Tom Scott (later a well-known poet) introduced Urquhart to them in London in 1944. Urquhart liked to tell the story of how, on one of the occasions when he and the Roberts were staggering from pub to pub in Soho or Fitzrovia, MacBryde clung onto a packet of mince. Back at the studio MacBryde proceeded to cook the mince, ignoring the fact that Colquhoun was drunkenly chucking his own paintings down the stairs.

Julian Maclaren-Ross recalled that he thought Urquhart 'was perhaps the only writer who could do them justice', but when he asked if he was going to write about them, Urquhart replied, 'Ah well, you know Julian it's not so simple to do Colquhoun and Macbryde [sic]. They may look easy but they're difficult to do.' [24] Here Urquhart does them as a composite character. Urquhart noted that Kenneth's partner, Davina Weir, 'is based on Nessie Dunsmuir, the poet and wife of another poet, W. S. Graham. Both Nessie and I were members of the Roberts' set for many years in London.' [25]

The famous artist Kenneth shares the drunkenness of his originals, which makes it comically ironic that he is invited to open a new reservoir in his home town: 'You that never touches water outside or in!' as Davina, also a famous artist, says to him. Urquhart depicts the ensuing events amusingly, including Kenneth's parodic celebratory sword dance. He contrasts the artists' bohemian gusto with the narrow-minded constraints of both a former colonial policeman and small-town Scotland, but there are hints that the pair's chaotic lives will end tragically, as did those of the Roberts. Kenneth's alcoholism, in particular, is clearly self-destructive, and the reference to money being more difficult to obtain than it was five or ten years earlier reflects the Roberts' experience. After a brief period of fame, they fell out of fashion in the 1950s and both died relatively early. This knowledge gives the title of the story a tragic irony.

The second of the stories described by Massie as a 'masterpiece' is 'Princess McDougall', a deeply moving example of Urquhart's ability to portray an entire life in the space of a long story or, as in this case, a novella. He works by the steady building up of detail and by conveying an awareness of how time passes for an individual. The story begins with ship stewards discussing Mrs Wilkie ('Princess') on what must be her last voyage from Canada to Scotland, then we return to her childhood in Granton, when she was Alice McDougall. Features from Urquhart's life there are mentioned, as so often in his work – West Cottages, where his grandparents stayed; the ferry boat the *William Muir*, of which his great-grandfather was the skipper – but he can always create a throng of different characters and life stories in that setting.

Alice receives her nickname because of her fastidious ways, and she continues, in a rather pretentious way, to aspire to better things. Urquhart selects the details that illustrate precisely her character and way of life: her affected accent, her job as a buyer in a Princes Street department store, her friendship with the equally superior Miss Cochrane (they never address each other by their first names), the entertainments they attend. Eventually Princess marries a Canadian, but she is not completely content with her life in Canada. With an almost hypnotic effect, she keeps sailing between Canada and Scotland, unable to settle in either country for various reasons; in all, she crosses the Atlantic sixteen times (not including a possible posthumous voyage). Gradually, all her aspirations come to nothing; Alan Bold wrote about Urquhart's 'emphasis on the way dreams are defeated by hostile circumstances', [26] and this story shows that such a defeat can come even to someone who had seemed to be successful.

The *donnée* here, as in much of Urquhart's work, came from his own family. He wrote, 'Alice McDougall . . . was suggested by the life of my mother's cousin Liz Christie, who was born in Granton, became a buyer in Jenner's in Princes Street, married a Scots-Canadian in her middle age, and spent most of her later years travelling backwards and forwards across the North Atlantic.' [27] However, the real person is transformed into a symbolic, almost mythic figure. Urquhart gains the reader's sympathy for Princess, despite her faults, partly by showing how badly she is treated by her family, partly by showing her attachment to a lost way of life, and partly by the suggestion that she may not be able to find peace even in death. As in all of the stories in this book, Urquhart demonstrates his ability as a master story-teller to illuminate and help us to understand the lives of others.

Colin Affleck

Notes

Documents in The Papers of Fred Urquhart in the Special Collections of Edinburgh University Library are indicated by 'EUL'. Other unpublished material is from Urquhart's personal archive.

1   Maurice Lindsay, *History of Scottish Literature* (1977), p. 416.
2   Obituary by Giles Gordon in *The Independent*, 28 December 1995; at http://www.independent.co.uk/news/ obituaries/obituary-fred-urquhart-1527539.html (accessed on 25 May 2014).
3   This volume was originally to contain 'Two Lives: 1914' and 'The Life and Death of Aberdeen Jock', but it was too long, so Urquhart omitted them, in order that 'Camp Follower' could remain; see Urquhart's letter of 26 December 1979 to Janet Law of Quartet Books. These two stories, which were eventually collected in *A Goal for Miss Valentino* (2014), are situated far from the kailyard.
4   Urquhart wrote an article called 'The Problem of Time in Fiction' – published in *The Writer* (March 1954), pp. 6-8 – in which he described his favoured fictional structure involving 'a kind of beginning at the end and swinging backwards', which 'takes us very near to the "stream of consciousness"'. He explained that he began to write *Time Will Knit* chronologically, before realising that the story would be better told by starting in the present and moving into the past. Although he does not mention it, it is possible that, as an avid film-goer, he was influenced by cinematic flashbacks.
5   Reviewing Urquhart's *Full Score* in *Chapman*, 61-2 (Autumn 1990), p. 190.
6   Typescript headed 'TRUE CHARACTERS in the work of FRED URQUHART'. 'Once a Schoolmissy . . .' is included in *The Last Sister* (1950).
7   'Auld Mother Claus' and 'Princess McDougall' in this volume are examples of stories where the first draft was more chronological and Urquhart then moved text about to avoid starting at the beginning. See EUL MS 2807 and 2804.

8   Alexander Reid, 'The Voice of the Lonely' in *Scotland's Magazine* (February 1958), p. 56.

9   Collected in *Proud Lady in a Cage* (1980).

10 See Notebook 1973-91. Urquhart saw the picture in his copy of *Francisco Goya: Paintings, Drawings and Prints*, selected and introduced by Philip Troutman (1971), where it is Plate 36. Other genuine paintings by Goya are mentioned in this story.

11 Carbon copy with alterations and comments in EUL MS 2805.

12 Mrs Hyslop's further adventures can be found in 'Luke's Lucky Dip', collected in *A Goal for Miss Valentino* (2014).

13 See Urquhart's correspondence with Maurice Fleming, editor of *The Scots Magazine*, 10 May to 10 August 1976.

14 This is an example of Urquhart's habit of thinking up a title before finding a story to fit it; some time before he wrote this story, Urquhart began a completely different one with the same title, about a repressed-homosexual soldier and a German prisoner of war who reminds him of Willy Fritsch. Only two pages of this exist among Urquhart's papers.

15 Fred Urquhart, 'Growing Up with Films' in *Tribune* (5 September 1947), p. 23. For the Alsatians, see Urquhart's typescript headed 'NOTES for ALAN BOLD'S Literary Guide to Scotland', pp. 2-3.

16 'Growing Up with Films', p. 23.

17 Scenes from *Ein Walzertraum* (1925), the German silent film directed by Ludwig Berger and based on an Oscar Straus operetta, can be viewed on YouTube: http://www.youtube.com/watch?v=WGrrustzVAM (accessed 16 June 2014).

18 Conversation with Urquhart.

19 See Renée Houston, *Don't Fence Me In* (1974), pp. 143-4, 148, 157.

20 EUL MS 2806.

21 Postcard dated 4th [July 1970].

22 See entries for 3 to 15 July 1970 in Urquhart's Journal for 3 July 1970 to 8 September 1987.

23 Typescript headed 'TRUE CHARACTERS in the work of FRED URQUHART'.

24 Julian Maclaren-Ross, *Memoirs of the Forties* (1984 [1965]), p. 199.

25 Draft of typescript headed 'TRUE CHARACTERS in the work of FRED URQUHART'.

26 Alan Bold, *Modern Scottish Literature* (1983), p. 212.

27 Typescript headed 'TRUE CHARACTERS in the work of FRED URQUHART'.

Pilgrimages to the Old Manse

I made my second pilgrimage to the Old Manse nineteen years after I made the first. The first time, Teenie Peebles, the maid who had been with Agnes Inglis for so long, was acting as custodian of the house, which had been turned into a museum since the author's death. I don't know why I expected the old woman, who was getting on for seventy then, still to be there on my second visit; but I did, and I said as much to the woman who opened the door.

'Miss Peebles is dead and gone,' she said. 'I have been in charge these ten years.'

She was every inch a châtelaine, a stout, full-bosomed woman in her late forties, wearing a smart black wool jersey dress. Her closely-shingled blue-rinsed hair looked as if she had just stepped out of the hairdresser's. Her black eyes were bold behind horn-rimmed glasses, the tops of which were studded with brilliants and curved upwards like a satyr's eyebrows.

Her shrewd gaze swept past my grubby cyclamen slacks, my old government surplus anorak and my headscarf, even though it had been bought at great cost at Maggy Rouff's in Paris, and settled on my husband. She scrutinized his expensive tweed suit, his short silvery hair, his distinguished appearance, his air of authority. She was satisfied. Every bit of his six feet three inches and sixteen stones proclaimed that he was a gentleman.

'I am Miss Selkirk,' she said to him in a pseudo-genteel accent. 'Would you be writing a book about Agnes Inglis, sir?'

I laughed. Teenie Peebles had asked almost the same question. My poor husband, who practically never opens a book, except a third-rate adventure story, and who thinks Raymond Chandler is highbrow!

'Mary Selkirk?' I asked.

Her eyes became wary. 'Yes, my name is Mary,' she admitted.

Before I could stop myself I cried: 'You were another abandoned child.'

I was about twelve or thirteen when I discovered the novels of Agnes Inglis. I started to read voraciously when I was seven. I read everything I could lay my hands on. We were an Edinburgh working-class family, so there was only a handful of books in the house; mostly school prizes of my mother's and a few paper-covered Nat Goulds bought by my father in his bachelor days. I was an only child. When I went with my parents to visit their friends, whose houses had as few books as our own, I borrowed what I could: *The Girl of the Limberlost*, Jean Webster's *Daddy Longlegs*, Edgar Wallace, Tarzan and Annie S. Swan, all were seized eagerly and chewed to a pulp. Apart from Annie Swan, a name breathed with reverence in almost every Scottish home of that time, the only other Scottish woman author I'd read until I discovered Agnes Inglis was Mrs Oliphant, and I didn't care much for her. It was not until I was in my late teens that Elinor Dalziel introduced me to Naomi Mitchison's historical novels, and then I was so ignorant that for a good long time I thought she was English. Elinor, whose family knew the Haldanes, did not, for some weird reason, enlighten me otherwise. So, until I discovered that the author of *The Conquered* and *The Corn King and the Spring Queen* had been born in Edinburgh, Agnes Inglis was the only Scottish woman writer who mattered a damn to me.

I found her purely by chance in the public library. I did not know about public libraries until I went to Broughton Secondary School, but soon I was visiting the one in Mc-Donald Road, the branch nearest the school, two or three times a week. My reading was catholic. I went doggedly from P.G. Wodehouse to *Anna Karenina* and *Resurrection*, taking a pot shot at Edna Ferber on the way. H.G. Wells, Compton Mackenzie, Margaret Kennedy's *The Constant Nymph*, Galsworthy and Turgenev were all tumbled like ingredients in a pudding into the mixing-bowl of my brain. Nobody had ever spoken to me about Agnes Inglis; I'm sure I'd never seen her name in a newspaper or magazine. I found her because I was looking for O. Henry in the library. Our English teacher had recommended him and Kipling as 'masters of the short story' and, in my anxiety for culture, I was going to give O. Henry a going-over. I had already tried Kipling and found him wanting. I read *Kim* and *The Light That Failed* and *Stalky & Co* without enjoyment; and any time I have tried to read Kipling since I came to what is called maturity I still find him wanting. He and Laurence Sterne are among the great Unloved Ones of my literary life. That day I was looking for O. Henry none of his books was 'in', but instead, in the wrong place, there was *A Laird in Old Siena* by Agnes Inglis. Critics say this is one of the poorest of her novels, but because it was the first I read it has always been a favourite of mine. Of course, the story about the handsome young Scots aristocrat who goes to Italy to try to cure his tuberculosis and falls in love with a doctor's daughter is banal. But what is not banal is the elegance of the writing: the complexities of what is now called her Jamesian or Proustian style. And Elena, the heroine, is a much stronger, much more natural character than some of the book's denigrators think. I picked the book off the shelf out of curiosity. A quarter of an hour later I was still standing in the same position, having got to the end of the second chapter. I moved only when a young woman librarian tapped my shoulder and said 'Excuse me' so coldly that I jumped and nearly made her drop the bundle of books she was going to put into their niches on the shelves. There may have been an O. Henry among them. I didn't wait to look; I took *A Laird in Old Siena* home and finished it that night. Next day I went back to the library for another Inglis.

Agnes Inglis's world of urbane, cultured Scottish aristocrats who moved leisurely from Italy to Spain, from Provence to Baden-Baden or the Black Forest, was so different from my own that it charmed me completely. It was a gracious, gentle world where money was never mentioned, where evidently it was unknown. But it was also something more than that. After all, I could read about nearly the same kind of world in the romances of other authors like Ouida or F. Marion Crawford. But no, Agnes Inglis had something, she gave something that Ouida never could: a nobility, a sensitivity, a truth, a fundamental rock-bottomedness. I knew, young as I was, that she wrote about *real* people, and the others didn't. I soaked myself in Agnes Inglis, and by the time I went to Edinburgh University I had read and re-read everything she had written and had found out everything I could about her.

I went to the university much against the grain. It was my father who insisted upon my going. He had 'bettered' himself, as they say, by becoming a small tradesman, of whom there are legions, and he wanted to better his daughter. I really didn't learn anything at what pretentious snobby students called the Varsity that I wouldn't have found out for myself, but I did get a degree. And that, I discovered afterwards, came in very handy; it impressed folk when I went after jobs. My qualifications alone were of no use; it was the degree that did the trick. Businessmen think everybody with an M.A. must be clever. More fools they! Some of the biggest dolts I've ever met were plastered with M.A.s and B.A.s and B.Sc.s up to their backsides. Nevertheless, businessmen who are so sharp they could sell old dog bones to cannibals are always more prone to hire a

12

drear with an M.A. than a bright boy without one. I remember a friend of mine telling me that Edwin Muir, who was a friend of hers, could get only a clerical job in the Ministry of Food in Dundee after the war started because he didn't have an M.A. Even though Edwin was a well known poet and critic, a revered figure in the academic world of St Andrews, he didn't stand an earthly when jobs for the literary boys were being handed out in the Ministry of Information and other so-called 'intellectual' ministries because he didn't have that necessary wee bit of paper. My friend, a schoolteacher who had an M.A., told me: 'I said to him, "Edwin, I'll lend you mine. It would be better with you than gathering dust in my cupboard or holding up the sash of the window." But he just laughed and said: "It's very kind of you, Poppy, but I expect I'll survive without it." '

The only important thing about the university was meeting Elinor Dalziel. We became friends because of our mutual admiration for the work of Agnes Inglis. I don't suppose I'd have met her otherwise, for she belonged to the landed gentry. Apart from Elinor herself and what her friendship has meant to me over the past thirty-five years, it was through her that I met her cousin Robert who became my husband: Robert, who hunts and shoots and fishes, yet who withal (a lovely word that Agnes Inglis loved to use) is as gentle as the legendary dove, General and ex-Governor of a colony though he is.

I met him in the August soon after my nineteenth birthday. It was at Elinor's home in Perthshire, the family estate. My father was so proud when I told him I was to stay for a week in a castle. It is only a small castle, hardly worthy of the name, but its turrets and wings and balconies grew in number every time he spoke about it to his friends. As for me, it was my first experience of gracious living, and I seized it avidly.

When she was young, Elinor's mother had known Agnes Inglis. She had been brought up on an estate in Dumfries-shire near one belonging to the Inglis family. Agnes was an only child. She was twenty years older than Mrs Dalziel, so they'd had few contacts; Mrs Dalziel mostly remembered her as a pretty young woman who had kept a small child well supplied with cakes and biscuits whenever their parents met at tea parties. Agnes's parents had died when she was about thirty. She had turned the family house into a home for foundling girls and gone to live in an old manse. She was still living there, and now — in that year 1937 — she was a spinster of seventy-seven. 'She's never married, poor thing,' Mrs Dalziel said. 'She seems to have been content with her romantic friendship with Mr Henry James.'

I said: 'I've read some of their letters.'

'A sad exchange,' Mrs Dalziel said. 'You should write to her, you and Elinor. I believe all writers like to get fan mail or whatever it's called.'

Elinor and I composed a letter, asking if we might visit Miss Inglis to express our admiration for her work by word of mouth. Nearly a month later we got a short typewritten note saying she lived the life of a recluse and saw nobody. The signature looked illiterate.

In 1939 Agnes Inglis published her last novel. I meant to write and tell her how much I'd enjoyed it, but war came and Elinor and Robert and I were swept into it. When Agnes Inglis died in 1942 I did not hear it on the wireless, if it were announced, and I never read about it in a newspaper. The war was almost over when I heard.

In 1943 I married Robert before he went to North Africa. When the war ended he was posted to Germany and I joined him; we lived there until 1949. Then we went to Saudi Arabia where he was military adviser to King Ibn Saud. Except for short visits, we didn't get back to Scotland, to settle on Robert's estate in Kincardineshire, until the spring of 1952. At the end of October my husband had to go to London on War Office business, so we stayed with Elinor in her flat at Rutland Gate. Like myself, Elinor had become 'a novelist of distinction', as they say, though what it really means is that your books don't sell and are read only by one in a million.

On our way home I asked my husband to go by the west coast route, via Carlisle, so that we could stop in Dumfries for the night and I would, at last, be able to visit Agnes Inglis's home. By this time, Agnes Inglis, unknown to the majority in her lifetime, had become a cult figure. She was sometimes called Scotland's Charlotte Brontë. Volumes of essays about her work, biographies and critical studies were being published every few months. Her letters to Henry James had been published. His to her, of course, had been printed in the 1920 edition of his Letters, edited by Percy Lubbock. Several books about their literary friendship had appeared. The Old Manse, where she had lived for over fifty years, had been turned into a museum with Teenie Peebles, her maid, in charge. 'Dear faithful Teenie, whose devotion to me I can never properly describe,' Agnes Inglis had said in one letter to Henry James: 'Teenie, who to me is nurse, mother, child and stern guardian rolled into one. I could not exist without her. What a treasure she is!'

The treasure was now a dumpy little woman of about seventy, dressed in the style of Queen Victoria, sitting bolt upright on a green velvet chair in the drawing-room. A gawky servant girl with sly black eyes ushered us into the 'presence'. Without waiting for us to introduce ourselves, she said to my husband: 'I am Miss Christine Peebles, who used to be Miss Inglis's companion. I'll be glad to answer any questions you might like to ask. Would you be a professor, sir?'

Robert laughed. 'No, it is my wife who is the professor in our family. My wife is a great admirer of Miss Inglis's books.'

Teenie Peebles gave me the briefest of nods. She knew instinctively that Robert was gentry and I was not; she knew I belonged or had belonged not so very long ago to the same class as herself, even though I had not had time yet to open my mouth. I am not sure how she knew; for on that first pilgrimage I was still young, if you can call thirty-four young, I was still quite pretty and I was very smartly dressed in a costume I'd bought in New York.

'My wife writes books too,' Robert said. 'Novels.'

'I never read novels,' Miss Peebles said. 'I have neither

15

the time nor the inclination. When I was younger, of course, I read all Miss Ness's. She always gave me the manuscript to read before she sent it to her publisher.'

'How wonderful for you,' I said. 'How wonderful to have read *Dona Lucia's Second Husband* and *The Moon Over the Tiber* before anybody else.'

'There was nothing wonderful about it,' she said. 'It was a bit of a trauchle, if you must know the truth. I really didn't have time to pander to Miss Ness and her daftness. I had too many other things to take up my attention. A house like this doesn't run itself, you know — though maybe you don't, being young.'

I said: 'I manage to run quite a large house.' I was going to add that it was really a castle with well over fifty rooms but, seeing the look in my husband's eye, I desisted.

'She manages to run me successfully, too,' he said. 'Forby finding time to write her books. She's a busy bit lassie.'

Although Teenie Peebles did not actually sniff at what she evidently considered our bad breeding — mine for my claim to be a good housekeeper, and Robert's for his overfamiliar, perhaps condescending use of the vernacular — she implied that she would have sniffed if she hadn't had better manners than either of us. She pushed open a connecting door and ushered us into Agnes Inglis's study.

'Miss Ness spent most of her time in here,' she said. 'When she wasn't sitting at that desk staring into space, she was standing looking out of the window. It wasn't that often she'd be writing when I opened this door. It used to give me a fair scunner sometimes when I saw her empty-handed. "If only ye'd do a bit dusting, Miss Ness," I'd say. "It would take up your time and attention. All these knick-knacks and these books take such a long time. It would save me, and it'd give you something to do." But she never heeded me. She seemed to forget all the housework I had on my shoulders, forby the cooking in the hinterend.'

'My wife's not a bad cook,' Robert said. 'I'll give her her due. She's a dab hand at scrambled eggs.'

This time Teenie did sniff. 'Miss Ness couldn't even be

16

trusted to boil a kettle. I often said to her: "I'd like to ken what would happen to you, my lady, if ye were ship-wrecked on a desert island. Ye'd never manage to survive." '

I said: 'Probably she would. She would have had her eight records to sustain her.'

Teenie gave me such a fishy look that it was obvious she had never heard of, far less listened to, the programme 'Desert Island Discs' on the wireless.

'If you don't mind, Miss Peebles,' my husband said, 'I'll go and walk in the garden. I'll leave Lady Dalziel in your good hands.'

While Teenie was showing Robert out, I examined the room that was already familiar from many descriptions by biographers and critics. Apart from all the ornaments and books, unchanged from Agnes Inglis's time, there were several glass cases in which a selection of her letters and manuscripts were displayed. Some of Henry James's letters to Miss Inglis were in one case with a card saying they had been found only recently and had not been published yet. I was studying them when a sentence leapt out: 'It is, indeed, I think, the very essence of a good letter to be shown; it is wasted if it is kept for *one* . . . I give you full leave to read mine aloud at your soirées!'

But surely this was not an Inglis letter? Surely he had written it to some other correspondent? (Who I couldn't at that moment remember.) Then I realized that James had written it *twice* (perhaps more?) to make sure that one, at least, of his correspondents cherished it for posterity. Also to make sure, or to try to make sure, that these corres-pondents did not throw away or burn his letters.

'You would be a clever wee girl?' Teenie Peebles said behind me.

I turned and said I supposed I was.

'I was never able to learn my three Rs,' she said. 'I didnie have much chance at the Home. We were all put out to work as soon as they thought we were big enough and strong enough. I was thirteen when I came into Miss Agnes's service. I was an abandoned child.'

I murmured sympathetically.

'Most of the orphans were,' she said. 'I was found on a doorstep in Peebles. They aye cried us after the towns we were found in. The glaikit lassie that showed ye in, Mary Selkirk, she was an abandoned child too. Abandoned in more ways than one. I often wish I had the courage to tell her to pack her bags and get weaving.'

Miss Peebles took a crumpled packet of Woodbines from her cardigan pocket and offered it to me. 'I like a fag now and then,' she said, striking a match for both of us before I had time to get out the gold lighter Robert had given me for my last birthday. 'That lassie steals my fags,' she said. 'She steals mair than that. But what can I say? I need somebody here. I'm ower auld to manage on my lone. I suppose I'll just have to thole her thievin' and her imperence.'

Teenie angrily puffed her cigarette. 'I'm hard put to it whiles not to draw my hand across her lug at the things she says. Especially at what she says ahint my back. She thinks I'm deaf, but I'm no' as deaf as all that. Ach, but I suppose I'll just have to grin and bear it. I've put up wi' imperence all my life, and I daresay I'll manage to survive a bit more before the Lord calls me.'

She gave another angry puff. 'Miss Ness could be right imperent, too, y'know. She could be a real madam when she took a huff. But I had my own methods o' dealing with her. "Now, Miss Aggie," I'd say. "Enough o' that. We'll have no more of it." She hated being cried Aggie. She was aye cried "Miss Ness", except, like I say, she forgot herself and I had to put her in her place.'

Teenie stubbed out her cigarette. 'It was Miss Ness that taught me to smoke. I remember it fine. It was after one of her huffs. She'd had a letter that mornin' from Mr Henry James and somethin' in it had garred her gorge rise. I think it was somethin' about yon Mrs Wharton, a woman Miss Ness and me could never abide. Whatever it was it put Miss Ness in a right paddy, and she was very imperent to me when I brought in her breakfast. But I wasn't havin' any. I planked down the tray and I said, "Look ye here, Miss Aggie. One mair wrong word frae you and I pack my valise and go." So she laughed then and said: "Och, Teenie, whatever would I do without you? Here, have a cigarette and that will cool you down." Well, I'd never had a smoke, so when she pressed me I indulged for the first time. Many a quiet fag me and Miss Ness had after that when things were on top of her and she wanted a wee crack with me about her writin'.'

Before Teenie had time to reach into her cardigan pocket, I offered her my Gold Flakes. 'I shouldnie chainsmoke,' she said as I lit it for her. 'They say it gi'es ye lung cancer. But ach to hang, I'm ower auld to care now.'

'It wasn't often that Mr James's letters upset her,' she went on. 'In fact, I'm sure that was the only one that ever did. Though there was aye great excitement when one o' his letters came, of course. She would sit all mornin' readin' it again and again, and in between whiles she'd stare into vacancy as if she had a want. You'd never have thought to see her then, looking like somebody in a loony-bin, that she was sic a clever woman. Then next day she'd make up her mind to answer it, and she would sit for maybe an hour without havin' written a single word. "What can I say to him, Teenie?" she would say. "He writes such beautiful letters. I feel that mine could never hope to be as good and beautiful as his. Oh, what will I say!" So I would say: "Ach, tell him about auld Mattie McLauchlin's white hen that's aye layin' in our hedge," or something like that. Of course she would never write to him about sic daft things. I've often wondered what she did say to Mr James. They tell me her letters to him were printed in a book a while syne, but I've never read them. Nor could I ever be fashed reading Mr James's letters to her, though she left them lying all over the place.'

I remembered an Agnes Inglis letter to the Master: 'Sitting at this old woodwormed desk, which my parents had delegated to the attic but which I got my gardener to bring down after they died, I noticed, looking out of my window, wondering, as I always do, at the beauty of the river valley, which I can glimpse between the tall fir trees, a large bird of dazzling white drifting along beside the hedge,

19

and as I watch this domestic animal (or should it be fowl?), for it turns out to be a hen belonging to a neighbour, I see her disappear into the undergrowth . . .'

I moved over to the window. The branches of a rowan tree tapped against the panes. Beyond it a dark mountain of a monkey-puzzle shut out most of the sky. I could dimly see fir trees behind that, but no sign of the river; the garden was crowded and closed in with greenery.

'I see the trees have grown a lot since Miss Inglis died,' I said.

'Och, not that much,' Teenie said. 'The garden's aye been like this — hemmed in by thae big trees. The laddie that comes and does the garden lops off branches every now and again, but it never seems to make much difference. It was near enough like this when I came here as a lassie.'

'But Miss Inglis has described the view of the river from this window so often,' I protested.

'Havers! We've never been able to see the river from here. She must have imagined it. She had nothing else to do.'

The door opened suddenly and the servant girl poked her head around it. 'Please, mum, will ye be wantin' tea, Miss Peebles mum?'

'You know fine we'll be wanting tea. I would've thought you'd have had it ready by this time.'

'The kettle's boilin' and everything's ready, mum,' Mary Selkirk said. 'But the gentleman — will he be wantin' tea, too, mum? He's sitting in the car.'

'Tell Sir Robert when tea's ready,' I said. 'He'll come quickly enough.'

'Will ye be wantin' biscuits forby the Dundee cake, Miss Peebles mum?'

'Ay, of course, we'll be wantin' biscuits,' Teenie said. 'Bugger off now and bring it in.'

Miss Peebles turned to me with the aplomb that duchesses are supposed to have but often don't. And then she grinned and winked. All pretence was dropped. We understood each other now. We were local girls who had made good. She was an abandoned child who'd become châtelaine of a museum; I was a working girl who'd hooked one of the gentry and gotten herself a title.

There was an old fashioned typewriter on a stool beside the desk. 'Did Miss Inglis use that much?' I asked.

'No, she could never be doin' with it. Miss Ness was ower impatient to learn to work it properly. She tried to do it sometimes with two fingers, but she aye gave up and said she was quicker with her pen. She garred me take lessons on it, though. A lassie in the village came here three nights a week for a while to teach me, but I never made any headway. What was I needin' to type for, anyway! Miss Ness thought of course it would be handy and that she could dictate her stories to me to save herself the hard work of putting pen to paper. But nothing came of that ploy, I'm glad to say.'

The door opened again, and Mary Selkirk looked in. 'There's more folk come to look at the hoose,' she cried. 'What will I say to them, mum? There's three auld ladies and a man. What'll we do? There's no' enough Dundee cake for us all.'

'Tell them the place is shut for the day,' Teenie said. 'Tell them to make an appointment and come another time. Tomorrow afternoon will be suitable, or the next day.'

'Right, mum!' The door banged.

'Really, this place goes like a fair now,' Miss Peebles said, accepting a Gold Flake from my case. 'But when Miss Ness was alive we didn't have so many visitors. She couldn't be bothered with folk. She was feared of them.'

'I don't blame her,' I said. 'Did she go out at all?'

'She never went anywhere, except maybe once a month for a drive in the carriage to Dumfries. That was when we had a carriage, of course: a carriage and pair. And a coachman. That was when I was still a young woman, mind. As we got older Miss Ness never went over the doorstep.'

'She travelled a lot when she was young,' I said. 'Italy and France and Spain. It was in Italy that she met Henry James. Did you ever go abroad with her?'

'For God's sakes no! What would I be doin' abroad? Anyway, she'd done all her travellin' by the time I came here. She was nearly forty and had settled in her groove.'

'Did Mr James ever come here?' I asked.

'No, I never set eyes on hair or hide of him,' Teenie said. 'But that Mrs Wharton came once. An American lady. She was chums-a'-bubbly with Mr James. She didn't half put Miss Agnes through the mill. She speired her right, left and centre, asking how she wrote this, why she wrote that, how often she did this, what did she think of that. Puir Miss Ness! Mrs Wharton near enough asked her how often she went to the lavvy.'

'When was this?' I asked.

'Och, I cannie mind the year. It was afore the first war, though: that I do know. It was in the days when moty-cars weren't common. Mrs Wharton came in a big one, with her chauffeur, Mr Cook. Such a nice man! I can see him as though it was yesterday. Him and me and the other two maids had many a good laugh in the servants' hall at Mrs Wharton and her capers. Now there's nobody to sit in it but that glaikit cratur' Mary Selkirk, who doesn't ken what a good laugh is. Ah well, them were the days, as Harry Gordon used to say! D'ye mind o' Harry Gordon? Yon was a grand comedian. I aye listened to him on the wireless.'

'I remember him,' I said. 'I was brought up on him and Tommy Lorne and Will Fyffe.'

'I kent ye were a sensible lassie.' Teenie Peebles sighed nostalgically for the glory of a lost time. 'To revert to Mrs Wharton,' she said. 'She stayed for three days, and she insisted on taking Miss Ness out in the moty-car for a drive to Ecclefechan to look at a house some auld author was born in. Och, what a palaver there was! Miss Ness had to put on a moty-veil, tied roon her hat. And Mrs Wharton had on one, too, of course. When they came home I asked Mr Cook why he didn't wear one, because there was no show without Punch, and he laughed and said: "Miss Peebles, you're a real devil!" I'll never forget that. Oh, me and Mr Cook got on fine. But yon Mrs Wharton was a different kettle o' fish. Her man was what was called a "neurasthenic" and was in a private hospital. He was really a daftie, ye ken. His name was Teddy. She was gettin' ready to give him the heave when she was here. Miss Ness was scandalized at the cold-blooded way she talked about him. It seems the poor man didnie ken what a tartar he'd gotten in tow with. He called her "Puss". Puss! I ask you. She was a real scratchy auld cat right enough.'

The door opened and again Mary Selkirk poked her head around it. This time she looked directly at me and said: 'Please yer ladyship, the gentleman – I mean the lord – he's no' in the car. This wee note was lying on the seat.'

The note said. 'Have gone for a walk along the river. Back in one hour. R.'

'That's fine,' said Miss Teenie Peebles. 'We can have a better wee crack without the men-folk. The gentry men dinnie really like tea, anyway. They'd rather have a good glass of the hard stuff.'

'Bring in the tea, lassie,' she said to Mary. 'And bring in the whole Dundee cake. You can get a bit o' what's left. Ye've got plenty o' biscuits in the kitchen to fill ye up.'

She accepted another Gold Flake and sat in the easy-chair beside the empty fireplace, the chair Agnes Inglis had always sat in when she'd grown tired of sitting at her desk. 'The General'll enjoy his wee dander by the river while we enjoy our wee crack,' she said.

'But how did you know he's a general?' I said. 'We never told you.'

'I read the papers, Lady Dalziel, and I've a guid memory for faces. I mind seeing Sir Robert's photygraph in a paper when he saved yon King from bein' killed by some wild Arab heathen.'

Mary Selkirk came in with the tray and placed it beside the old woman.

'Now, Lady Dalziel,' Miss Peebles said. 'Will ye have milk in yer tea, or are ye that new-fangled that ye want lemon? If ye want lemon ye'll have to go and look for one.'

'Milk,' I said. 'No sugar.'

'Attagirl!' Teenie said. 'I could never abide sugar in my tea, though it hasnie kept me frae getting fat.'

She handed me a cup, then she nipped out her cigarette, still three-quarters unsmoked, and placed it carefully in the ashtray. 'That'll come in handy later,' she said, giving me a wink. 'Waste not, want not!'

She sipped her tea. 'Yon Mrs Wharton!' she exclaimed. 'What a limmer she was! She stayed here for three days, and it felt mair like three weeks. By the end o' it puir Miss Ness was near demented. She had to take to her bed and bide in it for a week after "Puss" left. Puss indeed! She divorced that puir Teddy two three years after that. Miss Ness was more than scandalized. I mind she wrote a long letter about it to Mr James. She read bits out to me and kept askin' my advice. Oh, she was in a right tizzy about it.'

I did not know this letter. It was not in their published correspondence, so it looked as though Mr James had not preserved it, probably for his great friend Edith Wharton's sake.

I said: 'It's funny that Miss Inglis never married.'

'What's funny about it?'

'Well, she was a pretty woman,' I said. 'She was a clever woman. In fact, she was a brilliant woman, one of Britain's greatest writers. And I imagine she was a charming woman?'

'Oh, Miss Ness was charming all right. She could charm the backside off a wheelbarrow.' Teenie filled her mouth with Dundee cake, chewed for a few seconds and added: 'But she had no inclination for men.'

'Surprising,' I said. 'She writes so well about them. She understands them completely, and she obviously admired them. Did she never have a great love affair? Before you knew her maybe? Did she never talk about some man she'd loved when she was young?'

'The only man she ever talked about was Mr Henry James. I suppose he was a young man when she met him?'

'Reasonably young,' I said.

'Mind you,' Teenie said, taking another large slice of Dundee cake and shoving a good proportion of it into her mouth, 'I aye thought Mr James was a bit of an auld wife. I never met him, but Miss Ness would insist on reading his letters out to me, and between ourselves I didnie fancy the sound of him. Too much talk! I cannie thole men that talk too much. That was what was wrong with yon imperent young doctor that set his cap at her.'

'What young doctor was this?'

Teenie swallowed the remains of her cake, restrained a belch, wet the tip of her pinkie and mopped up the cake crumbs from her plate.

'Well, he wasn't really as young as all that,' she said. 'He'd be in his middle thirties. But he was cried "the young doctor" to show the difference between him and auld Dr Blackie. His name was Murdie, Dr Thomas Murdie. We aye had Dr Blackie at the Manse, but once when Miss Ness was ailing and there was something wrong with Dr Blackie at the same time -- he was getting gey doddery by then – the young doctor came instead. There wasn't a great deal wrong with Miss Ness, ye ken, but she got notions into her head that she was ill and dying. Oh, this was when she was about forty-five: I daresay she was near the change o' life. Well, I was young myself then – twenty or so – and I didn't have much time for her aches and pains. I thought most o' them were put on. But young Dr Murdie played up to her, pampering her as though she was a bairn. He was a well set up man, and I daresay he was good-looking in his way. I didnie fancy him myself, but it wasn't long before I found that Miss Ness did. Foolish cratur' that she was, to be taken in by such a callant! Howsomever, there it was. He was in and out of the house two-three times a day. I fair lost patience wi' him, and wi' Miss Ness for encouraging him, for I kent he had other patients that needed his attention far more than she did. Then, not content with sitting for an hour sometimes, holding her hand and whispering to her, the pair o' them giggling like a couple o' bairns, he took to taking her out in his gig for wee drives. "To blow the cobwebs away," he says to me. "Miss Inglis doesn't get enough fresh air." This was a lot of blethers. Miss Ness had her own carriage and pair if she wanted to go out jaunting, and she could aye get plenty o' air and exercise in the garden. Howsomever, there was nothing I could do about it; I just had to watch her making a fool o' herself. But when he started sending letters I was able to put a spoke in his wheel.'

I held out my Gold Flakes. Teenie glanced at the half-smoked cigarette in the ashtray, pursed her lips and took a fresh one. She lit it and said: 'The doctors employed a half-daft laddie to run their messages, and one day he came with a letter to Miss Ness from Dr Murdie. I opened it. I had nàe scruples about it. I soon put an end to it at the back o' the kitchen range. The imperence o' the fella to presume that a lady like Miss Ness would even look at him.'

I blew a mouthful of smoke into the air and said: 'Well?'

'It was a note to say he couldn't call for her in the gig at three o'clock, like they'd arranged, but he'd call for her the next day at the same time. I said nothing when Miss Ness got herself all dolled up, with a hat and veil, after lunch and sat in the drawing-room with a book. I kent she expected me to say, "And where are ye off to, Miss Ness?" But I said nothing. Half-past two came, three o'clock, half-past three and still she was sittin' there with her hat on. The village is two miles away, as ye ken, so naturally she'd never dream o' walking there to meet him. She was never what ye might call a walker, anyway. At four o'clock she went up the stair, and I didnie see her again until six o'clock when she came down and sat at that desk.'

Teenie lifted the teapot and shook it. 'Would ye like another cup? This'll be well stewed by this time, but I can get Mary to make a fresh pot.'

I shook my head. 'No, thank you, Miss Peebles.'

'I dinnie think I'll bother either. I dinnie fancy the dregs.' She put the teapot down with a little bang and said: 'Well, the next day I got Miss Ness well out o' the way long before three o'clock. I made some suggestions to her about answering a letter of Mr James's, and she was firmly closeted in here, writing away, when I made it my business to go down the drive and pick some flowers. I was picking away —

leisurely, ye might say — when Dr Murdie drove up in his gig. I stood just inside the gate so that he couldnie drive his horse in — unless it was over my body, and even he who wasnie a gentleman would never have dared do that. "Oh, are ye lookin' for Miss Ness, sir?" I said. "She's away to Dumfries for the day. She went this mornin' with a friend Mr Henry James, a famous author though ye may no' have heard o' him. I don't expect they'll be back till late. The gentleman's going to bide here for a few days."

'So that was that,' Teenie said, helping herself to another of my Gold Flakes. 'He said nothing — what could he say? — and he turned his horse and drove away. But the next day the daft laddie came with another note and said he expected an answer. I tellt him to tell Dr Murdie that the answer would be sent by hand. It never was. I burned Dr Murdie's letter after I'd read it — oh, it was that lovey-dovey it near garred me bock! — and then I suggested to Miss Ness she might go to Dumfries in the carriage to buy the new hat she'd been talking about. So off she went, and she wasn't long away before Dr Murdie arrivèd all in a dither. But he met his match. If he thought he'd frighten Teenie Peebles he had another thought coming. I tellt him Miss Ness and her friend were away to Locherbie and they would probably be bidin' the night there. "And who knows?" I said. "Maybe wedding bells will be ringing." So that was that. For a week on end he sent letters every day, either by the daft laddie or the post, but they all ended up in the kitchen range. Miss Agnes knew nothing about them, so he never got any answers that might have ended up in the *Collected Letters of Agnes Inglis!*'

Teenie laughed and said: 'The upstart, to think he'd be able to hang up his hat with a bonnie, rich lady like Miss Ness! I got a doctor frae Dumfries the next time she thought she was ill, and we had him for a wheen years. In the hinterend, though, we had a lady doctor, and she attended both Miss Ness and me until the end. It was her that made out Miss Ness's death certificate. She died very peacefully, I'm glad to say. She was sitting up in bed eating her breakfast, and she'd just said to me: "There's never anything in the post these mornings, Teenie, there's never been anything worthwhile since poor Mr James died," when she gave a funny wee cry, and lo and behold she was awa' wi' it. I coffined her myself. There was no need for the undertakers. I told them to lay the empty coffin on the bed beside her, after I'd laid her out, and I got a woman friend from the village to help me lift her into it. No man had touched her while she was alive. I was determined no man was going to touch her when she was dead.'

I never saw Teenie Peebles again. I wrote to her, but she never answered; I don't think I expected a letter. I got Robert to send her a brace of pheasant, and I sent Christmas cards for several years. I often thought about her, though the book I'd started about Agnes Inglis never progressed and I gave it up, at last, as a bad job; I realized I was a novelist, and that a novelist is neither a good biographer nor a critic. I always meant to go back to the Old Manse to see her, but I never managed, for when Robert was made Governor of a West Indian island we stayed there for a good many years, and what with this and bringing up two boys and a girl I had time to write only an occasional novel. (Elinor in Rutland Gate did so much better.) But now that the children had grown up — or what they considered grown up — and had left Robert and me on our own, to live our lives without them, we were back in Scotland, and so, driving again from London to Kincardineshire, we made another pilgrimage to the Old Manse.

'What do you mean, madam?' Mary Selkirk said. 'I was never an abandoned child. I can prove it. I still have an old mother alive in Glasgow. And my father died there a few years ago. I don't know where you got the idea.'

'But Teenie Peebles told me,' I said. 'She told me . . .'

'Teenie Peebles said a lot more than her prayers,' she

said. 'She was a bit of a gabber in her old age. I gather from this that you have been here before?'

'Many years ago,' my husband said.

'Will you please sign the book, sir? And step this way. There is a charge of half a crown for each of you. The money goes to a good cause: The Agnes Inglis Home for Orphan Girls.'

While Robert was signing the visitors' book a girl of about sixteen with long straight fair hair, dressed in tight blue jeans and a crumpled floral blouse, came and leaned against the newel of the stairs. 'Will I make a cuppa, mate?' she asked.

'I don't think so, Dawn,' Mary Selkirk said. 'I don't think the lady and gentleman will be staying that long.'

She glanced at the book: 'Oh, Lord Dalziel!' she exclaimed. 'It isn't often we get such a famous visitor.'

'Don't you remember when we were here before?' I said. 'It's nineteen years ago, but I remember you perfectly.'

'I'm afraid I don't,' she simpered. 'But then, I have a poor memory for names and faces.'

'But you recognized my husband just now.'

'Oh, but that's because he's been so much in the news lately. I've seen him on television. The ceremony about handing that island over to the natives. What was it? Self-government . . .'

'I was in the ceremony too,' I said.

I laughed and said: 'But of course, I was done up for the occasion, with false eyelashes and a big lace hat and a mink stole and what-have-you. Mutton done up as lamb!'

'Oh, I wouldn't say that, my lady,' she said.

Mary Selkirk was the kind of woman who would never really be embarrassed, but in case she was, I said: 'Can I see Miss Inglis's study? It's through this door, isn't it?'

Robert said: 'I'll wait in the car, dear.'

The room was the same as I'd remembered it, except that a large photograph of Teenie Peebles, with a permanent wave and a glazed smile, in a silver frame, was on Agnes Inglis's desk in the place where the photograph of Henry

James used to be. I walked about the room, peering at the books and the letters in their glass cases, all of them in the same places, and then I found the Henry James photograph half-hidden on the wall at the back of the door.

'I felt it was only right,' said Miss Selkirk behind me, 'that Miss Peebles should take a front place on Agnes Inglis's desk, for after all, it was Teenie Peebles that was the driving force behind her. We must give credit where credit's due.'

'Oh, but Miss Peebles has always been given due recognition in Agnes Inglis's letters and in most of the books written about her,' I said. 'I don't think anybody could ever doubt the important place Miss Peebles had in Agnes Inglis's life.'

'That's as it may be,' Mary Selkirk said. 'But in my opinion Miss Peebles has never been given her rightful due. It was her that really wrote most of Agnes Inglis's books. Aggie Inglis was a silly woman without a thought in her head. All she was good at was sitting with her head in her hands staring out of that window. It was Christine Peebles who was the driving force.'

'But Teenie Peebles was uneducated,' I said. 'I gather she could hardly write her own name.'

'She was far cleverer than she let on,' Miss Selkirk said. 'She gave Aggie Inglis the ideas, and in the long run it was her that dictated the stories and Miss Inglis just wrote them down and put her name to them.'

'But that's nonsense!' I cried. 'I had a great admiration for Miss Peebles, but nothing will make me believe this. She was a totally unlettered woman.'

'Teenie Peebles was a sore trial before she snuffed it,' Miss Selkirk said. 'In fact, she was a cantankerous old bitch, and I had to put up with a lot of her lip — she had a very nasty tongue — when I nursed her in her last days. I have no cause to love her. She treated me very badly when I came here as a young lassie. But you must remember that I lived with her for years and she talked a lot to me. She told me all the ins and outs of Agnes Inglis's books, the way they were written, and how this was changed and that was changed when Aggie and Teenie Peebles couldn't agree. And so I maintain — and I'll maintain it to my dying day — that it was Teenie Peebles who wrote most of Agnes Inglis's books.'

'Well, don't you think it's funny that Miss Peebles never wrote anything in the twenty years after Agnes Inglis's death? It stands to reason that if she was as gifted as you say she was, she would have done something to show it.'

'I remember you now,' Mary Selkirk said. 'I remember the time you and your man came here, and you and Teenie sat in this room and drank tea and ate cake without ever giving a thought to me, sitting there on my lone in the kitchen. You thought you were Lady Muck. But I had the size of you. Even if Teenie Peebles hadn't told me afterwards that you came from the Gallowgate in Glasgow, I knew that you were just a jumped-up wee keelie who'd got too big for her boots. I mind what a grand laugh me and Teenie had when you had the cheek to send her a couple of pheasants. I never touched them. I gave my share to the cat.'

'Good afternoon,' I said, walking out.

As I closed the door very gently behind me, I thought: Keep your cool. You're a working-class girl who's become a baroness. You must behave like the rest of the gentry. You mustn't lose your rag.

And I thought what a pity it was that Robert had been made only a life peer. I would have liked our oldest boy to be the second Lord Dalziel. Howsomever, as Teenie Peebles would have said, he would be the eleventh baronet. Nothing and nobody could take that away from him, even though, long haired and bearded as he was (temporarily we hoped), he kept swearing he would renounce the title.

I was sure he would change his mind long before the time came, and I made up my own that Robert would not send a brace of pheasant to the Old Manse this season.

The girl in the tight jeans was sitting in the back of the car.

'This is Dawn,' Robert said. 'We're going to give her a lift to the village.'

'I've got to do some shopping for the auld wife,' she said. 'At the pub, y'know. A bottle of gin. Oh, she'll be well away tonight and I'll have to listen to her life story all over again.'

She leaned back luxuriously and said: 'Smashing car you've got. I'm going to have one like this — only I want a pink one. Yours is too drab a colour.'

'I didn't know that beige was drab,' I said.

'My name's Dawn Hawick,' she said. 'I'm an abandoned child like the rest of them. I was found in a go-cart in Woolworths in Hawick. My boy friend tells me it's a stigma. But I don't mind. I think it's kinda kinky, don't you?'

I said: 'It's nothing to worry about.'

'Aw, I'm not worried,' she said. 'But auld Selkirk's worried. She thinks it'll keep her out of the next world. Can you imagine! At her age thinking the pearly gates'll open wide and the Lord God'll receive her with open arms and say: "Is it you, pet? Come away in." That was all right for Miss Christine Peebles and auld fogies like her, but you'd have thought Mary Selkirk would have more gumption. However, if she believes it, good luck to her!'

She put her elbows on the back of the front seat and leaned over between Robert and me as he manoeuvred the car out of the narrow drive.

'Can I tell you something?' she said. 'It's the biggest laugh of all time. All them books that are supposed to've been written by Agnes Inglis were really written by Miss Christine Peebles, and she never got a penny for them, nor a bloody thank you. I tell you what it is, missis, it's like it says in the papers: A prophet is without honour in her own country.'

A Diver in China Seas

Now that I feel death's cauld hand crawling over me every night I keep turning my mind to the corpses I've seen in my day. Not that I have seen that many. I have aye tried to give them a wide berth, and I can mind of a few I declined to look at, though hard pressed by their nearest. In all, I've seen maybe seven or eight.

The first was Bobby Leitch. It was when he was eighteen or nineteen that I remember him best. He was a braw lad with yellow hair and big sad-like eyes that would suddenly light up and blaze like blue lamps when he saw a joke. Not that it was often he saw a joke; he was awful serious, and I mind him best with a sad face. When I was sixteen I took a great fancy to him. He was a shunter on the railway down at Granton. I was working myself then as a nursemaid to some swells at Trinity, so whenever I got the chance I hurled the pram with the two wee Ritchies in their white fur bonnets along to Granton, and I would parade beside the railway lines between the Middle pier and the West pier in the hope of seeing Bobby. Whenever I did he would just give a bit wave and cry: 'Hey, Carrie! How're ye gettin' on in the pugs' parlour then? Are ye still eatin' vinegar with a fork and holdin' out yer pinkie when ye sup yer tea?' And then he would laugh and give a string of wagons a shunt with his pole. He would leap on the nearside buffer of the last wagon and ride away with a wave.

Whiles it seemed senseless to walk all that way to Granton, putting up with the greeting of the Ritchie bairns, who were terrified of the steaming engines and the rattling of the long goods trains, just for the sake of hearing Bobby make the same auld joke and give the same wee wave. But I was in love, and when you're in love you'll put up with a lot.

And then one day my Auntie Annie brought the news that Bobby had been killed. When he was coupling some loose wagons onto an engine pulling other wagons the engine had come quicker than he'd expected and it had crushed him between the wagons. My Auntie Annie took me to see Bobby in his coffin. There was upwards of a dozen folk in the Leitch's house. Most were women, but there were some men too, and Mrs Leitch was dispensing tea to the women and drams to the men with a lavish hand. 'He's a lovely corpse,' Auntie Annie said when we looked at Bobby with his smooth bonnie face and his yellow hair brushed like a golden helmet. 'He's beautiful.'

Mrs Leitch, like a good hostess, agreed with her guest. She even went a bit farther. She said Bobby was that lovely she could have sat and looked at him all day.

I was fell taken with Bobby's corpse, and I've never forgotten it, though I can't rightly see his features after all this time. It must be sixty years syne, and you can't blame a body for forgetting the face of the first lad she fancied. It's only because I tell myself so often about his blue eyes and yellow hair that I remember them.

The corpse I mind best is auld Jessie Meiklejohn's. It must be about forty years since she passed on. It was before the war, anyway, in the days when it was not so fashionable to be cremated or for the corpse to be taken away to the undertaker's mortuary.

I was married to Harry Henderson when I became acquainted with Nora and Jessie Meiklejohn. They were a couple of auld maids living in a basement in a street off Leith Walk. I met Nora because of an accident. Harry and me were living in a tenement near there, and one forenoon coming out of the Co-op grocery this elderly body who'd gone out in front of me suddenly slipped on dog-shit and went down with a wallop. I was the first to reach her, and I helped her up and put the packet of tea and a few other things that had fallen out back in her basket for her. 'There ye are, missis,' I said. 'Are ye all right, hen?'

'I've twisted my ankle,' she said.

'Lord love us!' I said. 'Will ye be able to walk at all?'

She took a wee step and fell against me. 'I doot I can just hirple,' she said. 'Can you give me your arm as far as my door, dear? It's not far. It's just the next street, about a hundred yards away.'

I took her home, and I met her sister Jessie, and we all got very friendly over a cup of tea and a slice of Dundee cake. After that we became pals-a'-bubbly and I was as often in their house as I was in our own. Harry was unemployed at the time, and there wasn't room in our pokey wee but and ben for both him and me. So I used to leave him alone with his grievances and his eternal wireless — he switched it on loud as soon as he came in, and I believe he would have nicked me with his razor if I'd as much as raised a hand to put it off. There was no wireless at the Meiklejohns. A wireless would never have stood a look-in there. Nora and Jessie often talked thegither and they hardly ever seemed to draw breath — except when they were listening to me. They were aye delighted to see me. 'It's fine to have a bit of young life about the house,' Jessie said.

Young life! Me that was turned thirty-four at the time and feeling every day of fifty. My mother and father died when I was a bit bairn and I had no recollection of them or their corpses. I was brought up by my Auntie Annie. I'm never likely to forget her, the sanctimonious auld bitch, forever grasping for every penny I earned. So I was fell glad to have two decent women like the Meiklejohns to be friends with, even though they were getting on for forty years aulder than me. Their father had had a wee plumber's business and had left a bit of money. They weren't rich, nothing to put up bills about, but they were quite comfortable. They were very good to me. One or other used to slip me five bob or a ten shilling note nearly every time I saw them, telling me to buy something nice for myself. Not that I ever did. Anything they gave me aye went on food or on fags for Harry. It was their company I liked best. They were a lively pair of auld besoms.

When Harry was unemployed the first time I did some charring in the West End, and even after he got other jobs I kept it on, for the extra money was very handy. I cleaned a lawyer's office in the early mornings, then after I'd had a cup of tea and a natter at what used to be called a cabby's shelter near the Caley Station, I did the rough work at some gentry's house in Randolph Crescent. On the way back from my work I usually looked in at the Meiklejohns before going home. By the time I'd kent them a couple of years this was a daily habit. There was aye a bite waiting for me. They either kept something warm in the oven or they waited till I arrived to have their own lunch. I never needed to hurry home till it was time to make Harry's tea.

And then when Harry died after he got pneumonia through getting soaked one night in the last job he took as a night-watchman at a brewery the Meiklejohns were kindness itself. They wanted me to give up the but and ben and go and live with them. 'This is sic a big flat there's plenty of room for three,' Nora said. 'Especially since we all agree with each other so well.' But I put my foot down about this; I felt it was better to have a haven of my own, even though it did seem a waste to pay rent when it wasn't necessary. Still anon, it was better to be independent.

But sleeping in my own house was my only independence; otherwise the Meiklejohns and me lived in each others' pockets till Jessie died. I ate all my meals at their house, except my breakfast and that was just a couple of cups of tea and a bap spread with marge. They wouldn't take anything for my keep, but in return I did all their shopping and most of their housework. And I kept them entertained.

The Miss Meiklejohns liked a joke. When I met them first Jessie said: 'I don't hold with jokes that are dirty for dirtiness' sake. But I don't mind if a joke's not clean so long as I get a guid laugh.' I remembered this, and I was aye careful not to go over the score when I told them anything I'd heard in the cabby's shelter. Some of the jokes the taxi-drivers and the other chars told were gey near the knuckle, but as time went on and the two auld maids and me were letting our hair down more and more, I repeated some of these jokes when they pressed me. And we had so many good laughs that by and by I didn't trouble to beat about the bush but told them everything I heard.

One day I told yon one about the kilted sodger running like mad to catch a tram, and the auld English lady who clapped her hands and cried: 'Heah! Heah!' when he caught it. Jessie laughed that much at the kiltie's reply she complained afterwards of a pain in her back. 'I shouldn't have laughed so hearty,' she said. 'But oh, that's a guid yin, isn't it? Ye're a right comic, Carrie. I don't know how you mind them all, but I'm glad you're not blate in comin' out with them.'

Next afternoon Jessie was in bed complaining about her back, saying the awful pain in her left shoulder wouldn't go away and she felt a kind of numbness spreading from it. But bad though she was, she asked if I'd heard any good jokes that day. 'I've been laughin' again at yon yin ye tellt yesterday,' she said. 'I can just hear that kiltie sayin' "What did ye think ye'd see, mem? Ostrich feathers!"' And she laughed and laughed again, and gey near choked herself. At night she got that bad I went for the doctor. She died a wee while after he arrived.

I went then for Mrs Forsyth, the laying-out woman, and I let the undertakers know. I stayed the night with poor auld Nora. Next morning I didn't go to my work; I phoned one of the snooty wee typists in the lawyer's and told her I wouldn't be in because of a death in the family.

Then I chummed Nora, who was beginning to revive, to Patrick Thomson's to buy some black clothes. We had lunch afterwards at Mackie's in Princes Street.

When we got back in the late afternoon Mrs Forsyth was there again. The undertakers had been and Jessie, in her best blue nightgown, was in her coffin on the bed. 'She looks right bonnie,' Mrs Forsyth said, admiring her own handiwork.

Nora gave a few wee snuffles, then she said: 'Ay, our Jessie was aye a bonnie lassie. She could've married, y'know. There was no call for her to be an auld maid. She had plenty of flames and several guid offers.'

'Why did she turn them doon then?' Mrs Forsyth asked.

Nora said: 'God alone knows.' And she went to the dressing-table and tried on the black hat we'd chosen in P.T's. She stood back and looked at herself, cocking her head from side to side. 'D'you know,' she said, 'I don't think I like this hat. I don't think it suits me.'

'But ye liked it in the shop,' I said. 'Ye look lovely in it.'

'That's what yon sales-lassie said, but I'm beginning to think she was telling a lie. Not that I'm accusing you of bein' a liar, too, Carrie. I just don't fancy myself in it.'

Mrs Forsyth said: 'Ye look awful nice in it, Miss Meiklejohn.'

'It's the kind of hat that would've suited Jessie,' Nora said.

'Ach, ye look jist as nice as yer sister in it.' Mrs Forsyth's hand went to her mouth. 'Ye ken what I mean, Miss Meiklejohn.'

Nora raked her with a fish-like eye.

'See how it goes with the coat,' I said.

Nora put on the new black coat and paraded up and down, preening herself. 'How does it look, Carrie?' she asked.

'I tellt ye in the shop,' I said. 'It's a right braw rigout.'

'It doesn't go with this hat,' she said. 'I wonder if Jessie's mourning hat would go with it?'

She brought Jessie's black velour from the press and put

it on. 'There!' she cried. 'This is the very dab. It suits me better. In fact, though it's myself that says it, it suits me a damn sight better than it ever suited Jessie.'

'Puir Miss Jessie,' Mrs Forsyth said, giving her bleary eyes a bit dicht with a dirty hankie. 'She'll never wear a hat again.'

'Ah well, she'll have a halo instead,' Nora said. 'Like enough, anyway, if all we read in the Bible is true.'

She took another turn up and down in the coat and the black velour, then she sat down forenent the mirror and admired herself.

'One of Jessie's auld beaux was a diver in China seas,' she said. 'Davie Nasmyth. He went there after she'd turned him down three times. But he's back bidin' in Edinburgh. At Tollcross. He came home five years ago, and we saw him once or twice. But he stopped comin' when Jessie refused him again.'

Mrs Forsyth looked into the coffin, sighing: 'Oh, Miss Jessie, if ye'd jist played yer cards right you could've been a lady of leisure in China and them other foreign places. Ye would jist've needed to clap yer hands and the wee blackies would've come runnin' to do yer biddin'.'

'It's more likely that it would've been Davie Nasmyth that was clappin' his hands and Jessie that would've been runnin' at his bidding,' Nora said. 'Though, mind you, if Jessie had been the marrying kind I don't think she'd have chosen Davie. She had plenty of better flames.'

I had heard of this man Nasmyth before. 'Will he be comin' to the funeral?' I asked.

'I don't know. I suppose I'd better invite him. I'm sure he'd want to see Jessie off on her last journey.' Nora sighed. 'It must be four years since we saw him. I wonder if he's changed much. He's just a year aulder than me.'

'Ye should hang up yer hat with him, Nora,' I chaffed her.

'Ay, ye should grab him while the goin's good,' Mrs Forsyth said with a laugh. 'There's nothin' like a funeral for bringin' folk thegither. It's wonderful what a few tears on a lassie's cheek'll do to the menfolk.'

'I'd never thocht o' it,' Nora simpered. 'But it's an idea, isn't it? He must be lonely. As for me, God kens what I'm going to do without Jessie. Ay, I suppose I've got to the age when I need a man's strong hand behind me and his broad shoulders to fall back on.'

'Well, ye'd better get in touch with him right away,' I said. 'If ye write him a letter I'll go out and post it. We cannie depend upon him seein' the funeral notice in tonight's *News*. No' everybody reads the hatches, matches and despatches.'

'Ach, I cannie be fashed writing,' Nora said. 'I'm too tired and worn out. Maybe you could phone him tomorrow morning, Carrie, from your work? I'll be glad to have a man's support at the funeral. Davie hasn't got a phone himself, but if you phone the newsagent three doors away they'll give him a message.'

Next morning when I set off for the West End I was intending to phone this newsagent as soon as I got into the office, but on the way I decided phoning would be an awful trauchle. I decided, too, I wasn't going to bother about going to work. A death in the family was surely good for three days off.

I went to the big Co-op drapery in Bread Street and bought a pair of winter drawers. I knew how cauld it could be standing beside graves and hanging around churchyards. Then I went to Tollcross. I was curious to see what a diver looked like; to the best of my knowledge I'd never seen one.

Mr Nasmyth was tall and very thin, with a terribly wrinkled face the colour of cold coffee. He looked ninety but I knew that, if Nora was telling the truth, he was only seventy-three. His hands trembled. He looked a right gawk, but there was nothing gawky about his voice. It was loud and very self-confident and sounded as though he was used to giving commands.

I told him Nora was wondering if he'd like to come and see Jessie before she was nailed down. 'No, no, no!' he cried. 'I've seen enough corpses in my day, Mrs Henderson.

I have no desire to see any more.' Nor would he accept Nora's bidding to the funeral. 'I'm feared of funerals,' he said. 'Will you give Miss Meiklejohn my apologies and say — well, I can hardly say a previous appointment, can I? Better say I'm not well. Tell her it's my malaria. It's not really a lie. I'm liable to get my malaria at any time without much warning. I hope, Mrs Henderson, you won't mind telling a wee fib for me?'

'Of course no',' I said. 'I'm delighted to be of any service to ye, Mr Nasmyth. Ye've jist to say the word.'

'Well, maybe you'll not mind coming back and telling me how the funeral goes?' he said. 'Will you come to tea the day after?'

In those times women didn't often go to the graveside, but if there had been no women there would have been hardly anybody at Jessie Meiklejohn's. Besides the undertaker's men, there were only two old men cousins. And seven women, all competing with each other to see who wept the most.

I told Mr Nasmyth this the next day when I went to tea, and what with this and other things I garred him laugh a lot. He was like auld Jessie, he liked a joke. He asked me to tell Nora he'd pay her a wee visit soon to offer his condolences.

I don't think he ever made that visit, though. Soon after the funeral I stopped seeing Nora so often, and stepping in only occasionally instead of every day meant that I didn't hear about everything she was doing, except that she was out on the ran-dan a lot. She joined a Whist Club and got very pally with another auld maid like herself.

Neither did Mr Nasmyth ever mention he'd been to see her, and as he took me into his confidence it doesn't look as if he had. Not that I cared whether he saw her or not. It was Jessie that was really my friend. And Mr Nasmyth's too, if it came to that.

After we'd been courting for about six months me and Mr Nasmyth got married. He died when he was seventy-six, the same age as I am now, and left me a good pickle siller.

His was the last corpse I saw. I did hear that Nora Meiklejohn lived until she was ninety, but I never saw her after I married Davie, nor did I see her corpse or go to her funeral. And now I'm thinking, with death's cauld fingers plucking at me, how lucky she was to live till ninety, even though she wasn't lucky enough to hang up her hat with Mr Nasmyth.

Camp Follower

I

Whiles, on the march, if they were not harassed by the Frenchies and whenever the Bavarian sergeant-major was out of sight at the head of the column, Willem would take Kirsty up behind him on his horse. These stolen rides were near as hard to thole as the rocky tracks and the dust. Bouncing on the charger's crupper, holding her pack with one hand and clinging to Willem's belt with the other, aye on the alert for the sergeant-major and ready to slip off at the first sign of his big chestnut's white blaze, Kirsty often wondered if all the trouble was worth it. If only her feet were not so sore she would rather have walked the endless Spanish leagues. Her shoes had worn through long syne, and she kept tearing strips off her petticoats and binding them round her feet to try to keep the flapping soles from falling off.

The sergeant-major had a down on the camp women and he was a martinet about horses being over-burdened with baggage. Kirsty was in the fore-front of his black books because of Willem. It would go hard on her if they were caught. Even though he was one of the Bavarian's favourites Willem would suffer too. There was no fear of him being tied to the wheel of a gun-carriage and flogged in front of the regiment, but the Bavarian had his own methods of dealing with good-looking young soldiers who misbehaved. Instead of reporting them to an officer he would administer his own punishment. Willem had no wish to be taken to a quiet corner and ordered to drop his britches and get beaten like a bad wee boy.

The Bavarian was in the mid-thirties, a handsome man with light brown yellow-streaked hair and a russet complexion, the skin stretched so taut across his cheekbones that it looked as though they'd burst through. His eyes were large, cold and pale green, so pale they were near enough the colour of phlegm and as distasteful. He exuded coldness, and Kirsty thought there were few women who would want him. He gave her the grue. She was feared of him and kept out of his way as much as she could. Although he was a strict disciplinarian he let his favourites call him 'Hansi'.

There were whiles when Kirsty wished she was back in Edinburgh. The cobbles of the High Street and the Grassmarket were surely not as hard and cauld as the Spanish rocks. Yet it was her own fault she was here, so she maun make a kirk or a mill of it. She should have listened to her mother. When Kirsty had gotten tired of being a servant to Lady Pringle in yon big house in Abercrombie Place, deeved by the auld wife's eternal wheenging about her ailments and her grievances against this body and that, her mother had urged her to wed big Geordie Tait, the fisherman, and settle in her own but and ben and be at nobody's beck and call. But although Kirsty listened to one bit of Mistress Gloag's advice and gave Milady Pringle quick, short notice, she did nothing about big Geordie; she had no desire to become a Newhaven fishwife like her Auntie Annie, going with a creel on her back round the doors of the gentry in the New Town crying 'Caller herrin' and 'Fine fresh fish frae the Forth'. Instead, she settled in to looking after the Gloag home in a tenement in the Lawnmarket, keeping her young brothers and sisters in some kind of order and helping her mother make the mutton pies, sheep's brains and sheep's head broth she sold on her booth at the mouth of the close. Mistress Gloag did a roaring trade at nights with the sodgers from the Castle garrison, as well as with the fine young gentlemen who sauntered up and down the Royal Mile in daytime. Kirsty did a fine trade with some of them too. Oft-times one of the Gloag brats running unexpectedly up the stairs would dash in and discover his eldest sister earning a shillingsworth with some buck whose appetite had been whetted by partaking of Mother Gloag's dainties. At night, after the pies and broth had all been consumed and Mother Gloag had gone upstairs to count her brats and see them bedded or was in the grog shop across the street swigging Dutch gin, Kirsty would stand at the close-mouth with some girls of her own age and inclinations and bandy words with strolling soldiers of the 3rd Battalion of the Royal Scots from the Castle. And often she would walk with one of them down the Mile, past dark Holyrood and its ghosts of Queen Mary and King Charles who'd had their heads chopped off by the English, and they would comfort each other for youth's eternal longing and loneliness on the banks of springy turf beneath Salisbury Crags.

It was on one of these nights that she'd taken up with Rob Copeland. He had stopped at the close-mouth and, after catterbattering gaily for a while with her and her companions, she had accompanied him down the Mile for a sixpennyworth of love. It ended in Kirsty giving herself for nothing.

Even yet, though her love for him had brought her to this foreign land and all the tribulations that beset her, she had never regretted falling in love with Rob. He was a well set up callant with merry blue eyes and red hair that kept sticking out from under his Royal Scots bonnet. He was a likeable cratur', cheery and gallus, and, in the darkness of the close, his hands would grope beneath her clothes even though there were other folk there. He would laugh at her protests and coo: 'Och, Kirsty, ma wee doo, they're a' that busy wi' their ain ploys they've no' got eyes for what you and me are up to.'

Then one dark night, while slashing rain was being driven into the close by a high wind from the North Sea, he told her in the midst of their canoodling that the Regiment had got its marching orders. 'We're bound for the Peninsula,' he said. 'We're to join Sir Arthur Wellesley's troops at Cork. We leave in three days, hen, so we hinnie much time left.'

'I'm comin' with ye,' she said.

Early next morning she walked to Newhaven. Her Auntie Annie already had a full creel of fish on her back, but when she heard what Kirsty had to say she handed it over to her eldest daughter and told her to do the daily round. She took off her fishwife's shawl, put on her Sabbath bonnet and set forth to introduce Kirsty to her friend Collie Menzies, the sutler in Leith. The upshot was that Menzies hired Kirsty to gang and help him with the provisioning of the Royal Scots.

Mistress Gloag skirled and screaked like a demented seagull trying to fly against a gale. 'So ye're awa' to the wars to be a sodger's doxy, are ye, ye graceless besom? Leavin' yer puir auld mother in the lurch wi' all thae bairns to feed. Ye'll come to a bad end. Ye dinnie need to come hirplin' back here when the war's ower and yer sodger has let ye down, ye sinful slut, or ye'll find a shut door in yer face.'

Kirsty took no heed of her mother's ranting. She put her few duds in an old Paisley shawl, slung it over her shoulder and begged a lift on a cart down to Leith.

The weeks on the troopship were the happiest Kirsty ever had. Collie Menzies kept her and the other women he'd hired hard at it, cooking sheep's head broth, sheep's brains and tongue and mutton pies, and she was glad of all she had learned from her mother. Yet she found time to snuggle down with Rob in hidden corners, and he was aye ready to comfort her with strong arms and merry face when sickness overcame her in Biscay or when she was hard pressed by the bitchiness and spite of the other women aboard, some of them soldiers' wives, others lassies like herself, all following their men.

They disembarked in Portugal, in the Bay of Mondego, on 8 August 1808. Kirsty was never likely to forget that date, for it was the day after her nineteenth birthday, the last day you might say she'd ever truly had Rob to herself. It was the day she discovered that following Rob to the war was not what she had thought. She had never expected it would be plain sailing; she knew there would be hardships and danger, discomfort and the constant fear of death. But she'd aye thought Rob would be close beside her giving his cheeky laugh when the guns boomed, and she'd aye have his wide shoulders and his waist to cling to while she hid her face on his chest. Instead of marching alongside Rob, though, carrying his knapsack and seeing it was full of prog for them both, as she'd often imagined, she saw so little of him there were times when she might as well have been home in Edinburgh — except that in Edinburgh she would not have had to work so hard, nor would she have been deeved by all the noise and confusion and smothered by the smoke and constant dust. Rob was aye away at the top of the long column, marching with the other sodgers towards Lisbon, while she was at the hinterend in the baggage train with the women and other camp followers.

She rode in a mule wagon with Collie Menzies and his wife Ellen and two Leith drabs, big Mary with the squint and Cherry-pie Poll who was cried that because she was sic a dab hand at making this dainty. At nights, when he was not on picket duty, Rob slept with the other redcoats in bivouacs; while, away at the other end of the camp, Kirsty slept in the back of the wagon with Mary and Cherry-pie, a canvas curtain separating them from Collie and Ellen. Often in the small hours Kirsty could hear Collie grunting and snorting through his thick pockmarked nose, and she was thankful it was Ellen and not her who was having to put up with his cauld sweaty hands. And it was at sic times she longed with heart-sickening pain for Rob.

They saw each other only in the evenings. It was then that they managed sometimes to be alone long enough for a quick kiss and a cuddle. They had no opportunity for longer daffing. It was hard to find a quiet corner in a camp of more than ten thousand folk. And it wasn't safe to slip away into the darkness beyond the picket lines because of stray Frenchies and Portuguese blackguards ever ready to club you down for any coins you might have. Not that Rob or Kirsty were worth robbing. The Royal Scots had gotten no pay for a good long while. Every night Rob and other sodgers came to the prog shop and wheedled Collie Menzies into giving them mutton pies and lamb chops on tick: prog they needed to supplement their army rations, which were slender because the Portuguese would not supply the army with enough victuals. A lot of the Portuguese did not like the English invasion, even if it was to help them drive out Boney and his men, so they made trading difficult. Collie Menzies managed, though, by bribery and his smarmy tongue to buy sheep and hens and fresh meat from some of the natives, so his prog shop was aye well stocked. His wife and Kirsty and the two Leith women were kept so busy they had no time for looking at the country they were passing through or for knowing how the war was progressing, unless the artillery fired sometimes closer than they liked.

After the British defeated Marshal Junot and his Frenchies at a place called Vimeiro there was no sign of Rob for a couple of days. Kirsty thought he'd been killed, and she was near demented. It turned out that he'd gone off with a foraging party, and he came back laden and unrepentant. Kirsty was that relieved to see his dirty grinning face that she forbore to upbraid him for scaring the lights outen her, and she cooked the goose and the hens he and the other coves had slipped into the camp ahint the backs of their officers.

By this time Kirsty could not hide her condition. It led to endless lewd chaff from big Mary and Cherry-pie. What between this and the anxiety caused by snitching pies and other tit-bits, hiding them in a bag sewn into her petticoats to feed Rob and his friends, Kirsty had no inkling of whether they were winning or losing. They would march for a few days, then they would remain camped in the same place for maybe a week. She heard talk of the pass of Torres Vedras, and Cintra and an armistice, trouble with the Portuguese juntas, and Duro Wellesley with his long nose going back to England and Sir John Moore taking command in his place. Then they were on the march again, going into Spain. In a smaller column this time, many brigades and regiments being left behind near Lisbon. The rainy season started. The rain got heavier and heavier. And the heavier it rained the quicker they pressed on to Salamanca.

There was no time to rest. The bairn in her belly tired her by its kicking. She could think of nothing else, wondering how she and Rob could ever rear a bairn in conditions like this. There was sic torrential rain it was hard to keep dry even under the canvas of the wagon. The dust in Portugal had troubled them sorely, but now they were in a greater trauchle among the Spanish mud, slithering and sliding. The mud got so bad that eventually the women had to get out of the wagon and walk to help the mules; often pushing the wagon when it stuck. And it was when she was struggling to make one of the back wheels turn that Kirsty slipped and rolled into a ditch, bringing on her labour long before its time. Mistress Menzies and the two denizens of Leith delivered her with ribald laughs and rough words of comfort. The baby, born dead, was the spitten image of Rob. Kirsty wept with abandon: a mingling of sorrow and relief.

They were at Valladolid for Christmas. The rain turned to snow, and it was bitterly cold. And then they heard that Boney himself, with fifty thousand men, was coming from Madrid. Sir John Moore gave the order to retreat. And so they started on the long walk to the North West and the town of Corunna where ships were said to be waiting to take them home. Many a camp follower struggling through the snowbound hills, and some sodgers forby, lagged behind to die of starvation and exhaustion or to fall into the hands of the French.

Kirsty never knew how she reached Corunna, but reach it she did, and she'd regretted it ever since. The very name garred her eyes blear and her bowels churn with anguish. Adverse January winds had kept the English ships from winning into harbour. Soult and his Frenchies were close behind; Moore's men were caught like rabbits in snares. Sir John gave the order to turnabout and advance out of the town to face Soult's vanguard. In the battle Sir John himself and a wheen other brave sodgers were killed. One was Rob Copeland.

That night, after the sounds of heavy guns and musket fire had died away, Kirsty left the wagon where she'd cowered all day with big Mary and Cherry-pie Poll and went to the battlefield to look for Rob. She searched all night among the dead and wounded, asking everyone willing to listen if they'd seen him. It was just before dawn when she found his corpse. Like many others, Rob had been stripped by vandals of his red coat and Hunting Stuart tartan trews.

Hours later she was still cuddling his dear dead head in her arms when a Scottish voice said something close by. She had become so used to the night noises of the wounded and dying calling for their comrades or their wives or their mothers, so apathetic since the dreariness of dawn had fallen over the field, a pale wintry sun lighting up the carnage, that she paid no attention. She went on keening and kissing Rob's face until the man spoke again: 'I'm sorry, lass, but ye'll have to leave him. We're goin' to lay him to rest.'

Two sodgers of the Royal Scots were bending over her. The younger, Paterson, a waggish fellow, had sometimes played cards with Rob. They were carrying spades. Looking wildly around, she saw that many corpses were being carried towards a wood, and men were digging beside it.

She clutched Rob against her and screamed: 'No, no, no!'

'Dinnie be silly, dearie,' the older soldier said. 'He's got to be buried.'

She went on screaming and she struggled to hold Rob when they took the body from her. She stumbled after them, pummelling Paterson's shoulders. About halfway to the wood she was hitting him so hard he nearly dropped the body.

'Get awa', ye daft bitch!' he cried. 'Let'm go. He's nae damned guid to ye noo.'

When they reached a grave that already held several bodies, another Royal Scot held Kirsty while Paterson and his mate dropped Rob's body in beside the others and started to shovel earth on top of them.

'Now now, lassie, dinnie take on like this,' the sodger said. 'It comes to us all in the long run. Maybe his has been shorter than it should, but ye never ken . . . maybe he's weel out o' it.'

Kirsty went on screaming until the grave was filled, then she threw herself on top of it. She remembered lying on the grave, but she had no memory of what happened afterwards until she came to her senses in a hovel with an old Spanish woman looking after her. Paterson and his friends had left money for her keep. All the English had sailed away in the fleet that had arrived after the battle was won.

She stayed with the old woman for two-three days. Each day she went to the edge of the wood and knelt beside the grave she thought was Rob's. She could not be sure. There were so many graves. Some had rough headstones of wood, with names on them. She found Rob's name nowhere. And among the unmarked graves was the one she thought was his.

She was crouching beside it one day, keening, when a horseman drew up alongside and spoke. She did not know what he said. He went on speaking, but she paid no attention until he dismounted, put his hands under her oxters and lifted her to her feet. 'Can you get on the horse, my lass?' he asked.

His English voice sounded so kind she burst into tears and clung to him. 'Rob,' she sobbed. After a while, mur-

51

muring in a soothing way, he lifted her on the horse, got up behind her and they moved off into the woods.

II

Willem was a trooper in the 19th Light Horse. A platoon of his regiment had got separated from General Moore's army and it was preparing now to retreat towards Portugal, to avoid the Frenchies and join the Spanish guerillas. Willem was a country boy from Sussex. His mother had been a farm labourer's daughter, his father a Dutch dragoon who had gone away. Willem had been on a little foraging foray of his own when he saw Kirsty.

She had been his woman for about two years now. No longer did she ride in a wagon in luxury. She trailed along, her back aching under its pack of blankets and clothes, the dangling camp-kettle and frying-pan forever bumping against her backside. Yet the ache in her back and her feet was not as great as the other ache in her heart. She could not forget Rob. Whiles, she thought of slipping away from the army and making her own way to the sea, but she could never get further than thinking about it, for she knew she could never leave Rob behind in his foreign grave.

Willem was a big sonsy fine-looking lad, but he was not much of a catch for a girl like Kirsty. He was so pleased with himself he had need for nobody. He kept stroking his muckle hams with his cowman's red hands, a smile that was almost a smirk on his small thick-lipped mouth. Even when on horseback, his free hand was aye busy smoothing his thigh or pleasurably easing his buttocks off the saddle. He was kind and good natured, but he was not like Rob. Kirsty pined for Rob's warmth and his gallus Gallowgate laugh.

Once, in the mountains among the guerillas, she had seen a Spanish muleteer wearing a red jacket and a pair of Hunting Stuart tartan trews. Kirsty had looked so long the muleteer thought she fancied him. Crouching beside the fire, frying pork chops for Willem and a couple of his mates, Kirsty had watched the muleteer swagger towards her, a grin of assurance splitting his dirty face. She could not be sure, but she felt . . . she *knew* . . . the trews were Rob's. When the muleteer came close she saw the darn on the left thigh. One night at Valladolid a gunpowder spark had made the hole, and she'd darned it while Rob jumped up and down in his sarktail to keep his doup and his shanks warm. The muleteer leered and tipped his sombrero.

'*Vaya!*' she spat. And she lifted the frying-pan so threateningly that the man backed in terror, mounted his mule and kicked it away swiftly.

After biding for months with the guerillas they had won back to Portugal and joined long-nebbit Duro when he'd returned to Lisbon to lead them again and keep the thieving Spanish and Portuguese in order. Willem and the other camp followers and the Bavarian sergeant-major, who'd been as big a thorn to the guerillas as he was to Kirsty, were mad with joy when they saw Duro; but Kirsty cared for him as little as she cared for the war. She never had much notion of how it fared. Sometimes the English seemed to be winning; sometimes the Frenchies were screaking on top. She drudged along, cooking for Willem, choking over smoky fires with a camp-kettle, trying to spin out the starvation rations, sleeping beneath a hedge or in a ditch. For months there were clouds of dust and burning heat; and then there was rain falling relentlessly, and mud and yet more mud. Kirsty had not time to look at the country, her head was aye down and she could see little but the legs and rumps of mules and horses, the wheels of gun-carriers, the thigh-boots of troopers and the gleam of sabres and bayonets. She heard names like Ciudad-Rodrigo and Talavera and the Almeida, but they meant nothing to her; neither did the news that Duro was now to be called Lord Wellington.

The hunger in her belly was as great as the hunger in her heart. The Spanish looked sourly at the English who'd come to help them, and they would not give supplies to the troops. Food was so scarce the sodgers were as often scrounging and foraging as they were fighting. Some days they had no prog beyond the handful of flour rationed to each man. Willem and his mates were dab hands, though, at winning hens and ducks and wee pigs offen the sulky-jawed Spanish, and they brought their pickings to Kirsty who made many a tasty stew and baked pies almost as rich as auld Mother Gloag's in the faraway Lawnmarket.

But after the battle of Busaco when they fell back and entrenched in the lines of Torres Vedras, Duro came to some arrangement with the Portuguese, and the sodgers' food improved so there was no need for them to gang foraging for meat. Not that there was much they could thieve, for Duro had garred the Portuguese lay waste the country between Beira and Torres Vedras. All the cattle and sheep were driven ahint the lines, so the French couldn't get them and had to take their share of starvation.

The winter of 1810—11 seemed long to Kirsty. On the march there was action and hardship, constant movement to keep her so busy that memories of Rob did not trouble her often. But in the camp on the heights of Torres Vedras there was little to do except cook for Willem and try to avoid Bavarian Hansi with his cold disciplinary eyes; though this was difficult because he was aye coming, when off duty, to have wee fatherly chats with Willem and a new special friend Willem had made: Alfie, another big handsome childe with sleepy eyes from Sussex, who was so donnert he made even Willem seem brainy. Whenever Hansi came to their camp fire and sat, knee to knee with Willem and Alfie, Kirsty could not abide sitting opposite and seeing his green eyes watching her like a fox's through the flames. He frightened her. So she aye made excuses about having some ploys to attend to. Sometimes she went to the bivouac Willem had rigged up for her and himself, and either she went to sleep or she did wee jobs like darning and sewing on buttons. Sometimes she walked round the camp. She did not do this often, however, for she had randy drunken sodgers to contend with, or, what was even worse, their women-folk forever ready to pick a quarrel if their jealousy made them imagine Kirsty was after their men.

Kirsty had no truck with the other camp-women. Whiles, the older ones invited her to join in their clish-clash around the fires when they sewed or played cards or combed the lice out of each other's hair. But she aye refused; she had as little time for them as the Bavarian had. Indeed, if the worst had come to the worst, she'd rather have sat across the camp fire from the sergeant-major and closed her eyes.

There was one woman especially she did everything she could to avoid: a bold-eyed bawd from Fife, Bell Mitchell by name. Bouncy Bell, who'd been an Irish soldier's doxy until he was killed, ran a travelling knocking-shop and she was aye trying to enlist Kirsty's services. 'If ye like, we could share the profits,' she said. 'I wouldnie poach on yer favourite sodgers, dear, and ye'd be a great help in recruitin' willing lassies.' Although Kirsty steadfastly refused and did her best to jouk Bell, she was aye running into her, and Bell would say: 'Why can twa bonnie Scottish hizzies like us no' hing thegither, dear? Ye'd be better doin' a fair trade alongside o' me, pickin' and choosin' whae ye like, instead o' haudin' sae close to that muckle sumph Willem. He maun be nae guid to ye, he seems that fond o' his ain bum. Every time I see him he's pat-pat-pattin' it till he makes me want to spew.'

Kirsty refused Bell that often she couldn't find fresh words to express her reasons. And it was this refusal to be part of the camp's great gregarious hen-party that was responsible largely for her ending up with her neck clamped in an iron collar at the end of a short chain shackled to a wall in a village near Ciudad-Rodrigo.

III

At last the long winter on the Torres Vedras hills was over. Both Spanish guerillas and English scouts had brought word that the French were starving, so there was little surprise when they heard, at the beginning of March, of Marshal Massena's orders for the French to retreat.

The English set off in pursuit. What was left of the 19th Light Horse and other regiments followed Duro northward towards the fortress of Ciudad-Rodrigo. And Kirsty went in their train riding a donkey. Like hundreds of others, sodgers and their women, she had been laid low with the dreaded Walcheren fever. She was still weak and droopy, and the thought of trailing again on a long march made her wish she was dead and lying beside Rob at Corunna. So she was near flabbergasted with joy when, just before they set out, Willem brought her a little brown donkey. She suspected that Willem and Alfie had stolen the beast, even though Willem boasted about how much he'd paid for it, but she thought it wiser to say nothing. She was only too glad to put herself and their pots and pans and blankets on its back and ride away from Torres Vedras.

The country they moved through had been devastated by the Frenchies. It was so bare that even the seasoned, ever-optimistic English soldiery, tramping along in rags, regarded it with eyes as apathetic as the oxen they'd commandeered to drag the big guns because so many horses and mules had been killed or had died of starvation and sickness. But enterprising scroungers like Willem and Alfie were still able to smell out pickings. At nights, well away from the glow of the fires, Kirsty would pluck the poultry they snitched from under the noses of vigilant señoras, and next day, miles away, she'd cook them on the same fire as her protector's ration of rotten beef which gave such a whiff it overpowered the aroma of the stolen fowls. It was a nerve-racking business, though, and worse even for her than for the men.

Willem and big Alfie carried out the thefts with ignorant braggadocio and smirking Sussex peasant cunning infinitely slyer than its Spanish counterpart. They swaggered back to Kirsty with the spoils, often inviting some of their cronies to partake of the feast before it was cooked. Sometimes

Kirsty thought it might be better if they asked Hansi to be a guest instead of aye keeping their eyes skinned for him. Hansi could not have been a more dangerous participant than some of the stupid oafs Willem and Alfie favoured. Kirsty, cursed with a much vivider imagination than any of the sodgers, kept speculating upon the consequences of discovery, brooding over them and wondering how long it would be before somebody clyped to the Bavarian or to one of the officers. That Captain Hamilton Smyllie maybe? A stout sanctimonious wee man aye so keen to have evil-doers strung up and lashed or, better still, hung by their necks on a makeshift gallows. Duro had decreed dire penalties for rape and looting and murder. Wee Hammy Smyllie would be quicker than a stoat at a rabbit to seize any culprits in his teeth and shake them till they'd been given their just reward.

Jogging along on Peppy, the brown donkey — what the daft excitable Spanish called a *burro* — with the pots and pans clattering, Kirsty often wondered if she should give Willem the go-by. She did not need yon Bell Mitchell to tell her he was nae guid to her. She could feel in her marrow that she'd rue the day she ever set eyes on him. Should she maybe slip away some night on the gentle wee beast and hide till Willem had safely moved on with the regiment? Then they could fend their way north to Corunna and hope some kindly man-body would take them under his care. She did not want to leave Spain and dear dead Rob. At the same time, tired though she was of Willem and his self-satisfied swagger, she wondered, too, what would happen if he got killed. Would she be forced to fall back on big Alfie and put up with his stupidities? If only she and Peppy could get away from the army and the fighting and the Frenchies and the quarrelsome Portuguese. Peppy was a sweet wee cratur' and she loved him dearly. Now Rob was gone there was not another living soul she was fond of. Not that Peppy was likely to have a soul, him not being a kirkgoer but an outcast like herself.

She was still pondering on ways and means of winging

free of Willem when, at the beginning of May, moving at a quick lick, the English army caught up with the Frenchies, and Massena had to turn and take a stand at a village called Fuentes d'Onoro. The battle lasted two-three days. Kirsty never saw Willem all that time. She and Peppy and a couple of Irish women, *vivandières* she could thole better than most of the camp appendages, sheltered in the boggy woods beside the battle-field, taking kettles of hot black tea to the sodgers between scrimmages and bringing back wounded and patching them up as best they could before passing them on to the medicos. The confusion, the roar of the big guns, the charging cavalry, the shouted orders, the screams of some of the dying, the smoke and the heavy falls of rain, all kept Kirsty from thinking of Willem.

Several hours after the English had won she found Willem unhurt and Alfie with a superficial sabre-cut on the shoulder. Each was smugger and fuller of bravado than ever. Kirsty was so relieved to see them she turned a blind eye to their empty-headed boasting of what they'd done in the battle, and she thought no more of slipping away northward with Peppy. Willem and Alfie brought Kirsty a souvenir, a French knapsack containing an ivory fan, a piece of badly cooked pork, the corpse of a tough old cockerel and a gold necklace. Willem took back the necklace for safe keeping, and Kirsty never saw it again.

A week afterwards, camped outside a village on the road to Ciudad-Rodrigo, with a company of German hussars to which the 19th Light Horse was now attached, Willem and his mate brought back a dead sheep. They had stolen it not so much for its meat as for its fleece. It was a fine merino, which Willem coveted, hoping Kirsty would be able to fashion it into a jacket. 'And what are ye needin' with a thick sheepskin jacket in the summer?' Kirsty cried. 'It's hot enough already, God knows, and it'll get hotter and hotter.'

'The jacket can be carried on the burro's back till the winter. Come winter, my lass, you'll welcome a warm jacket as much as I will.'

58

'Little hope I have of ever gettin' to wear it with you here,' she said bitterly. 'I can see ye already — prancin' like a popinjay wi' it slung across yer shoothers.'

'Ah, Kirsty dear!' he said, chucking her under the chin. 'Think how proud you'll be to see me wearing it.'

'And what about the carcass?' she said. 'Are ye expectin' me to cook it all? There's enough here to feed the whole regiment.'

In an excess of boastful *bonhomie* Willem and Alfie invited several soldiers to help eat the sheep. Its skin dried slowly beside the smoking fire while Kirsty grumbled and laboured to boil the mutton. Before the skin was dry, though, they had to hide it in the bundle of blankets. They had got a whiff of rumour that the camp was to be searched.

The sheep had belonged to the village mayor, a jumped-up peasant already imagining he was an hidalgo. The mayor complained to Captain Hamilton Smyllie. Sniffing like a scavenging rat, already savouring the sight of striped flesh, Hammy ordered the Bavarian sergeant-major to take a squad and seek out the culprits. Hansi went to Bell Mitchell's knocking-shop to enlist two German hussars, favourites of his, for the squad.

'Michty me, sergeant-major!' Bell greeted him. 'What an honour to see ye here. I ken ye've no' come as a customer; I ken ye aye have other fish to fry. But mind, if ye ever do need a helpin' hand I'll be only too willin' to accommodate ye. I'd be glad to make arrangements to get ye whatever ye crave for.'

'No sank you, madame,' Hansi said. 'I kom to get Ridel and Gosch for duty.'

'Weel, they're busy the noo,' she said. 'Can I offer ye a drink while ye're waitin'? A wee nippie rum?'

'No sank you. Fetch them.'

'They'll no' want to be disturbed just yet,' Bell tittered. 'Besides, they've been bidden to a feast, and Fritzi Gosch has invited me to gang wi' him. Will ye be goin' to this feast, sergeant-major?'

'Vot feast?'

'Oh dear!' Bell put her hand to her mouth in exaggerated alarm. 'Have I spoken out o' turn? I was sure ye'd have been bidden, you that's so chief with Willem, such a great pal, like.'

'Villem? Oh, so? Fetch Ridel and Gosch. At vonce.'

'I'm sure I didnie mean any harm,' Bell said. 'I'm no' one to clype on folks. Still anon, Kirsty Gloag's a cauld-hearted coo and she's aye been ready to lead yon big saft Willem astray. If there's any blame, ye havenie to gang farther than her door to find it.'

Alfie had sloped off to eat some of the baked meats in secret by the time Hansi and his two German hussars came to the bivouac shared by Kirsty and the burro and, some-times, Willem. Most of Kirsty's mutton pies had gone already; they had been thrust into the hands of invited guests and they'd been told to fly as if Boney was at their heels. But the pot of sheep's head broth was still on the fire. Willem had supped more of it than he wanted, and his mouth was burning. Hansi bent over the pot and sniffed.

'So?' he said.

He nodded at Kirsty and said to the hussars: 'Take her to Captain Smyllie.' Then he tapped Willem on the haunch with his riding switch, jerked his head towards the darkness beyond the camp and said: 'Kom.'

IV

The June sun was merciless. She was dying of thirst. She had sucked her lips till they were cracked and bleeding. She'd been hanging here since six o'clock this morning when the farrier had soldered the iron collar round her neck and riveted it to the chain attached to the wall.

It was mid-afternoon, and not a soul among the crowds who'd come to gape had offered her a sup of water or a bite to eat. For the first few hours she'd managed to stand upright, but at last, overcome by exhaustion, shame and starvation, she had sagged against the wall. The chain was too short to allow her to sit on the ground. She was being strangled slowly by the iron collar. Her hands were manacled behind her, and she could do nothing to ease the burning iron away from her neck. She kept trying to stand upright, but her legs, sagging with strain, were weaker than her will.

Before handing her over to the mayor and the two big gaolers who'd taken such a delight in twisting her hands ahint her and holding her head for the farrier to clamp on the collar, Captain Hamilton Smyllie had taken snuff; then he had offered her the box with a sneer and said: 'Best have a little pinch, m'dear. It may be all the nourishment you'll get before our Spanish friends send you into the hereafter. In England we hang people for sheep stealing. I believe they use the garrotte here. Have you ever seen a garrotting? Such an unpleasant death, m'dear.'

Kirsty had spat on his snuffbox. Then she had spat in his face.

She wished now she'd saved that spittle. She could be doing with it. A drop of water. Only a drop of water . . . If she could just get that before she died . . . She knew she would, very soon now, be dead from hanging. They wouldn't need to trouble about the garrotte.

She'd been collared to the wall for three hours by the time the English army started to march out of the village. Thousands of sodgers and camp followers passed in front of her, and not a one raised a hand to help her. Some had stared as if she were an animal tethered because it was wild and dangerous; some had glanced with disdain, and a group of foppish young ensigns had ridden right up to her, reined in their horses and discussed her points as though preparing to bargain for her in a brothel. Others had looked at her slyly, speculatively. A great many, and their number was much in excess of half the English horde, had not even noticed her sagging there. Some she knew, like the German hussars and others who'd often guzzled her mutton pies, affected not to see her, talking loudly and looking everywhere but in her direction.

When the 19th Light Horse went by, most of the

troopers stared straight ahead. The Bavarian rode between Willem and another favourite trooper. Willem turned his head towards her in a shamefaced way and mouthed something. It looked kindly meant and, likely, was supposed to be encouraging, but she could not make it out. It meant nothing now, anyway. The Bavarian, staring coldly through her, dug his spurs into his horse to make him prance and plunge. He spoke sharply to the beast, and the other favourite trooper laughed. Willem bowed his head over his horse's neck. Big donnert Alfie, riding close behind them, had smirked, jerked up his thumb and given her a wink.

She had gazed sullenly at the camp women and, give them their due, most had passed in silence. One or two had shouted words of sympathy or encouragement. Bell Mitchell, driving her mule-wagon in the rear, had leant forward and cried: 'I'm vexed to see ye in sic a sorry state, hen. Ye should've come into partnership wi' me when I asked ye. I hope things'll turn out all right for ye in the hinterend.' She put her head round the canvas cover of the wagon to shout back: 'I'll pray for ye, dearie, when I get hame to the kingdom of Fife.'

Kirsty did not hear Bell's last words. Through her half-shut eyes she had become aware suddenly of the donkey tied to the back of Bell's wagon.

'Peppy!' she choked. 'Peppy . . .'

The small brown backside with its thin tail was soon swallowed up by the dust of the wagons that followed. Kirsty closed her eyes, and tears trickled down her cheeks. But they dried before they could reach her tongue poked out instinctively to receive them.

The people she'd known, auld acquaintances some of them, were all gone now, and she'd never see them again. The sun was at its hottest, and she knew she couldn't last much longer. Her neck seemed ready to burst into flames under the red-hot collar, and she felt that blood from the chafed skin was running down her breasts. There was a haze over her eyes, and she kept losing consciousness. Once, the sound of music made her senses quicken, and she opened her eyes. A muleteer was playing a guitar and, standing beside him, a cat-faced girl with a water-jug on her shoulder was swaying slightly to the tune while she ogled him. She laughed when she saw Kirsty's eyes open, and she said something that made the muleteer laugh too.

The next time her eyes opened there were three monks in brown habits with thick white ropes round their waists, sandals, and hoods over their shaven skulls, murmuring in churchy tones beside her. One monk made the sign of the cross, then they all bowed their heads and said a prayer. She lost consciousness again; then she was aware that something hard was touching her face. The tallest monk was holding a crucifix so that she could kiss it. She turned away her head and whispered: 'Papish . . . awa', awa', ye deevil . . .'

The next time she opened her eyes the sun seemed to have lost some of its dazzle. An elderly stoutish gentleman wearing a green long-tailed coat with gold buttons, an embroidered waistcoat, a pale yellow cravat and a tall narrow-brimmed black hat, was sitting on a stool a few yards away, sketching her on a pad. A swarthy-faced manservant held a grey umbrella over the artist's head. Beyond was a coach and a coachman standing beside two bay horses.

Seeing she was conscious, the artist said something to her. It sounded friendly. There was such kindliness in his round, highly coloured face that she whispered hoarsely: 'Save me, sir. Oh, for God's sake, save me . . .'

'One moment! Only one moment more, then I shall demand your release,' the gentleman said in English.

He drew a few more lines, held away the sketching pad, studied it through half-shut eyes, looked at her again, then at the drawing. He nodded briskly, handed the pad to his servant and said something. The servant brought his master a flagon of water from the coach.

The gentleman poured some water into his left palm and, dipping his right forefinger into it, moistened Kirsty's lips. 'A little, señorita,' he said. He continued to dab her lips with the water for some time before he allowed her to sip slowly from the flagon. Whenever she showed signs of trying to gulp, he withdrew the flagon and said: 'No, no, slowly, slowly.' His other arm held her firmly round the waist, keeping her upright, so that the iron collar did not drag on her neck so much. As soon as he considered she'd had enough water, the gentleman took the umbrella from his servant and gave an order. The man disappeared from Kirsty's view. She could see nothing but the artist's florid face, full of compassion, as he held her against him and put the umbrella over her, shutting out the blazing sun.

Kirsty sank into a daze against his chest. She was roused by voices from behind the umbrella's wide arc. Peering round it was the loathsome face of the mayor, and behind him the hulking piggy-eyed farrier. She moaned with terror. The gentleman took away his arm from her waist, produced some documents from his breast-pocket and flaffed them in the mayor's face with a great show of authority, bursting forth into a stream of Spanish. Vaguely Kirsty could make out every now and then, for they were repeated so strongly, the words *El Rey* and *Primer Pintor de Cámara*. The mayor began to look frightened and he kept genuflecting and saying '*Si, si, señor*'. Kirsty was not aware of much else until the evil-smelling farrier came close and started to file the collar off her neck. She screamed with pain and fainted.

The jogging of the coach revived her. She was lying on a velvet cushioned seat, her head in the gentleman's lap. His right arm supported her head. Seeing her eyes open, he held a flask of brandy to her mouth and let her take a few sips.

The documents with the official seals were lying on the opposite seat. He laughed and said: 'One is my paper from the last real King of Spain, Carlos the fourth, appointing me Chief Painter to the Court. The other is an order from the usurper, Joseph Bonaparte, commanding me to gather together as many paintings as possible for the museum he has started in the Buenavista Palace. They are documents of little real value. But enough to pull wool over the eyes of that rogue, the mayor. The farrier cannot read, and the mayor can read only the simplest words. The fool thinks I am taking you to a dungeon in the Retiro and that King Joseph himself will supervise your execution. Droll, eh?'

Kirsty closed her eyes. She had no comprehension of what he was talking about. She knew only that she was safe. She was as safe with him as she would have been with dear laughing Rob. The swaying of the coach lulled her into unconsciousness again. Even the great jolts it gave when the coachman strove to guide his horses past the ruts on the road to Madrid failed to rouse her. Francisco Goya held her firmly against his shoulder and looked down at her with pity. Then, as he gently touched the inflamed mark the iron collar had ground into her neck, his eyes hardened with contempt and hatred for the cruelties of humankind.

V

'A little that way, Christina. *Por favor.*' Goya signalled with his hands, and Kirsty inclined her face a little to the left. Although she'd been a member of Goya's household for five years and had learned enough Spanish to make herself understood she still did not know left from right. Her Spanish was so poor and Goya's deafness was so bad that often they made connection only by signs. She could not always understand his English; her own had got thick and clotted through lack of use, and when she got excited and gave tongue she always lapsed into such broad Scots that she had to translate the words into English before trying to translate them into Spanish.

She stood patiently, unmoving now he'd got her into the position he wanted. She did not look at him while he painted; she was so accustomed to him that she never noticed what he was doing, how often he stood back and looked at the canvas, how often he made gestures of despair, how often, after standing with shut eyes, he would attack the painting again and, sometimes when he was pleased, hum a flamenco she didn't know the words of although the tune was as familiar to her now as her own face in a mirror.

She had been the old gentleman's model that many times she wondered no longer what he'd paint her as next. He had made so many sketches of her in different positions that she'd lost count. Many she'd never see again after he'd shown her the drawing at the end of the sitting. He had drawn her as a water carrier; he had drawn her sitting on a donkey. Often he had used her body as a model and then put another face on it. Once he had even got her dressed as an auld wifie and drawn her in such a way that, in the hinterend, she didn't recognize herself. Some pictures she could remember better than others. Three she would never forget.

There was yon first drawing of her chained to the wall. He'd redone it last year with a brush; now it was standing facing the wall of the studio, with 98 marked in the top corner. On it, too, Goya had written *Por Liberal,** making out she was a girl guerilla captured by the Frenchies. And there was a big oil on canvas called *La Carta* where he'd painted her reading a letter (though she couldn't read) while another young woman held an umbrella over her. It was hanging in King Ferdinand's museum in the Prado Avenue alongside other pictures Señor Goya had painted years before she knew him. Kirsty had been to the Prado Museum two-three times to look at it, every time wondering how he'd managed to make her look so young and carefree, and still relieved because he'd garred her wear the ends of her mantilla across her neck — like she was wearing this black mantilla now — to hide the mark left by the iron collar that occasionally, even after all this time, burned like a fiery brand.

And, above all, there was the time he'd painted her naked because he wanted to finish a picture he'd started

*For being of generous spirit.

years ago of his great love, the Duchess of Alba, and had never finished because the Duke had found out. Señor Goya had had trouble about that painting with the Inquisition. It seemed that the Inquisition had been done away with during the war, but wee King Ferdie had revived it, and the priests had been at Goya endless times questioning him about that painting and two he'd done of another naked woman called the Maja. The priests had questioned her too, accusing her of being the model for them all. And, although Señor Goya had managed to persuade them in the long run that the Maja was another woman, a woman long before her time, Kirsty had had to do penance for that one picture of herself naked. For of course she'd become a Catholic. Old Señora Goya, God rest her soul, had begged her to turn when Kirsty was nursing her in her last days.

The Holy Fathers, as you had to call the Inquisitors, had accused her of being Francisco Goya's paramour. Like enough, more folk than them thought she was Goya's fancy woman, but this wasn't the case. She and the auld man were fond of each other, but that was all. She had acted as his housekeeper ever since his wife, poor body, had passed away. Goya was seventy this year, auld enough to be her father, auld enough to be her grandfather if it came to that, the Spaniards marrying so young. It was dreadful the way folk clashed, making up scandal and spreading it without cause. Even though he'd painted her without a stitch on, Señor Goya had aye behaved like a perfect gentleman. Better than many of the so-called English nobility she'd met in the days when she was stravaiging with the troops; like the young sprigs of officers with their grand loud voices and foppish ways only too willing to give her a tumble in the dark where nobody could see them, but looking at her as if she was cauld parritch in broad daylight.

Though there were some fine English gentlemen too. You had to give them their due. Duro Wellington now, there never was a finer nor a more noble man. Yon time he'd come to the studio, after the relief of Madrid, for

Señor Goya to paint his likeness, he'd been very gracious and had tried to speak Spanish to her. Kirsty could not but laugh, he was so solemn bowing over her hand, that she'd had to hide her face ahint her fan. She'd taken to carrying a fan to put foment her mouth after her teeth started to fall out. Her teeth had never been the same since yon brute of a guard had given her a dad on the mouth to make her hold still for the farrier to clamp the collar round her neck. There were such gaps now, so many decayed teeth, that she dare not open her mouth to smile. She aye just curved her lips. It gave her a kind of pussycat look, but that wasn't to be helped.

Even if he'd noticed her lack of teeth, the Duke was too great a gentleman to take heed. He had been the soul of courtesy, treating her like a queen — him that was sic a great man now the Spanish had made him Duke of Ciudad-Rodrigo. Little did he ken that once upon a time she'd been one of the humblest of his camp followers.

Ay, Duro Wellington was a far greater, a far more royal man than that daft cruel crookit wee dwarf, King Ferdinand the seventh, who'd come creeping back to Spain as soon as Duro had made it safe for him. Instead of being king, Ferdie should be the court jester. He was a sleekit wee bauchle, bigoted and full of tricks. Señor Goya had painted his picture twice, so she'd been close enough, handing him wine and cakes and fruit, to have a good look at him, though she'd kept her head bent low, of course, like the señor had warned her. She didn't like the mannikin, royal blood or no royal blood. He was like a vicious wee dog. He wagged his tail in sic a friendly fashion, then when you put out your hand to stroke him he caught it in his teeth. And he was that conceited into the bargain. He'd taken exception to Señor Goya's portraits, saying they made a mock of him.

This, after Señor Goya had gone to sic a peck of trouble to make the cratur' brawer and bigger than he really was! He had trauchled sorely over these paintings. It had been easier with the one of Ferdie on the horse; the horse was that big that Goya had been able to make the dwarfie's legs far longer than they really were, and nobody had noticed, for they'd looked at the horse more than at its rider. But although he'd cloaked the king's daft-like simper in both pictures, he had not been able to hide the mad glaikit look in his eyes. The king had been furious, and both Goya and Kirsty kenned full well that it was him, his royal Catholic Spanish Majesty, that had put the Inquisition on to them. 'Put not your faith in princes,' Goya had said as much to himself as to her, and then when he saw her look he'd told her it was a quotation from a long time back.

Not only had the king been furious at his own likeness not being as grand and awe-inspiring as he would have wished, he had been angry because Señor Goya had painted a picture of the usurper king Joseph Bonaparte that had made Joseph look far more like a king than wee Ferdie, and he had got the Inquisition to accuse Goya of collaboration with the French. And, going a step farther, he'd done away with the museum of pictures Joseph had started in the Buenavista Palace and had them shifted to the Museum of Natural History in the Prado Avenue. Ferdie was so full of spite that even the priests of the Inquisition seemed like bairns in comparision.

But the storm had blown over, and Señor Goya had weathered it so far. Still anon, Kirsty did not trust wee Ferdie and she'd be glad when she was able to get as far away from his clutching hands as she could.

Although the war was long over and Boney had been put away on an island somewhere, she had no wish to gang back to Edinburgh. Her heart was here in Spain with Rob. And here she would bide until she joined him on the other side. Even though she might not bide much longer with Señor Goya. She would have liked things to go on the way they were, she liked looking after Goya and his house and acting as a model whenever he wanted, but he was showing far too much interest for her liking in a queer brazen body he'd just met, Doña Leocadia Zorrilla. Even though the señor was getting on and you might think he'd be long past it, Kirsty knew the signs too well to let them pass unheeded. She kenned fine that before long Doña Leocadia would be invited to bide here as a guest, and soon she'd be so well installed there would be no shifting her. And Kirsty was not prepared to bide in a household ruled by Doña Leocadia. She had her own plans made. There was a baker a couple of streets away who was a widower and needed a helpmate. He and Kirsty were keeping company, as you might say, though Señor Goya did not jalouse this yet. When the time was ripe Kirsty was ready to move her duds to the rooms above the bakery and settle down to make mutton pies for the citizens of that quarter of Madrid.

Mind you, life with the baker would not be like life with Rob. Nobody would ever be like Rob. It was sad that they'd had sic a short time thegither. It seemed almost like a dream now — though sometimes, through the night, she'd waken up crying after seeing him so clearly she'd tried to grip him. A while back Señor Goya had taken her in the coach to Corunna, but she hadn't been able to find Rob's grave. The place looked different. She had searched and searched, but nothing looked like what she remembered. She had seen the grand monument that Marshal Soult had erected in memory of Sir John Moore and all the gallant men who'd died with him, but although this showed she hadn't dreamt it all, it wasn't much consolation. No monument, nothing or nobody would ever be any consolation for Rob and the wonderful months they'd had together. Howsomever, Jaime the baker was a fine-looking young childe — he was a year younger than herself, and she'd make sure he never found out — and he was generous and good-natured, and she kenned full well she'd be happy with him.

Goya put down his brush and stood back, hands on hips, from the painting. He smiled and nodded with satisfaction. '*Muchos gracias*, Christina,' he said. 'You have great patience.'

Kirsty stretched her arms and gave a wee sigh of relief. She moved towards the easel. 'Looky now, eh?' she said, and she nudged Goya. '*Por favor, señor*? A wee keek?'

Goya bowed elaborately and extended his hand towards the painting. Kirsty looked at the likeness for a long time. It was her as she'd been seven years ago. He hadn't painted in the lines around her eyes. Only the cat-like smile, not showing any teeth, belonged to the here and now. She was beautiful again.

'Whaty calla?' she said in a loud voice, leaning towards him and mouthing her words. 'Whaty you name, eh?'

Goya pursed his lips until they stood out like a rosebud in his plump pink face. 'Spanish lady in a black mantilla?' he asked.

'But I'm no' Spanish,' she protested.

'You look Spanish,' he said, with an expansive shrug. 'Who is to know the difference?'

'But even if I was Spanish, I'm no' a lady, *señor.*'

Goya looked at her, he looked at the painting. He smiled tenderly and took her hands in his. 'You are a Scottish lady,' he said, bowing to her. 'A Scottish lady of great and warm and noble heart.'

Auld Mother Claus

Late on Christmas Eve the bazaar in the basement of a large store in Princes Street was still doing a roaring trade. Worn-out assistants kept looking at the big wall clock while frenziedly wrapping up parcels. There was a queue at Santa Claus's Corner waiting to dip into the two sacks labelled *50p a dip* and *75p a dip* stacked on either side of him on his sleigh.

'Ma, I want another dip,' a child yelled.

'Ye're not gettin' another dip,' his tired mother said. 'Ye've already had two dips. It's time we were home and ye were in yer bed.'

'I'm not goin' till I get another dip,' he said. 'I'm goin' to yell and yell and yell till I get it.'

Without waiting to see the effect, he joined the queue. His mother sighed with resignation and stood beside him, putting down her loaded shopping bags with relief.

When they reached Santa's sleigh, the little boy did not bother to listen to Santa's greeting. He thrust his hands into the seventy-five pence sack and started to rummage around.

'Haven't you been here before, dear?' Santa said.

'Ay, this is his third dip,' his mother said. 'Here, Rikki, it'll have to be the fifty pence bag this time. My money's about spent.'

'Well, why let him have another dip?' Santa said tartly. 'Twa dips is enough for any bairn.'

'Ye've got a point there,' the young mother said. 'Stop rakin', Rikki. Santy says ye've had enough.'

'What's Santy got to dae wi' how many dips I have?' Rikki cried belligerently.

'Because it's Santy who's in charge here,' said the stout figure in the red coat and red hood and white woolly whiskers. 'If Santy says "No", Santy means "No". Ye've had yer fair share o' dips, son. We're goin' to close up shop for the night.'

'Belt up, ye silly auld skate,' Rikki shouted. 'I'm havin' another dip.'

'Rikki!' his mother cried. 'Say ye're sorry to Santy.'

'You belt up too.' Rikki rummaged again in the seventy-five pence sack. He pulled out a toy and said: 'I'm havin' this.'

'What ye're goin' to have, ma bonnie wee man, is a ding on the ear,' Santa said. 'And I'm invitin' yer mammy to give ye one.'

'Oh dear,' the mother said ineffectually.

'Go on, hen, give him a guid clip,' Santa said. 'It'll do him the world o' good. As head of this department, I give ye full permission to clip him one. If you'll no', I have a guid mind to do it masel'.'

'You and who else?' Rikki said. 'Belt up, ye auld jessie. Ye talk like a jessie. Doesn't he, Ma? Are ye a jessie, Santy?'

'I'll jessie ye, ye snippy wee shaver!' Santa cried. 'Any more cracks and I'll scud yer hint end for ye.'

'Oh dear,' the mother said again.

'Give him the money and let's get away hame,' Rikki said. And he reached up and pulled off Santa Claus's beard.

'It's a wumman, Ma!' he cried.

'Ay, it's auld Mother Claus,' said the female Santa. 'And if ye don't buzz out o' this bazaar quick I'll dig ma claws into ye. Hard.'

She took off her hood and shook her short grey hair. 'It

was ma grandchildren that drove me into takin' this job,' she said to a bystander. 'By God, if I'd kent what I would have to put up with, I'd have stuck to bingo in the hope o' makin' a bit extry for Christmas.'

It happened because Harry and Lesley were hostile when their father told them he had invited their grandmother for a week at Christmas.

'What d'you want to ask her for?' Harry said. 'She'll just make everybody miserable, interfering the whole time. It's not that I mind myself, mind. I'm so involved with my own thing, I'm quite impervious to her. It's Ma I'm thinking about.'

'Ye don't need to worry about Ma, son,' Geordie Hyslop said. 'Ma is quite capable of looking after herself. In fact, it was Ma who suggested it.'

'She was just being polite,' Lesley said.

'I tell you, Dad, it's just not on,' Harry said. 'The old lady doesn't go down well here, and you know it. It's no skin off my nose if she stays for the New Year as well as Christmas. I won't be in much to be bothered by her; I've been asked to a lot of parties. But what I'm getting at is — I wanted to ask two-three pals from the athletic club for a wee get-together on Christmas Day, and I can't do that if the old lady's here. She'd drive us all round the twist. You know what she is: aye poking in her neb. Even at the funeral she couldn't avoid saying my hair was too long and telling me to get it cut.'

'Well, if it comes to that, son,' Geordie said. 'It's ower long for my taste too.'

'It's my hair,' Harry said. 'I need my hair like this to preserve my image in the sporting media.'

'The sporting media!' Geordie laughed. 'God help us! You said two sentences when you were interviewed on the telly, and you spoke for three minutes on the radio when you described how you won the under sixteens' swimming championship.'

'Well, it was a start, wunnit?' Harry said. 'I'm aiming to be a sports commentator when I'm finished on the athletics scene.'

'Finished on the athletics scene!' Geordie laughed so much that he spluttered. 'D'ye hear that, Ma? Oh, this is rich!'

Jean Hyslop looked up from darning a cigarette burn in a sheet and smiled. She said nothing.

'You've only got one toe on the athletic scene so far, son, so stop haverin',' Geordie said. 'Anyway, that has nothin' to do with your granny comin' for Christmas.'

'Oh, but it has. I tell you, Dad, it'll be a big mistake to have Gran here for any length of time. A few hours every second Sunday is bad enough, but to be deeved by her for three whole days — aw, we'd all end up in the bin.'

'Besides, she makes such a noise supping her soup,' Lesley said. 'And it's me that's always got to sit next her. Such a great privilege. She'll insist on having soup at least twice a day, and she'll say "It puts marrow in your bones" about a dozen times at every meal.'

'That's enough from you, miss,' her father said. 'We can do without your one-and-ninepenceworth.'

'It's Freudian, Dad, that's what it is,' Harry said. 'You must still feel you want to be tied to her apron-strings.'

'Any more of your lip, my man, and I'll draw my hand across your jaw. In fact, I'll do more. Big as ye are, I'll take down yer breeks and put ye across my knee. Ye wouldnie like folk to see ma finger-prints on yer bum the next time you're swimmin' on the telly, would ye?'

'Now, Geordie,' Jean Hyslop said. 'As for you, Harry, less of it. Upsetting your father. Remember his blood pressure.'

'What's my blood pressure got to do with it?' Geordie cried. 'I'll give this young pup a guid lammin' if I get any more o' his gas.'

'Take it easy now, Dad,' Harry said. 'Don't say anything you'd regret.'

'Regret! Dear God . . . '

'Not another cheep out of either of you,' Jean Hyslop said. 'I'm ashamed of you, Harry. Going on like that about your poor lonely old granny. Begrudging her a bit of happiness.'

'Well, she doesn't dig us, and we don't dig her.'

'Enough!' Jean held up her hand. 'She's coming for Christmas, and that's that.'

Mrs Margaret Hyslop was seventy. She had been a widow for six months. She lived in a tenement overlooking what had been the London and North Eastern Railway when she got married about fifty years ago.

'I'm like yon French detective that Rupert Davies played on the telly,' she told Nan Finlayson, a friend she'd made recently at bingo. 'He wrote a book *The Man Who Watched the Trains Go By*. I read it out the library. Well, I'm the woman. I can sit at my kitchen window quite jecko for hours watchin' the trains. I ken a lot o' the engine-drivers to wave to. Oh, I get fair thrilled when I see the London trains whizz by, and often I wish I was on them, on my way to Piccadilly to live it up.'

'Well, why don't you go for a wee trip?' Miss Finlayson said.

'Couldnie afford it, m'dear. Anyway, it wouldnie be like what it was when we used to go to London when poor Tam was alive. Often when I was nursin' him in his long illness I longed to get my horns out, but now he's gone it wouldnie be the same. So I play bingo instead and content myself with thinkin' about all the guid times we had.'

'But is bingo enough?' Miss Finlayson said. 'Surely ye need somethin' else to take up your attention? After all, ye're still a young woman and full o' go.'

'I ha'e my dreams,' Mrs Hyslop said. 'Another cup, m'dear?' And as she poured the tea, she sang: 'Meet me tonight in dreamland, sweet dreamy dreamland, there let my dreams come true . . .'

She was not enamoured of the Christmas invitation

either. 'I don't want to go, Nan,' she confided. 'I feel it's my duty, but I'm not keen. My grandchildren give me the pip.'

'Och, Meg, what a like thing to say about your only son's bairns.' Miss Finlayson was genuinely shocked. 'You're lucky to have them. How'd ye like to be like me — on my own, with nobody to turn to in moments of stress? I wish I had grandchildren.'

'No' if they're like mine,' Mrs Hyslop said. 'If I could get rid of mine in a raffle, ye'd be welcome to them.'

'What's wrong with them?'

'Everythin',' their granny said. 'To be quite honest, we're in different classes and don't see eye to eye. My son Geordie's an insurance agent and has a very posh bungalow at Blackhall. He's gone up in the world. He's never had to dirty his hands. Not like his puir father. My husband was with the Corporation. He was a refuse official. Not to put too fine a point on it, he was a dustman. A scaffy, y'know. He started with a horse and cart, but when he got aulder he was transferred to the depot to do administration.'

'A most useful and necessary job,' her friend said. 'And most arduous.'

'Ay, it was arduous all right,' Mrs Hyslop said. 'He was on the job night and day. Always at it. He was a most conscientious man, aye thinkin' about my welfare. I miss him sorely.'

'I'm sure of it, dear.' Miss Finlayson oozed sympathy. 'There, there, ye mustnie greet.'

'Ay, my son has gone up a step in the world, like I was sayin'.' Mrs Hyslop dabbed her eyes with her hankie. 'And his son wants to rise even higher. Harry's seventeen and still at the school. He's goin' to the Varsity next year, but that's only to keep him frae takin' a job. He's mad keen on sport and he's aimin' to be a head bummer in the sportin' world so that he'll never need to do a hand's turn all his life. There'll be no holdin' him if he gets all he's hopin' for. He talks awful tosted breed, if ye unnerstan' my Morning-side accent! Like Tom Cable said in a pantymime once when we were young. D'ye mind o' Tom Cable? Oh, he was a great comic, Tom Cable.'

'Him and Tommy Lorne,' Miss Finlayson sighed. 'And don't forget Harry Gordon.'

'Will I ever?' Mrs Hyslop sighed too. ' "Them were the days," as he aye used to say. There are no comedians like them now. The folk billed as comics wouldnie make a cat laugh. The best comics are the unconscious ones like ma grandson. His pan-loaf accent would make ye die. He's gettin' ready, y'see, to be a great sports commentator on the telly after he's made his mark in athletics. He's got it all marked out. He was near greetin' because he wasn't chosen to go to Montreal, to the Olympic Games. So was the coach at this athletic club he goes to. The coach thinks Harry's the whole cheese at swimmin', runnin' and the high jump, not to mention judo. He thinks so much o' him he's made Harry more swelled headit than he's any right to be. Harry spent the whole o' the Olympics sittin' in front o' the telly tellin' the others what to do. Mind ye, he had some cause. Britain didnie do as well as was expected in the Games, did she?'

'Did ye hear the auld woman on the wireless, Irene somebody — Nicholson, I think it was — who'd won a gold medal for swimmin' in the Olympics of 1912 or 1910 or whenever it was? She was awful good. They weren't all togged up in fancy uniforms in thae days. "Not even blazers", she said. There was nothin' swelled headit about her.'

'I wish ma granddaughter had heard her and taken a leaf out her book. She's as bad as Harry. She's only fourteen and she's a right wee madam already. She knows more than anybody else in Blackhall because she's been abroad a few times. Trips with the school, ye ken. Two days once in Belgium; then two days in France. And they went for a week last summer to Germany. Ye'd think she'd been all over the world. She's got a boy friend in Munich and writes to him every week. Long screeds in German. I've seen her writin' the letters, so I ken it's no lie. Oh, she's very clever and all that. Her head'll burst wi' all her knowledge one o' thae days. I hope I'm there when it happens. I'm lookin' forrit to seein' what comes out. What I'm no' lookin' forrit to is a week in her company and sittin' next her at the table. I ken she shudders at every bite I take, so I make a noise just for sheer devilment. "Must you sup your soup like that, Gran?" she says. "It's so common." I'd common the wee besom if I had her in my control for a couple o' days.'

'It doesn't sound to me like a very happy Christmas,' Miss Finlayson said. 'If I was you, I'd find some excuse for not goin'. Why don't you take a job in a shop? That would keep ye busy over the Christmas period.'

'It's an idea,' Mrs Hyslop said. 'But it's a bit late to think about it now.'

'Och no. I ken the thing that would suit ye a fair dab. They're lookin' for somebody to act as Father Christmas in the store where I have a part-time job in the canteen. They always have a man, but the last few years all the men they've had have gone on the bottle and frightened the bairns. So they'd be willin' to consider a woman this year.'

'Well, it's worth tryin',' Mrs Hyslop said laughing. 'It'll be a nice wee change for the bairns to have a Mother Christmas. More homely. I'm no' likely to frighten them. Nor they me.'

'I hadn't reckoned, though, on yon forward wee shaver and his kind,' Granny Hyslop said, telling her family at Blackhall of her unmasking, when, instead of coming for a week, she had graciously conceded to come for lunch on the first of the two government-ordained Christmas Bank Holidays. 'It's a pity they didnie live in Cuba where Fidel Castro has changed Christmas to the summer-time and has rationed each bairn to three toys. And cheap ones at that.'

They were about to take their seats at table when Jean Hyslop said: 'Will you sit across there, Mother, beside Harry.'

'Delighted,' Granny said, and she made a face at Lesley

as she sat down.

She turned to Harry and said: 'And how are ye gettin' on, son?'

'I'm tremendously involved in training for the next Olympics at Moscow in 1980,' he said. 'My coach says I've every chance of representing Britain in the 800 metres and one of the swimming classes and judo.'

'Good for you,' Granny said. 'I hope ye get a lot o' medals.'

'I expect I'll get one gold, anyway,' he said. 'The next four years are going to be very significant ones for me. They'll give me a great opportunity for learning all the technical points and help eventually to promote my career in the media.'

'Fancy that,' she said, unfolding her scarlet paper napkin. 'Well, I might come to Moscow to watch ye if I make enough money at bingo before then. Ye're not the only one, ye ken, son, that's involved in a great ploy. There's no future for me as auld Mother Claus, but by 1980 I have every hope o' bein' the Bingo Queen o' Edinburgh.'

Nostalgia for a Waltz Dream

Mrs Nance McQueen and her friend, Mr Whittaker, heard the noise a few minutes after they left the pub. Half way along the street Mrs McQueen clutched his arm and cried: 'Listen!' He nodded solemnly. Mrs McQueen pressed her lips together, and they quickened their steps. Mrs McQueen swayed against him as she teetered on her stilt-like heels, and she was hiccupping with exertion by the time they reached the front door. They were no sooner inside than the woman in the ground-floor flat appeared at her door and said: 'I don't want to complain, but reelly this is a bit thick.'

'Half a mo',' Mrs McQueen cried, brushing past her. 'Keep your wig on. I'll settle her hash in a jiffy.'

'Jean!' she shouted, rushing upstairs. 'Jean! Will ye stop it this instant!'

But the raucous roaring of rock 'n' roll went on. 'Jean, d'ye hear me?' Nance cried, bursting into the sitting-room.

The girl leaning against the radiogram glanced up in surprise. 'You're back early,' she said.

'Early!' Nance screeched. 'Not half early enough, if ye ask me. What d'ye mean by makin' all this racket? How often have I told you . . . ?'

'Racket, doll?' The girl switched back her black pony tail. 'There's no racket.'

'Well, what d'ye call this then? A quiet Sunday At Home?'

'Now look, doll,' Jean said, putting her hands nonchalantly on her green jeans-clad hips.

'Don't you doll me!' her mother cried. 'I won't have it.'

'Nance, Nance,' Mr Whittaker warned.

'What's he doing here?' Jean jerked her head in his direction, without looking at him. 'I thought we made a bargain that you could see him as often as you liked and anywhere you liked so long as he didn't come near the house?'

'Bargain! Bargain!' Nance nearly lost her breath. 'Oh, if your granny had just lived to see this day!'

'And what would your grandfather have said!' Jean jeered. 'Aw, don't hand me that line, doll.'

'I'll have less of your old-fashioned lip,' Nance said. 'Or auld as ye are I'll take ye across my knee and skelp your backside.'

'You'd have a job,' Jean said. 'Be your age, hon.'

She turned away and began to shuffle through the records of Elvis Presley, Tommy Steele, Frankie Vaughan, and Bill Haley and his Comets.

'Be my age!' Nance screeched. 'Oh!' She sat down, her heavy breasts sagging inside her smart black dress. She clenched her fists, then she opened them and, curling the fingers like claws, pushed them through her shoulder-length peroxided hair. 'Oh, you limmer! If I had *dared* to speak to your granny like that . . .'

Jean put another record on the radiogram, saying: 'I'll turn the volume down a bit this time, but farther than that I won't go. Get him out of here before I spew.'

'Come on, Nance, we'll go to the Seventy Club,' Mr Whittaker said.

'We'll do nothing of the kind,' Mrs McQueen cried. 'I'm staying right here to give this bitch a piece of my mind. And so are you.'

'Now, Nance,' he said.

'Get!' Jean said, without looking at either of them. She was staring straight ahead, her eyes like bits of black glass, her face expressionless, as she moved her shoulders and hips in time with the new cacophony from the radiogram. 'If you don't know how to lead your life, I know how to lead mine.'

In a taxi on their way to the Seventy Club in Soho ('It's well named!' had been Jean's parting shot. 'Just the job for a couple of beat-up old squares like you!') Nance repaired her make-up while Mr Whittaker clucked soothing monosyllables. She did not listen. Her mind was far away as she tried to smooth out the wrinkles around her eyes. Now, if I had talked to Dad like that, she mused, I'd have got a scud on the lug. Like the time we were biding in that room in Abercrombie Place and I went to the pictures to see Willi Fritsch . . .

Tears of nostalgia suddenly flooded her eyes and as she put up her hands to try to check them and crouched sobbing against Mr Whittaker's shoulder, Nance whispered: 'I wish I was a lassie again . . . I wish I could see *A Waltz Dream* again . . .'

The year was 1926. Nance Jeffrey was thirteen, and her father was on the dole. He had lost his job after the General Strike. The previous year the family had come to Edinburgh from Kirkcaldy. They had not been able to get a house and, while waiting for one in the new housing scheme near Granton, they had got a large unfurnished room for ten shillings a week in one of the sedate grey streets close to Princes Street.

'It's an awful price,' Mrs Jeffrey moaned to her friends. 'Ten bob for a wheen square yards o' bare boards. And one and ninepence a week extra for the use o' a gas-ring! It's fair profiteerin', that's what it is. If I wasnie feared to be flung oot on the street again I'd go to the polis aboot it. That auld Mrs Ritchie should be prosecuted for chargin' such a rent.'

As long as Mr Jeffrey was in the job he had got in a brewery, the family managed all right, though as Mrs Jeffrey kept saying: 'It's a tight squeeze. Five o' us in that one wee box mornin', noon and night. We'd near need a hurlie-bed ablow the bed!' This was a family joke. Nance was getting too big to sleep with her younger sister and brother in one of the two double-beds that were crammed end-to-end along one wall. And whenever she remonstrated, saying she would rather sleep on the slippery horsehair sofa, her mother always said: 'Be thankful you didnie live when your granny was a lassie. *She* had to sleep in a room a damned sight smaller than this. And there were eight o' them, laddies and lassies, and they had to have one bed in ablow the other, and it was wheeled oot every night before they said their prayers.'

But when Bob Jeffrey got the sack because the foreman in the brewery yard had his knife in him not so much for going out on strike with the others but for having heard him say that the foreman's head was 'as thick as shite in a bottle', conditions became more serious. Some weeks they were not able to pay the rent, and soon they were in arrears. Mrs Jeffrey tried to help the situation by sometimes getting jobs as a waitress for a large firm of caterers. On these spasmodic occasions – usually an all-night dance or a big dinner party – she would bring home some of the leavings. And at two or three in the morning when their mother came in, white-faced and exhausted from rushing about for hours from kitchen to table or buffet, the children would sit up in bed and watch while she unpacked her old black gladstone bag. This bag was intended for her cap, apron and spare pair of shoes; but these did not take up much space, so there was plenty of room for whatever food Mrs Jeffrey had been able to salvage. 'Mind you,' she often said, 'it's nothin' like as big a bag as some o' the waitresses have. Auld Miss McCaig now! She carts a muckle great portmanteau around wi' her. I've seen her stuff a whole chicken into it, forby puddings and tarts. She must be fair lapsided by the time she trauchles hame.'

Although Nance was inclined to be sniffy about her mother working as a waitress and terrified that anybody would find out — she lived in agony for weeks after Mrs Jeffrey told her that the mother of one of her school friends had been waiting at a banquet in the City Chambers — she had no scruples about eating her share of the jellies, slices of roast beef, and pieces of lemon meringue pie that Mrs Jeffrey brought home in grease-proof paper. These additions to the family larder all helped, but still they were always in arrears with the rent. Coming home from school in the afternoon Nance was always in a ferment, wondering if she would manage to get upstairs without the huge Alsatian dog from the flat beneath bounding out, barking and snuffling at her; but even that stomach-turning experience was nothing compared to her humiliation if she heard Mrs Ritchie's needle-sharp voice saying: 'I must have something on account, Mrs Jeffrey. Even a few shillings. It's not good enough. I have to put up with all the discomforts of having such a lot of strangers in my house, so I don't see why I shouldn't get some compensation.'

'She never thinks about what we've got to put up wi', does she?' Bob Jeffrey often said when he would come back in the evening after tramping from a builder's yard in Newington to a sawmill at Powderhall, and from there to Leith docks, in search of work, always to be met with the same story: 'Sorry, son, there's nothin' doin'. Try us again in another week or two.'

At the beginning of December Nance got a part-time job. After school she worked from half-past four to six or seven every evening as a message-girl for a firm of drapers in Princes Street. On Saturdays she went to the shop at eight in the morning and, after scrubbing the front door-step and cleaning the long brass plates beneath the windows, she delivered parcels at the houses of gentry in Morningside, Merchiston and Corstorphine, being warned every now and then to be sure to go to the back doors. Vaguely she resented this. But she did not resent the money she got for tram-fares, for she found that by calculating the distances between ports of call and walking part of the way to cheaper fare-stages she could save some of the money. In this way she sometimes made twopence or threepence in an evening, and more on Saturdays when she had more calls. Often, disregarding the manageress's reminder about 'Be sure and go to the tradesmen's entrance now, Nancy,' she would ring the front-door bell, and sometimes — if it were a gentleman taken with her pretty little pink face and auburn hair — she would get a tip of threepence or sixpence. She never told her parents about these small extras; she regarded them as her rightful due for her cleverness. Every Saturday afternoon she handed her wages of four shillings and sixpence to her mother, and got back sixpence for her pocket.

She was supposed to finish at one o'clock on Saturdays, but often it was much later before she thankfully handed over the last parcel. On the days that she finished on time, she went home for dinner, and then with her sixpence pocket-money went to a cinema matinée, paying either twopence or threepence, depending on how she felt about sitting in the cheap or the dearer seats. On the days she was late, sometimes she dashed straight to the pictures and got home in time for tea; other times she waited and went to the pictures in the evening. Occasionally, if she had had a good week from tips and tram-fares, she would go to the pictures twice on Saturdays, as well as her usual visit during the week.

One Tuesday evening, having told her mother she would go straight to the cinema after finishing her job, she went to the Savoy to see Gloria Swanson in *Madame Sans-Gêne*. When she got there she found long queues for all seats. After hovering for a few minutes, wondering if the queues would start to move, she decided to come earlier the following night — she had saved one shilling and ninepence, so felt she could lash out for once — and she hurried along to the Grand to see Ivor Novello in *The Rat*. But there were long queues at the Grand too. It was getting late, and

Nance calculated that if she stood in a queue she might miss the beginning of the film. Ach to hell, she thought, *The Rat*'s on all week, I can easy see it on Saturday. I'll take a walk up to Leith Walk and see what's on there. I'm not going home yet to look at Dad's sour face. Ma's out at some dance and won't be home till yon time. I might as well wait till the other kids're in bed.

Outside the Salon she lingered and looked at the stills. *A Waltz Dream.* It was a German film she had never heard of. Who was in it? Mady Christians, Xenia Desni and Willi Fritsch. Never heard of them. But gee, if that was Willi Fritsch he was right handsome and no mistake.

The last showing was billed for nine o'clock. It was just on that now, and on an impulse Nance scurried to the box office and put down fourpence. For the next two hours she sat entranced, even though it was an unpadded wooden seat six rows from the screen. She fell completely, madly and irrevocably in love with Willi Fritsch.

His blond good looks intoxicated her. The film was set in a Ruritanian kingdom, and Willi was a prince who had arrived to marry a princess he had never seen. Pretty, dark-haired Mady Christians was the princess, but Nance did not pay much attention to her. She craned forward, waiting impatiently for the scenes where Willi was the centre of attraction, and she gazed wide-eyed every time he was shown in close-up. Willi changed out of his smart, tight-fitting uniform, donned a lounge suit and a straw hat, and slipped out of the palace to wander incognito among the crowds who were making merry in the streets in honour of the engagement of their princess. In a shop window he saw a large photograph of himself in uniform, and he was looking at it when two big fat women jostled him rudely, and the subtitle flashed: 'Young man, take off your hat to Our Prince.' Which he did in a daze. Soon after that he met a dazzling, fair-haired girl, Xenia Desni, and they fell in love. Nance could not really concentrate on the story – it was a gay, light, sophisticated affair of champagne bubbles and Viennese waltzes – she was so carried away by Willi's flashing teeth, moist lips and glistening eyes. It was many years later before she learned of the effects got by glycerine, but that night she sat in a ferment of adoration. Willi dancing, Willi riding a prancing charger, Willi in one dashing uniform after the other . . . Willi making love, first to Xenia, and then to Mady (who got him in the end, of course), Willi, the gay, laughing prince . . .

Nance went home in a dream, waltzing through the dark Edinburgh streets in Willi's arms. She was jostled out of it when the Alsatian downstairs bounded out, barking furiously, and gripped the hem of her dress. She screamed.

'Maybe that'll teach you to come hame a bit earlier, my lady,' her father said after he had got her safely inside. 'What do ye mean by stayin' out to this time o' night?'

'But I was just at the pictures,' she gasped. 'Ye kent I was goin' to the pictures. I tellt Ma.'

'Ay, but ye should have been hame by half-past nine,' he said. 'Don't you dare stay out as late as this again or ye'll feel the weight o' my hand. We have enough to worry us wi'out you stravaigin' the streets as late as this.'

The next evening Nance went to see *A Waltz Dream* again, but she saw an earlier performance. She was tempted to stay and see the film through twice, but fear of her father made her leave soon after it had started again, also fear of the attendants hovering in the aisle, one of them likely to pounce and say: 'Have ye bought this seat, hen? Would ye like me to bring ye a pillow and blankets?'

She saw *A Waltz Dream* four times that week. Even Gloria Swanson and Ivor Novello, favourite stars of hers, were given the go-by in favour of the glamorous Willi Fritsch. During the next few weeks, all other films — except a few she felt she couldn't miss — were abandoned in favour of the one with the German charmer. She followed *A Waltz Dream* all over Edinburgh, scanning the advertisements in the *Evening News* to see where it was to be shown next. She saw it in a bug-hutch in Gorgie, in a flea-pit in Leith, and in an old tin-roofed shed, once a mission now a cinema, in Tollcross. Her savings from her tram-fares and tips were poured out lavishly on trips to the remotest suburbs of the city. By the time she had seen it more than a dozen times she knew Willi's every movement, every flashing smile, every wave of his crisp blond hair.

And then, after it had disappeared from her view for several weeks, and every daydream was full of its memories, she saw that it was paying a return visit to the Salon in Leith Walk. And so she saw it on the Thursday and Friday evenings. On Saturday she finished her job as quickly as possible, throwing her savings wildly around on tram-fares, and dashed to the matinée. Then she went home for tea, and was back at the Salon in time for the first evening showing at six o'clock. Instinct told her that this would be the last time she would see it, so, defying the thought of her father, and disregarding the attendants prowling up and down the aisles, she sat on and saw the entire programme again.

It was a quarter to eleven when she left the cinema. She scurried out, hiding her face in the collar of her coat in case Tim, the doorman, would notice her and remember how long she had been there.

As she was turning into Abercrombie Place a man leaning against the railings stepped out and grabbed her shoulder. She yelled. He slapped her face.

'How often have I tellt ye, my lady, to come hame in time?' Bob Jeffrey hissed. 'I've been out huntin' for ye for the past two hours.' And he gave her a blow on the side of the head. 'That'll teach ye to start walkin' the streets at your age.'

'As if we havenie enough to worry us without wonderin' about you!' her mother cried when they got in. 'I've been fair demented, thinkin' ye'd had an accident or — or — that somethin' bad had happened to ye. If I had dared stay oot as late as this when I was your age your granny would have skelped the skin off my backside wi' a belt.'

'Well, if I ever have a wee lassie,' Nance whined to herself, slipping into bed beside her brother and sister, 'I'll see that she gets to do what she likes.'

And now here was Jean, nineteen and a fair problem with all this rock 'n' roll. Two or three nights a week she went out with boys to jazz clubs, and the other nights she stayed at home and made the neighbours' lives hell with her radiogram. Nance didn't know what to do with her. Nance herself had got married in 1939 to Willie McQueen because he was the dead spit and image of Willi Fritsch. She had had other lads before Willie, but somehow or other none had come up to scratch, and when Willie appeared with his fair wavy hair and flashing eyes, Nance knew this was it. She'd been a bit disappointed when Willie went into the Navy at the outbreak of war, for she'd been looking forward to seeing him in a guardsman's tight uniform, breeches and top boots and spurs and all that, but she had to admit that he looked a real smasher in his bellbottoms. But he hadn't lasted long, poor soul, he'd gone down with the *Ark Royal.* And so Nance had been a bit surprised to become a widow with a tiny baby. She had stayed in Edinburgh for a while, then when Jean was old enough they had come to London, and now Nance was manageress of a baker's shop and doing very nicely, thank you. Sometimes she thought about Willie McQueen, wondering what would have happened if he'd survived the war, but mostly she didn't bother; she'd had the odd boyfriend now and then, and now she was going steady with Mr Whittaker, who had his own good-going little business but also a wife in an asylum so that he couldn't get a divorce. It was a pity, but there it was; there was nothing they could do except hope for the best, a quick despatch for Ada, the poor daft cratur'. It was such a nuisance that Jean didn't seem to care for Mr Whittaker, in fact she had taken a real scunner to him, and sometimes Nance was at her wits' end, wondering what to do. If only Jean would be a sensible lassie and give up all this rockin' and rollin' dirt and go to the pictures instead . . .

As she leaned against Mr Whittaker and gave her face another going over, Nance wondered what had happened to Willi Fritsch. Goodness, it was nearly thirty-three years ago . . . You'd hardly credit how time flew! Poor Willi, he must be bald and toothless by this time . . . if he had got through the war all right.* Thirty-three years . . .

For a moment Nance Jeffrey was a girl again, dancing with the glamorous Willi, watching the champagne bubbles disappear to the strains of a Viennese waltz. Tra la la la tra la la la ta dee dum dum . . . *I'm the merry widow of a gay deceased* . . . And then she was sitting in the taxi drawing up outside the Seventy Club. She giggled and struggled out, pulling down her girdle with a girlish squeal while she glanced coquettishly at the taxi-driver, who was young and good looking. And she giggled again, lurching against portly Mr Whittaker escorting her so gallantly across the pavement. But as they went into the discreetly lit entrance and their eardrums were almost split by the moaning of a glottal-stopped moron rendering a rock 'n' roll number, the giggle turned into a gasp, and Nance cried raucously: 'Aw no! No, I just cannie take it!'

*Willi Fritsch died in July 1973, aged seventy-two.

Dusty Springtime

'So this is the Boul' Mich'?' I said. 'At last! After all these years . . .'

Pat said: 'Nobody calls it the Boul' Mich', Gran, except stupid old hack writers.'

'And nobody calls me Gran except stupid young bitches.'

'Don't crab,' she said. 'What am I going to call you, then? I'm Addie's daughter and you're Addie's mum, even though you're dressed like a doll and acting like one.'

'Don't rub it in, or I'll give you a dad on the jaw,' I said. 'Call me what you used to call me.'

'All right, Miss Nell,' she said.

We walked on and on, me following like a wee dog, for she took that big strides, until at last she said: 'Let's go along here, to *Le Balzar*, for a drink.'

We turned into the Rue des Écoles. I was going to have a decko at the stills outside a cinema but Pat walked straight past it and into a café. She sat down at a long table, her back to the street, and opened the Paris edition of the *Daily Telegraph*. I sat opposite her but couldn't see the street because of a partition. 'What's the idea of sitting away back here?' I said. 'Why don't we sit at a table on the pavement?'

'Only tourists sit there.'

A young waiter greeted Pat in a gabble of French. All I could make out was her name: Madame Curtis. She stood up and they shook hands. 'This is my grandmother,' she said, waving at me.

He bowed. He didn't quite click his heels together, but it felt like it. *'Madame,'* he said.

'How are ye, son?' I said, fluttering my eyelashes.

Pat said: 'What would you like to drink, Miss Nell?'

Fancy asking me that likes a wee drop of the auld kirk such a daft question.

'You're not getting whisky,' she said. 'Try *un Americano.'*

This was a raspberry coloured drink in a glass that had ice all frosted around the rim. I tasted it. 'Not so dusty.' I took another sip and smacked my lips. 'In fact, it's right gorgeous. It has more than a touch of class, hen. Like me!'

'Don't call me hen,' she said.

'Why don't we sit outside?' I said. 'I didn't come to Paris to sit in the inner darkness of a place like this. I want to see what's cooking.'

'Have it your own way,' she said. And she got up and we carried our drinks to a table on the pavement. But Pat didn't look at life going by. She opened the *Telegraph* and held it in front of her like a shield.

'This is the bar Sartre and Simone de Beauvoir use,' she said. 'If we wait long enough you'll maybe see them.'

'Who're they when they're at home?' I said.

'Look Gran, don't pretend to be daft. I know you know. Remember I'm not the studio audience. I heard you last ‚week in that comic programme of yours pretending you'd never heard of Elizabeth Taylor.'

This programme I do every week on the radio is called *Glamorous Grannies Who Put the World to Rights.* The other grannies are old pros, too. Tilly O'Toole was on the halls and in revue, like myself, and April Maxwell was a musical comedy star. It's a kind of quiz programme, and us three old tarts take on all comers, no holds barred. Certain people are picked, beforehand, from the studio audience — well, maybe not really 'picked', I think they shove themselves forward — and they ask questions and argue with us. If they can stand the pace, that is. We're all supposed to be kept in order by Mary Munday, the quiz mistress. She's another old trouper. Only she was legit. She played the mother or the maiden aunt in drama for years and years before she got to be a high-head-one in the B.B.C. Most of those that ask questions are teenagers, students and the like. They ask the daftest things. Trying to take the mickey out of us, y'know. Questions like: What do you think about abortions? Should girls have intercourse before they're sixteen? Do the Grannies think a girl should marry a man older than herself? What would you do if you were walking along a dark lane and a man in a car offered you a lift? Tilly and me are not long in putting the kibosh on the clever dicks. April's a bit more ladylike, but she can give them a right sting too, when she's riled. By jings, we make the fur fly. But we do get into some very nasty corners occasionally. Like last week when this imperent wee madam with long hair reaching to the hem of her mini-skirt says to me: 'Oh, Miss Linton — you don't mind if I call you Elaine, do you? I seem to have known you on the stage for such a *long* time . . .'

I nipped in with: 'And just how auld are *you,* hen?' But she ignored it and went on: 'Well, Elaine, I know you're the youngest grandmother on this programme, so I think this is a question you should be able to answer without taxing your brains too much. If you were Elizabeth Taylor and you became the youngest grandmother in Show Biz, what would you do? Would you disown your son? Or would you laugh it off?'

'And who's Elizabeth Taylor when she's at home?' I said.

Mary Munday cried: 'Oh, Nelly!' She keeps butting in

like this to give us a chance, she says, to cover up awkward questions and give us time to think. 'Don't tell us you don't know who Elizabeth Taylor is.'

'Never heard of her,' I said.

'Oh, come now, Nelly! You must've,' Mary said. 'She's married to Richard Burton.'

'I know him,' I said. 'He's always been my dreamboat. Y'know, I was nearly in one of his films once. They wanted me to play an old bag that got left in a railway waiting room.'

The studio audience laughed. I like to keep them on my side, so I give them a bit of old camp sometimes.

'It didn't come off, though,' I said. 'My agent asked such a big fee that Dickie Burton said he wasn't proposing to buy me; he wasn't in the white slave traffic.'

After the audience had quietened down I said: 'Och, I remember Betty Taylor now. Isn't she yon wee girl that was in a film about a horse race when I was a wee girl? She won the Derby or something. D'you mean to say she's married to Richard Burton? I'm that glad to hear she's done so well for herself.'

'You can kid the public as much as you like,' Pat said now. 'Only don't try to kid me.'

'It's a pity you aren't a kid,' I said. 'I'd skelp your backside.'

She said: 'Now Gran, behave as you should, like a grand old lady of the English stage.'

'British,' I said, though I meant Scottish.

'What was it they made you?' she asked.

'An O.B.E.'

I should have been made a Dame. I didn't want to take their old O.B.E. I told Charlie that when I got the letter from Downing Street. Charlie's my agent. 'Don't be a b.f., Miss Nell,' he said. 'Take what you can get. It's always a step on the way.'

'A bloody little step,' I said.

'After all, you're too young yet to be a Dame,' Charlie said. 'Time enough to become a Dame when you're seventy.'

'Speak for yourself, son,' I said.

Charlie's been my agent since I went to him when I was twelve. I looked older, so I didn't fash about the School Board man getting on my track. It was the time of the General Strike and everybody was too busy to heed whether I was twelve or fourteen or twenty. Dad was on the dole, and Ma was too trauchled to care what I did as long as I didn't get under her feet. So I hitch-hiked to Glasgow. The young ones nowadays think they're awful clever hitch-hiking to India and Turkey and places like that, but they forget there were folks before them who were just as bright, if not a damned sight brighter. I was bright enough, anyway, to find this theatrical agency. I went in, and there was this young fella with the blondy quiff and the choker collar and the rimless specs. Charlie was only twenty and had just started, but at the time I thought he was older. Like me, he was putting on an act. I've always been gallus, though; I knew I could deal with him. Nae bother.

He said: 'What do you do, dear?'

'I sing,' I said. 'And I dance. And I do a wee bit of patter. I'm a comedienne.'

'Let's see,' he said.

So I did. 'Not bad,' he said. 'What's your name, dear?'

'Nelly Sturrock,' I said. 'Well, it's Ellen Sturrock really.'

He pursed his lips. 'Ellen — Elaine? Hmmmm. Where d'ye come frae?'

'West Linton.'

'Linton? Ummm. Elaine Linton . . . We'll change your name to that, lass. How's that?'

'It's got a touch o' class,' I said.

'A touch o' class, ay! Elaine Linton, the lass with the touch of class.'

And that's how I was billed. I started in the pierrots at

Anstruther. Then I went on a round of the small music halls: Dundee and Dunfermline and Leith, places where the cheapest seats were threepence. And the next summer I got a rise in the world; I was in the pierrots at Rothesay. Doon the watter! Oh, I'll never forget the Glasgow Fair Week and the way the boys whistled at me. Life'll never be like that again.

Another waiter came up and said: 'Allo, Madame Curtis.' Pat rose and shook hands with him. 'My grandmother,' she said, nodding at me. 'My famous grandmother.'

'*Enchanté, Madame.*' He took my hand and bowed over it.

'And 'ow is Mamma?' he asked.

'You haven't seen her?' Pat said.

He hadn't: not for several weeks. Pat and I looked at each other. 'Well, Miss Nell,' she said. 'That's that.'

My granddaughter Patricia has this long Alice-in-Wonderlandy hair, as straight as a poker, shed in the middle and down to her waist. She's like thousands of other girls today. She's nineteen, been married a year to Lance Curtis, who works in the British Council, and she looks about fourteen. She's as prim as a kipper. They say she's like me, but that I won't have. I never looked like her even when I was fourteen. I took damned good care to see I didn't look like anybody else.

Her mother's quite a different kettle of fish, though. Not to beat about the bush, my daughter Adelaide is an alcoholic. And she's something even worse. She can't keep her hands off men. At the drop of an eyelid she drops her drawers.

It was because of Addie I was in Paris now, for the first time, at the age of fifty-six.

Addie takes after her father. I was sixteen when I met him. A smashing wee fella he was too, billed as Dandy Isitt, the comedian with a twinkle and a winkle. He had more than a winkle, I can tell you. He was a real wee ram, and his name should have begun with an R instead of a D.

But you never think of these things when you fall in love, and, boy, was I in love! Three months after I met him, I married him. We got hitched up on my seventeenth birthday. 'We'll go to Paris for our honeymoon,' he said.

'Paris in the spring!' I said, and I hummed Mendelssohn's *Spring Song.* I've always been a girl for a bit of culture.

We didn't get to Paris, though. I might have known better than trust him to keep his word. We had three days in North Berwick instead. With that cold East wind and full of the nobs. I didn't half put on the swank myself, but it wasn't the same as going to Paris.

'Never mind, hen,' Dandy said. 'We'll go there later on for a holiday. Oh, I'll do ye proud! Maxim's and the Ritz and all that.'

But that day never came. We never had time for a holiday. We were kept that busy on the halls, one week in Newcastle, the next in Glasgow, then up to Aberdeen and down to Manchester. Soon after we married we went into a double harness act, but this didn't work out, and we went back to our own routines. Though very often we played on the same bill. This was grand as long as we were on the same footing and Addie was a bairn and we could all bide in the same digs. But it wasn't so hot when Dandy began to slip, what with drinking and betting and other capers, and I got bigger billing than him. The wee green-eyed monster showed its fangs. 'This is my wife,' he would say in a pub. 'The famous Miss Linton. Me, of course – me, I'm nobody. It's Miss Linton that's the big cheese in our household.'

Poor Dandy, he was his own worst enemy. He did everything to excess. He didn't know the meaning of moderation. He aye had to be the best at everything. And it was his downfall. He'd have been all right if he'd never bought that horse. But there he was, the friend of jockeys, a great betting man, aye at race meetings when he could find time between performance. He even brought racing patter into his act. 'I've got a sure thing for the two-thirty at Doncaster. I'm putting my shirt on it.'

It was more than his shirt he put on. Nothing would satisfy him till he'd bought a racehorse. Or a share in one. He and his bookie pal, Bob Wallace, bought this two-year-old, Sleepy Sailor, between them because it was going cheap. That should have made them smell the proverbial. Especially Bob Wallace who spent his entire life on the course. They didn't, though. Sleepy Sailor never won a race. It was a right rogue. Only Dandy, that cocksure, would ever have thought he was fit to ride it. Not in a race. Even Dandy wasn't big-headed enough for that. No, he just wanted to show off to his pals. He was drunk, of course, and smoking a big cigar.

That was how he broke his back. It was as simple as that. One minute he had mounted the horse and was showing off; the next, the horse had reared, whirled round and fallen backwards. Nobody knew how it happened. Some said Dandy stubbed out his cigar on Sleepy Sailor's backside; others said that when the horse gave the first buck the cigar fell from Dandy's mouth and landed on its hide.

Bob Wallace himself shot the horse. I often wish he had shot Dandy too. It would have been better for him than seven years in a wheel-chair. Mind you, Dandy never complained. And he never was really bitter. The nearest he came to it was when he said, as he used to sometimes after a few drams (for the doctor allowed him to take as much of the auld kirk as he liked): 'I'm sorry to be such a burden to ye, Nelly. I don't mind a kept woman, but I can't abide a kept man. I never dreamt I'd end up as one.'

Neither had I. Not that I minded. I was a star by then, in England as well as Scotland, and making big money. I was never off the boards. I never got the chance to 'rest', as we say. So I was able to keep Dandy in the style to which he'd become accustomed. A male nurse and a house-keeper and all that. Oh ay, we lived in the grand manner.

We moved down to England when I starred in a Cochran revue, and I bought a house on the river at Henley. It was easy reached from the West End in the plum-coloured Rolls I bought with my first film money.

We didn't have that car for long. I sold it when my next season on the halls started. I didn't feel like paying a chauffeur's wages for doing nothing. I couldn't travel from Aberdeen to Birmingham, from Sheffield to Dundee, in a Rolls every week. Besides, I liked the Sunday trains and all the dirt dished out on them when the profession got together.

I sold the Henley house after Munich. I thought Dandy had better be back on our native heath if we did get bombed, so we moved to a cottage in Dumfriesshire. But the male nurses and the house-keepers always girned and never stayed long because it was too quiet and they said they had no social life.

Dandy died in 1942. It was a relief. He was in continual pain, and I was away from home so much, doing my stuff in workers' canteens as well as on the halls, films and the B.B.C., I wasn't able to see how he was being looked after. In any case, Addie started to be a problem about then, and I had enough on my plate with her.

Addie was four when Dandy had his accident. By the time she was ten she was up to her tricks. I suppose Addie had a queer upbringing. She would never stay at any of her schools. When she was at home she got on Dandy's nerves, and she was always hanging around the male nurses. And when she came round the halls with me she was forever running in and out of the men's dressing rooms. She was that bad, some of the lads used to keep their doors locked.

As she got older there was no holding her. Some folk said: 'She's like her mother, man crazy.' That's not true, and it's not fair. I know my act was a bit blue sometimes, but I never went to the lengths of the late, great Nellie Wallace, bless her. Mind you, I was a bit 'suggestive', and I still am, when it suits me. In some halls, of course, you could get away with murder, so you fashioned your performance to suit your audience. The one I gave in the West End was different from the one I gave at the Met in the Edgware Road, and the Met's was different from the one at the Chelsea Palace. The way I acted on the stage isn't the way I act off it, though. I'm not the easy meat some folk think. I've always been faithful to Dandy. When I wink at some big gorgeous hunk of beef in the second row of the stalls and say 'Ooooh, what a man! Just let me get at you!' I don't expect him to run round to the stage door with his tongue hanging out. It's part of my act, and the audience loves it. I'd have you know I'm still a respectable widow. Not that any of the lovely big hunks ever do come round, it's only the wee creeps. More's the pity. But I'm always hoping for the best when I leer at the audience and cry: 'I'm all for *passion*!'

If I got a gorgeous big hunk I don't believe I'd know what to do with him. Not like Addie. She went through the boys like a dose of salts. She was that bad I often thought she'd land in the pudding club. But whenever I lost my rag, she would remind me that I'd got married myself at seventeen.

'If you get married when you're seventeen,' I said, 'I'll murder you.'

'I won't, Ma,' she said. 'I promise.'

She kept her word.

She was eighteen when she married Sonny Spence, the boxer. My granddaughter was a seven months baby, and she was barely a year old when Addie and Sonny parted. It wasn't Addie's fault, mind. I will say that for her. And she tried to keep the home together. She was willing to let bygones be bygones, but the bloke she'd found Sonny in bed with wasn't. He didn't want to share Sonny with a woman and a kid. So Addie parked wee Pat on me and hared off to Paris to marry Gaston Christophe, the artist, a man I never liked or trusted. He didn't like me either. So all the four years he and Addie were together I never got invited once to their home in Montparnasse. In fact, for most of the time I had to look after Pat because Addie and

Gaston were aye gadding away to Algiers or Persia and places like that where they couldn't take her. So Paris was still a dream, for I'd never been able to get there even after the Liberation to sing to the troops. The fellas in charge of E.N.S.A. sent me to the Outer Hebrides and workers' canteens in places like Burton-on-Trent and Workington. They were going to send me to Iceland, but I put my foot down. They were going to fly me there in a bomber, but I told them I wasn't setting foot in any bloody plane even though it set the war effort back ten years. Some of the boys in the back room who hand out the Honours must have remembered this when they dished me out only an O.B.E.

After Christophe divorced Addie, she married Jeremy, a wishy-washy American who pretended he was a freelance journalist. It was a good thing his old man had made a few millions in mineral waters, otherwise they'd have starved. The old man even paid my passage on the *Queen Elizabeth* when I went to stay with them in New York for a couple of months: the only holiday I ever managed to have, and that was because I'd made a nice wee packet out of a couple of featured roles in films.

Addie managed to spin out that marriage for three years, but Jeremy got wise to her in the long run. His old man gave her a big settlement to let Jeremy divorce her. After that Addie didn't bother with marriage licences. She just parked Pat on me and went off with the man of the moment. Pat and me got on fine. By that time I'd got this nice wee flat in Brighton, over an antique shop in the Lanes. It's handy for London. Though travelling on the train isn't what it used to be. I loved the Brighton Belle. Me and Larry often used to have a kipper together, and he's been to see me in my local several times.

It's funny. Though I never got to Paris myself, it's been Addie's spiritual home for years, if the likes of her can be said to have anything spiritual. Pat was there with her and one of her fancy men, getting her French brushed up, when she met Lance Curtis. Addie's been dotting back and forth to Paris ever since, staying with Pat and Lance in their flat in the Rue de Tilsitt, between lovers.

Pat's a canny Scot, like me, and never uses the phone if she can send a postcard instead. Some folk say I'm mean about this, but the truth is I'm as terrified of the phone as I am of aeroplanes, fast cars and horses. So I knew there was something very far wrong when I heard those French telephonists jabbering away. Pat's not one to beat about the bush. She said right away: 'Addie's gone.'

'What d'ye mean?' I said. 'Is she dead?'

'I dunno, Gran. She's just gone. Disappeared. We haven't seen or heard of her for a week.'

'Have you tried the police?'

'What's the good of *les flics*? If we go to them, there's no knowing where it'll end. They'd have me at the mortuary looking at bodies they'd fished out of the Seine.'

'D'ye think . . .?'

'No,' Pat said. 'She'll be with some man somewhere, or hanging around the bistros on the Left Bank. Will you come over and help me look for her?'

I phoned the B.B.C. and told them they'd have to get an understudy for me this week. Then I phoned Charlie.

'What do you want to go chasing away to Paris for, Miss Nell?' he said. 'Let the bitch sink or swim.'

'Listen, son,' I said. 'Addie's my daughter, and though she's a grown woman I feel responsible for her. Besides, it's a good excuse for me to see Paris. I've aye wanted to go to Paris in the spring.'

'You've left it a bit late, haven't you, hen? It'll be a gey dusty springtime. In case you're not aware of it, Nelly, it's July now. It'll be very hot in Paris.'

'Ah well, I'll just have to pretend it's spring.'

'Remember ye don't speak French, Nelly.'

'Keep your wig on, son,' I said. Charlie's as bald as an egg now. His blondy quiff went long years ago. 'I can oo-la-la and parlyvoo with the best of them. Tootleoo!'

Pat said much the same as Charlie when she met me at the Gare Saint-Lazare. I went by the boat from Newhaven, and on the train from Dieppe I travelled in the last carriage and got in tow with the ticket-collector. I was the last one off the train, all the other passengers were miles ahead as I trailed up yon long platform and saw Pat waiting at the barrier.

'Where've you been, Gran?' she cried. 'I thought you'd missed the boat or done something daft at Dieppe.'

'Och, I was just saying *adieu* to the ticket-collector. Such a nice young fella. He fair took a fancy to me and was teaching me French.'

'God, don't tell me you're going to turn out like Addie! Cradle-snatching!'

'Now look, hen,' I said.

'Don't call me hen, Gran.'

'I would have you know, Mrs Curtis, that I'm not cradle-snatching. I couldn't help the young fella taking a shine to me, could I? After all, in the spring a young man's fancy lightly turns to love.'

'So it appears does an old woman's,' she said, taking my suitcase. 'C'mon, let's get a taxi.'

While standing in the queue and I was watching an old lady dressed in black walking straight to the head of it and commandeering a taxi from right under a man's nose — really, the French are terrible! — Pat returned to the attack: 'Wearing kinky boots at your age! And what've you been doing to your hair? Why on earth did you let your hair-dresser dye it that pinky colour?'

'It's not pink, I'll have you know,' I said. 'It's russet, and I dyed it with my own hands.'

'I thought it looked homemade. It's about six different colours. From pale pink to yellow ochre.'

I said: 'It catches the boys' eyes, anyway. And that's something.'

By this time we'd crept to the head of the queue and Pat was opening the door of one of those funny-like taxis that don't look like taxis when I said: 'Here, wait a minute!

I'm not going in this one. I won't have a woman. Nobody's going to drive me but a man.'

It wasn't only the girl-driver. I didn't like the look of the big Alsatian on the seat beside her. Pat said something in French to the folk behind us, and they got in. They didn't seem to mind either the dog or the girl, but the French are funny. Pat and I got into the next taxi, and she said: 'You're worse than Addie. Man crazy! I can see I won't be able to let you out of my sight for one second.'

'You don't need to worry,' I said. 'I wouldn't thank you if Rock Hudson and Muhammad Ali were trussed up naked on a platter in front of me.'

Pat said: 'Chickens for an auld hen!'

I ignored this.

'I wouldn't trust you with them for five minutes,' she said.

'Well, they might come in handy,' I said. 'They could carry my bags when I go shopping. And they could protect me in the supermarket.'

'More likely you'd need to protect them,' Pat said.

I don't doubt it. There's a wee whippersnapper with a cockeye at the cash-desk in the supermarket who always calls me 'Elaine'. I could crown her when she cries: 'I thought you was ever so funny last night, Elaine. I laughed ever so — though I don't agree with what you said, of course. Ow, no! You're not in the groove, mate.' I have to grin and take it. One of my public. It would give me great pleasure to throttle the wee bitch. I wonder what Rock and Muhammad would make of her? Run for their lives, I daresay.

I adored Paris. Even with Addie on my mind, I couldn't help enjoying myself. Mind you, my feet were sore. We walked everywhere. Young Lance took the car to his office, so me and Pat had to pad the hoof. We took the Metro and buses and taxis here and there, but mostly we walked. On the Left Bank we kept dotting in and out of bistros and brasseries that Addie had been going to ever since she was married to Gaston Christophe. I wondered why Pat who isn't a drinker, God bless her wee soul, was so well known at *Le Balzar* and other places, then I realized it was because she'd been in them that often looking for her mother. It turned out this wasn't the first time Addie had disappeared. Only this was the longest. It turned out, too, that a lot of these places still called Addie 'Madame Christophe'.

The patron at one bistro made goo-goo eyes and greeted me as *'la mère de Madame Addie'*. And he gabbled away and gave us drinks on the house, saying: *'Je vous adore, madame, comme j'adore la Grande Dietrich.'*

'Oo-la-la!' I cried. And I sang *'Falling in Love Again'* for him.

In the evenings Lance took us around in the car, though he never believed we'd run into Addie. He knew as well as I did that if anything bad had happened we'd have heard before now. But it was a grand excuse for him to show me Paris, and I was only too delighted to give him the excuse. By the third evening I didn't give a hoot about Addie. After all, she was nearly forty and could do what she liked.

But Pat was fair dedicated to the search. If she had been terribly attached to her mother I'd have seen the force of it; but Addie had neglected Pat a lot when she was a bairn. I couldn't see the sense of such dedication.

Lance took us to Maxim's and Fouquet's and la Grande Cascade near Longchamp: all places I'd wanted to go with Dandy. Oh, it was like being young again! Though I knew, looking at all the dolly-boys and their birds, that I could never hope to be like them. Even though my heart was young and gay, my feet wouldn't let me, as my granny (and *she* never entered for the glamour stakes) used to say.

Day after day, Pat strode along, with me half running behind her. She hardly ever looked round to see if I was still there. She would sweep across streets, in front of the traffic, so that I had heart-failure the whole time. I was feared to stop and look at things in case she vanished in the crowd. And often against my better judgment I followed her right in front of cars, inches from their bonnets and their screeching horns, because I had to keep close to her.

The morning we went to the Ile de la Cité, Pat walked slower, though, and I was able to get a good look at the flower market and the Palais de Justice and the Aga Khan's house. We crossed the bridge onto the Ile Saint-Louis and had a drink in an Alsace café. When we went back to the Ile de la Cité, I was all set to go into Notre-Dame. I had a headscarf ready in my bag, to put on when I went in, for though I'm not a kirkgoer I believe in paying respect to other folks' religious observances. Live and let live has aye been my motto. I thought Notre-Dame was a wee bit spoilt by all the coaches parked outside, all full of tourists. We walked beside them, and as I looked from the tourists to the gargoyles on the walls I began to pull the headscarf out in readiness.

Pat doesn't hold with churches. 'We won't bother to go in,' she said. 'You've seen enough of it. And Addie's not likely to be inside, wherever else she may be.'

I said: 'I'm going in, hen. I'm not coming all this distance without seeing what it's like inside. Maybe we'll meet the ghost of Lon Chaney.'

'Who was he?'

'My God!' I cried. 'After all I've taught you about films! He was the Hunchback of Notre-Dame, of course.'

'You're wrong, Miss Nell,' she said. 'That was Charles Laughton.'

I gave up.

But I didn't give up about going inside Notre-Dame. I put on the headscarf and told Pat I'd meet her at a café near the Pont Neuf in half an hour. 'You wait for me there,' I said, 'while I have a wee word in the cathedral about your Ma.'

Even though Pat was always in a hurry I saw lots of queer

things. Two-three times I saw *gendarmes* making arrests, and I was horrified to see them punching the men they were arresting and driving them along with more punches. I couldn't believe my eyes the first time I saw it, in the Champs-Élysées, and I thought of the fuss if it had happened in London. And in the Luxembourg Gardens, where I'd got Pat to sit down for a minute so that I could rest my feet, I saw a middle-aged French woman tackling a couple of boys who'd laughed at her hat. I don't blame them. It was a terrible hat, and I wouldn't have worn it except at the Chelsea Arts Ball. But *madame* didn't think it funny, and she gave those boys biff. Pat laughed and said: '*Très formidable!*' And she translated what the woman was saying, not that I needed a translation. *Madame,* wagging her forefinger and following the boys like a bulldog bitch in heat, was enough.

I saw a lot of queer things in Paris all right. And the queerest of all was something I saw on the 14th July. I'd always heard Paris is a wicked city, but I really couldn't believe my eyes at this. Wicked? It was downright shameless.

Early in the morning, about ten o'clock, Pat and I went to watch the Bastille Day parade on the Champs-Élysées, at the Arc de Triomphe end, almost opposite Fouquet's. Early as we were, others were earlier. The pavements were jam-packed. I held Pat's hand as we stood in the crowd waiting for the show to begin. We couldn't move. I was glad we were close to two young *gendarmes,* for I thought if the crowd got too excited I might get swept off my feet, and a brawny arm would be handy, even if it did belong to a hated *flic.* We could see nothing because of the folk in front, except the tops of tanks and gun-carriers and what-ever other military vehicles they were. I heard afterwards there were soldiers and sailors marching between them, but I saw neither hide nor hair of them. Suddenly there was a terrific *zooming,* and flight after flight of different kinds of aeroplanes and helicopters came flying over the Arc de

Triomphe; they were so low they just skimmed the tops of the buildings, and they flew straight down the Champs-Élysées. I was terrified. I cooried down and hoped none of the planes would fall on me. The noise was deafening. Mind you, it was all very impressive. I'll hand the French that, they put on a very good show. The first flight of planes had red, white and blue smoke streaming out behind them. I really couldn't appreciate it all, though; I began to feel suffocated in the crowd. After a while, we squeezed our way through, into a quiet side street. Pat had coffee, and I had *un Americano* in a café. Parked near it was a 'Black Maria' (or whatever it's called in France) with a lot of young *gendarmes* mooching around it. Waiting to arrest folk, Pat said. Most of them were smoking. Some came into the café and had beer, and when two showed they wanted to get into conversation with us, Pat rose and said: 'Time we went, Gran.'

I wouldn't have minded having a wee crack with them, for they seemed nice-like fellas, but Pat strode off and I was forced to follow. By this time the parade had stopped, and the crowds were flowing into the side streets. We dodged through them, down past the Élysée Palace where we watched the diplomats drive in to lunch with the President. Then we passed an empty theatre that Mistinguette and Chevalier had played in in their hey-day, and the American Embassy, and then we drifted on and looked in Lanvins and other swanky shops, all closed for the day, and I saw a lot of wonderful, very expensive clothes I'd have liked.

At last we got to the Opera House, and Pat said we'd wait for a bus. I was thankful because of my feet. It was an awful hot day. There was a great queue round *l'Opéra*. There was to be a special performance of *Il Trovatore* and folk were allowed in only by invitation. Quite a lot of queer-like old girls, who looked as if they'd been hidden in garrets for generations, dressed in ancient rigouts, cloaks and cartwheel hats and moth-eaten furs, were being escorted across the street by *gendarmes* to their places in the queue. There was no punching going on here. Everything was very lovey-dovey and *après-vous-madame.*

Our bus came. I was sitting next the window, watching the crowds and the traffic, when I saw something I'd never expected to see in Paris or anywhere else. A car was running alongside the bus and, looking down, I could see right into it: a lot more than I could have seen from the pavement. I saw the legs and thighs of the driver. He wore very tight lilac coloured slacks and had his legs spread well apart. I saw the legs and skirt of the girl next him. I couldn't see their heads. What I could see, though, and only too plain, was the girl's hand clutching the man's crotch.

I nudged Pat and said: 'Lookit that, for God's sake!'

'That's nothing,' she said.

'It's disgraceful,' I said. 'It's a real disgust. By jings, if anybody belonging to me did that in public I'd kill her.'

'C'mon, Gran,' Pat cried, rising and heading for the door.

'But we don't get off here.' I knew enough about Paris by this time to know it was nowhere near our stop.

She was at the door. It had opened, and there was nothing for me to do but follow.

'What's up?' I asked on the pavement.

'C'mon,' she cried, and she hared away.

As I ran after her, I realized she was following the car that held that shameless bitch. The car couldn't go fast because of the traffic, and when she got near it Pat beckoned to me and cried: 'It's Addie.'

It was. Addie, sitting as brazen as brass, staring in front of her. Nobody on the pavement could have guessed what she was doing.

'Ye awful-like limmer!' I shouted.

Almost as if they'd heard me, the car toot-tooted, shot forward and got well ahead of us. We were running by this time. Pat was waving for a taxi and, lo and behold, one stopped and she bundled me in, crying: *'Suivez cette Renault.'*

Agitated though I was, I couldn't help thinking how cute Pat was to tell the make of the car at a glance. I never

113

know one car from another. Except a Rolls, I never miss them.

Pat said: 'I recognized her dress.'

It was like a film. We chased that car along street after street. We crossed the river, and on a bridge I said: 'Well, the only good thing is that we know now she's not at the bottom of the Seine.'

'Not yet,' Pat said.

We followed the Renault as far as the Boulevard du Montparnasse, and then we got stuck in a jam and it got away. We saw it turn into a side street, but when we got there it had disappeared. 'Never mind,' Pat said, paying off the taxi. 'I bet it's gone into some garage. This is a handy place for La Coupole and the Dôme and the Select and the Rotonde. They're all favourites of Addie's. She's always looking for a new young Hemingway or a Scott Fitzgerald. We'll try them all.'

She wasn't in the Rotonde or the Select. I wanted a drink, but Pat wouldn't let me. So I made up my mind crossing the boulevard that I'd have one in the next place, whether Addie was there or not.

We were no sooner inside the Dôme than somebody cried: 'Welcome, Miss Nell!' And there was this old queen I sometimes meet in the Salisbury when I go to St Martin's Lane, to Charlie's office. He was the last person I wanted to see, but *toujours la politesse*, as Pat says occasionally.

'How are you, Nelly love?' he said, getting up and pulling out a chair at his table for me.

'Not so dusty,' I said.

And then I saw this lovely big chunky man that was with him. I wondered at once what he was doing with this old queen, because if there's one thing I pride myself on it's knowing when a man is a *man*. 'This is Jack,' said the old queen. 'Jack — er — I've forgotten your other name.'

'It doesn't matter, she'll know it soon enough,' the big man said, standing to shake my hand. He was wearing lilac slacks. It must be the fashionable colour for men this summer, I thought.

'Oh, what a gorgeous big beast!' I said, giving my eye-lashes a good flutter. 'D'ye ken something, son? You're the spit and image of Marlon Brando. I go for him in a big way.'

Jack grinned, and then I saw he was grinning at somebody behind me.

There was a tap on my shoulder.

'Hello, Ma,' Addie said. 'At it again, are you?'

Like Arrows in the Hands of a Giant

Jess came from a Home when she was fourteen to be maidie to the Miss McGlashens. She was a thin, cantankerous quaen with dullish red hair, sandy eyebrows and lashes, and her light blue eyes were so pale they were almost like milk. But they were hard for all their milky-blueness.

Miss Sarah McGlashen was about sixty at the time, and Miss Alison was five or six years younger. They had come to Auchencairn as young women just after the Boer War and had aye kept themselves to themselves. Their father had been the doctor, and they had gone on living in The Laurels after he died, although it was too big for them. They had been V.A.D.s in the Great War, going to the Front with their father. They had no need to work, for the doctor had left them a bonnie penny. They were weird bodies who read a lot of books. They didn't mix with the local half-gentry and they had no friends except the minister's wife, and even she saw them only occasionally, for they didn't go to the kirk. They didn't interest themselves about the social life of the village, and so folk weren't pleased, for they thought that with so much spare time they should have helped to run the Women's Institute or the Girl Guides. Folk were fell curious about them, but they had never been able to get any change out of Aggie, the old maid who had been with them ever since they came to the village. So, now that Aggie was dead and lying beneath a fine marble cross in the kirkyard, folk were glad to get a chance of speiring young Jess when she went for the messages to Mrs Rintoul's wee shoppie.

And it wasn't long before Jess showed that she had none of Aggie's tight-mouthedness. Jess was glad of an audience. And many a queer tale she had to tell. Folk were flabbergasted. They had never believed that such on-goings could go on anywhere, far less in a respectable place like Auchencairn.

It started when Jess told them that Miss Alison took drink. 'I have to cart awa' at least a dozen bottles frae ablow her bed every week,' she said.

'What kind o' bottles, lambie?' Mrs Rintoul said.

'Port, I think,' Jess said. 'Ay, port. She gets it frae a grocer's in Aberdeen. She lies in her bed and puts in white tablets that fizz like sherbet. D'ye ken what I think?'

'Go on,' cried Mrs Mackie, forgetting to watch Mrs Rintoul weighing out her lentils.

'I think it's dope,' Jess said. 'I'm sure it's dope. Like that woman took. Brenda something that was in a' the papers and got the nick.'

'Did ye ever!' cried Mrs Beedie.

'Mind you, they were a long time in France,' Mrs Rintoul said. 'And ye ken what capers the French get up to!'

While folk were still digesting this, Jess came out with even more astounding details.

'They've started to beat me,' she whined one morning as she leaned against some crates of lemonade, eating the biscuits that Mrs Rintoul always gave her to keep her talking after she'd done her shopping. 'Every night they gar me kneel down and say my prayers, and then they lift ma nightgown and cane me across the bare arse. Miss Sarah gi'es me six, and then Miss Alison gi'es me another six. Every night! And they said if I tellt anybody they'd shut me in the coal-cellar.'

'Did ye ever!' breathed Mrs Rintoul, leaning on her counter like a lump of dough waiting to be rolled out and put in the oven. 'Did ye ever hear the like?'

'Show us the marks, Jessie,' said one of the admiring audience.

But Jess wouldn't. 'I'd be fair ashamed,' she said. 'No, no, I daurnie. It's bad enough havin' to bare my bum to thae twa auld limmers.'

'It's a disgrace, that's what it is,' Mrs Rintoul said. 'Ye should tell the polisman, Jessie.'

'Oh, I daurnie. If I did, they'd send me back to the Home — and worse things happen to ye there.'

'What kind o' things?' Mrs Beedie asked.

'Tell us, Jess,' cried Mrs Mackie.

But Jess wouldn't say another word. She finished off her biscuits, lifted her basket, and went back to The Laurels.

Word of such on-goings soon got round the village. It wasn't long before Mrs Ainslie, the minister's wife, heard the tale, put on her second-best hat and sallied along to The Laurels, and after some hemming and hawing over a cup of tea, she said: 'What's this I hear about you having to chastise Jess?'

'Chastise Jess?' said Miss Sarah, taking off her rimless glasses and pinning them to her bosom. 'I don't know what you're talking about, Kate.'

'There's a story going round the village that you — er — well, that you've caned her several times,' Mrs Ainslie said.

'Caned her!' Miss Alison giggled so much she nearly had hysterics. She was a delicate little woman, about half the size of her big stout sister, and everybody said she had 'a want'.

'There's not a cane in the house,' she spluttered when she got breath, 'and it would be a bit difficult, wouldn't it, to cane a girl of that size — even if one wanted to.'

'Well, I thought I'd better tell you,' Mrs Ainslie said.

'The nearest thing to a cane in the house is an old riding crop of father's that Jess unearthed from a cupboard the other day,' Miss Alison said, wiping her eyes. 'Now that I think of it, she said to me: "Did your daddy use to beat you with that?" ' She giggled again. 'What an imagination the girl's got!'

'It's no laughing matter, Alison,' Mrs Ainslie said. 'If I were you I'd pack her off straight back to the Home.'

'We couldn't, Kate,' Miss Sarah said. 'It was a dreadful place by all accounts.'

'By Jess's accounts maybe,' the minister's wife said.

'It wouldn't be fair to the girl,' Miss Sarah said.

'Well, I've warned you,' Mrs Ainslie said.

After the visitor had gone, Miss Sarah rang the bell. The maidie came unwillingly, for she had been deep in the pages of a lurid women's paper that she had spread over the kitchen table.

'Jessie, do you know what happens to girls who tell lies?' Miss Sarah said.

'Yes, mum,' Jess said sullenly. 'They go to the Burning Fire.'

'And do you want to go there?'

'Oh, no, mum. But I havenie been tellin' any lies.'

'I'm not so sure about that,' Miss Sarah said. 'A little bird has whispered about some of the things you've been talking about down at Mrs Rintoul's. I'm warning you, Jess, if there's any more of it — back to the Home you go!'

'Oh please, mum, please! Dinnie send me back there.' Jess began to snivel. 'The Matron would kill me if I was sent back. There was a lassie that got sent back once, and Matron shoved her in a bath o' boilin' water and dipped her head under a dozen times. Oh, I'll never forget the yells! She was skinned for weeks after it.'

'That's enough, Jess,' said Miss Sarah. 'Go back to the kitchen and if I hear another cheep out of you, you'll pack your kist and go.'

The following Sunday the minister announced that *Psalms* number one hundred and twenty-seven, verse four, was to be the text of his sermon.

'As arrows are in the hands of a mighty man, so are the children of his youth,' Mr Ainslie read quietly. Then he

folded his hands on the pulpit and said: 'I'll disregard the verse that follows – a verse that says happy is the man who has his quiver full of them. For that has nothing to do with what I am going to talk about today.'

He stopped and looked about him. 'Like arrows in the hands of a giant!' he cried so suddenly that a lot of folk nearly louped out of their seats and old Miss Patterson swallowed the pan drop she had just slipped into her mouth to keep her sucking through the sermon. 'A giant!' Mr Ainslie thundered. 'Just imagine if a giant appeared in Auchencairn and started to fire arrows among you! Think of the damage he would do!'

And then he fair let himself rip, saying that children with imagination were given to telling tales and that sometimes this was a good thing, but when they became downright lies it was something to be nipped in the bud; for, like arrows in the hands of a giant, they could be dangerous. It was a grand sermon and the folk in the kirk looked at each other and nodded as much as to say they knew fine who he was referring to. Jess was not at the kirk, and so Mr Ainslie's seed fell on stony ground, although she got a few digs about it from the women in the shop and for a while they would nudge each other and laugh when she started a tale.

After that Jess was more careful. She was learning quick, and she was learning more things than cooking and cleaning. She got to be a dab hand at hinting. She soon found that a word here and a word there was seed sown on far more fertile ground than any of the seeds left from Mr Ainslie's sermon.

Jess was twenty when the Second World War broke out. By that time she was well and truly established in The Laurels, and the Misses McGlashen couldn't do without her. The sisters were handless. Old Aggie had spoiled them, running after them like a hen after her chickens on a wet day, and they were nearly incapable of doing anything for themselves. They couldn't even make their own beds, and Jess said in the shoppie that if they were left to boil an egg it

121

would be a fully-hatched cockerel by the time they minded to take it out of the pot.

Jess still held court at Mrs Rintoul's, and for the first few months of the war the other wifies listened with bated breath to what she'd do to auld Hitler if she could just get her clutches on him for half an hour. Tearing off his toe-nails with red hot pincers was about the mildest thing that would happen to him.

Like many other Scottish towns and villages, Auchen-cairn soon got Polish soldiers. And the same Poles made hay among the village lassies while the sun shone on the local lads that were away facing Rommel in North Africa. Jess was one of the first quaens to drop her drawers after a handsome Pole with slanting eyes and a wee moustache kissed her hand. Jess had never had a lad before, and she could hardly contain herself with pride. Stefan practically took up his quarters in the Misses McGlashen's kitchen, and even Miss Alison would lift her nose out of her books to pass the time of day with him.

It wasn't long before the village wifies noticed that Jess had done more than pass the time of day with him, of course, but she never heeded when they gave her sly nudges. She had a boy a while later, a black slanty-eyed creature like his father, who by that time had gone to London and was never heard of again. The Misses McGlashen wanted to adopt the bairn. But Jess was for none of that. She thought she would lose some of her hold on the old ladies if the baby stayed in the house. Little Stefan was sent, when he was barely three months old, to the same Home where Jess had spent her childhood, and straightaway she forgot all about him. Some folk from the back of beyond in Ross-shire adopted him, and Jess signed the adoption papers quicker than a flea could loup from one old wife to another.

When the war ended the Misses McGlashen were getting doddery, but this didn't stop Miss Sarah from announcing one day that she was buying a second-hand car. The sisters had had a car when Jess first came, but they had never used it much and as time went on, with them hardly ever venturing out of doors, it had stood in the garage for years before they sold it. So it was a surprise to Jess when she found that Miss Sarah had kept her licence up to date.

'The sleekit auld hoor,' she said in the shop. 'Doin' a thing like that behind ma back. All thae years she's been doin' it and me none the wiser! A waste o' guid money!'

A week later Miss Sarah was driving an old Austin through the village. Will Garvie, the big fat policeman, nearly fell off his bike when he saw the way the car was wobbling from one side of the road to the other.

'I could have arrested her,' he told a crony, 'but, dear God, man, it would ha'e been more than ma job is worth if I'd tackled her. Auld Miss McGlashen would ha'e been on til me hook line and sinker, for she's got a damned nippy tongue in her head, although she's daft. I'd never ha'e heard the end o't.'

More than Will Garvie was scandalized. The village folk thought it was asking for trouble, but ever since Mrs Ainslie and the minister had gone to a better living in Glasgow there was nobody to carry their views to the old ladies. Jess was the only source of communication, and Jess, as folk knew fine, was not to be trusted. The new minister, a young student from St Andrews, was worse than hopeless. He'd paid one visit to The Laurels and was so terrified by his reception that he'd sworn he'd never go back.

Jess went her mile about it. 'If they must throw away their siller it would be wiser-like if they'd buy me a washing-machine,' she said. 'It would save me a lot of work now that Miss Alison's taken to peeing her bed and worse.'

Poor Miss Alison wasn't exactly senile, but she had got a bit forgetful about lots of things. Sometimes she forgot to come and eat, and whenever she thought Miss Sarah was safely out of the way, Jess would bawl up the stairs: 'Yer dinner's on the table, and if ye dinnie bloody well come and get it, I'll give ye howmanandy!'

Although she went her dinger in the shoppie, Jess was careful not to say anything about the car to Miss Sarah. Not that Miss Sarah would have cared. She put up with Jess's domineering so far but no farther, and sometimes after Jess had been more than usually outrageous, Miss Sarah would give a little secret smile. She knew that Jess thought it was more money spent that she wouldn't get when the McGlashens went to join the great majority, for they had no near relatives and the sisters had willed their money to Jess. The maidie had seen to that. She had delivered an ultimatum during the war, saying when the two old ladies were scared after some bombs had been dropped ten miles away: 'If ye dinnie leave me the money, I'll ging and get masel' a job somewhere else — and where would ye be then, ye fushionless auld craturs, if a Jerry landed in the garden? Ye wouldnie even be able to make him a cup o' tea!'

Miss Sarah was under Jess's thumb, but not all that under. She still had a spark of independence. And buying the car was one way of showing it. Miss Sarah wasn't in any way mechanical, but she had managed to learn something about gears and clutches years ago, and it wasn't long before Auchencairn got used to the sight of her and Miss Alison careering along in the old car. They could well have afforded a brand new car, and folk said they were even dafter than they looked not to have bought one and to have got a chauffeur. But the old car suited them fine. It gave them both a bit of pleasure, and God knows they had very little of that with Jess ruling the roost with a heavy hand.

Jess refused all invitations to learn to drive. 'I ha'e enough work to do,' she told the village wifies, 'without takin' thae twa silly auld hoors oot for an airin'. If they break their necks when they're gallivantin', I'm no' one that'll waste time greetin' at their funeral.'

Still, nothing happened to the old ladies, apart from running into a ditch and knocking down a gate and nearly killing a young bullock that belonged to Jock Meldrum of Little Cathlock. Will Garvie soon learned to turn a blind eye when they zig-zagged through the village, and he kept his fingers crossed that they'd never pluck up enough courage to drive all the way to Aberdeen, where the police

124

might not be as lenient as he was.

But a day came, when Miss Sarah was rising eighty, that Will was forced to have a word with her. It wasn't that Miss Sarah went fast. The trouble was that she drove too slowly. Sometimes there was a long procession of cars going through Auchencairn, with young drivers hooting and roaring because Miss Sarah was in front and right in the middle of the road. So a delegation was got up to ask her if she'd mind packing it in. Will Garvie led the delegation — he was feared to see Miss Sarah on his lone — and the up- shot was that she agreed that maybe the time had come.

She didn't mind very much, because Miss Alison had got tired of the car. Miss Alison had turned religious in her old age, and she was forever going to the kirk. Not only did she go twice every Sunday, she went two or three times during the week too. She asked Adam Mackie, the beadle, if she could get the key so that she could go in and sit and meditate, as she called it, whenever she felt like it. Adam was right annoyed. He thought the kirk should only be open on Sundays, for he didn't hold with the queer-fangled habit they had in England of keeping the kirk doors open all the time. However, as Miss Alison was a good customer, as you might say, he had to let her have her way. And many a fright he got after that when he went to dust and sweep the kirk and he'd find Miss Alison sitting in the corner of a pew in the dark. 'She's near scared the breeks offen me twa-three times,' he told folk. 'She's either sittin' in the corner like an auld witch, or she's kneelin' in front o' the pulpit singin' hymns.'

Apart from going so often to the kirk, Miss Alison took to wandering about the village or along the farm-roads. She seldom let on she saw folk; she just wandered along, muttering to herself, and sometimes she'd run into a hedge and try to hide when she saw anybody coming. If people did stop and force her to pass the time of day, she always said she was going to 'our other house'. Everybody thought this gey queer until old Granny Mackie, who was nearly a hundred and had been bed-ridden for longer than her daughter-in-law liked to think, said that maybe Miss Alison was talking about the house where she and Miss Sarah and the old doctor had stayed before they came to Auchencairn.

Miss Sarah was eighty-three when she was coffined. After the funeral Jess got the shock of her life when the prim lawyer from Aberdeen told her: 'Miss McGlashen made a new will shortly before she died. It's not a will I approve of, and I told Miss McGlashen so at the time. But she was stubborn and, as she was apparently in full possession of her faculties, I had to comply. She has left you two hundred pounds.'

'What?' cried Jess.

'Two hundred pounds. The rest of her fortune has been left in trust to Miss Alison, and on Miss Alison's death you will benefit in the following manner. Should Miss Alison die within two years of Miss McGlashen the entire estate will go to various charities which I won't trouble to name. Should, however, Miss Alison die at any time from two to five years of Miss McGlashen, and you have in that time looked after her with all due care and attention, you will receive the sum of three thousand pounds. The remainder of the estate will go to the aforesaid charities. If, however, Miss Alison should not die until between five and ten years after her sister, you will receive the sum of five thousand pounds, the remainder to go to charity. And, if by some wonderful chance — and I see no reason why this should not happen, for God is good — Miss Alison does not die for more than ten years after Miss McGlashen you will receive the entire estate — which I may say amounts to a very large sum indeed.'

'God is good,' said Jess, and she said it so low that the lawyer thought she was being as pious as he was himself.

But when Jess got back to the kitchen she yelled: 'Bested by that auld bitch!' and she beat her hands on the table until they were a lot redder than usual. 'Bested!' she yelled again, and she put her foot under Blackie the cat and kicked him right out the door. 'The twa-faced auld hoor! After tellin' me she'd left me all her siller! I just hope

126

she roasts.'

Still, there it was and she'd just have to thole it. Miss Alison was round about seventy-seven and there was no reason why she shouldn't see the ten years out. Not that Jess felt she should bother much about the 'due care and attention' bit. She was fed up slaving for them and cleaning up all Miss Alison's dirt after her. After all, she was not as young as she'd been either, and she didn't see why she shouldn't get help and live the life of a lady as long as she could. So, after she'd thought it out, she phoned the lawyer and told him she'd have to get somebody in every day to do the rough work. 'I'm an ill woman,' she said in a palavery tone. 'I've just kept going with Miss Sarah and Miss Alison because I was that fond of them, but I can't go on much longer on my own. I'm getting on for forty, you know, and I haven't got the strength to run after Miss Alison like I used to. This is a big house to run, and I can't manage. You can't expect me to do it.'

And so the upshot was that young Marlene Garvie, old Will's granddaughter, came to The Laurels every day to do the cleaning while Jess sat on her bottom and read the papers and watched the television. Jess only stirred herself to do a bit of cooking or to flight on Miss Alison.

'And what flightings she gi'es the puir daft auld body when she thinks I'm nae there,' Marlene reported in the village. It was Marlene's turn now to hold an audience in the shop, for Jess never set a foot outside the house. Old Mrs Rintoul had long since gone to her last home in the kirkyard, but her son's wife who ran the shop was always ready to listen with the other village wifies to Marlene's tales.

'She's a right queer one, that Jess,' said Marlene.

'She was aye a queer one,' said old Mrs Beedie. 'I mind when she came to The Laurels first you'd think butter couldna melt in her mou'. But she's blossomed forth since then. Ay, how she's blossomed! Ye nivir saw sic a change in anybody. The last time I saw her she lookit at me as if I was dust ablow her chariot wheels.'

'She's uppity right enough,' Marlene said. 'Do you ken

what she wants me to do now? She wants me to call her "matron".'

'Ca' her matron!' cried young Mrs Rintoul. 'I'd ca' her across the face wi' a wet haddie before I did that, if I were you.'

'Don't worry,' Marlene said. 'I just never let on I hear her.'

And so time went on. Miss Alison stravaiged the country roads more and more while Jess supped tea and watched the quiz programmes and cowboys on T.V. It was Marlene who always had to go and hunt for Miss Alison when she'd be away longer than she should, and it was Marlene who saw to it that she had a label tied to her wrist with her name and address on it. 'For it's nae safe for her with all thae cars whizzin' along as if they had the Devil himsel' after them,' Marlene said to her audience. 'They might think she was a scarecrow and just knock her doon for the fun o' it.'

'Sma' wonder!' Mrs Beedie said. 'I thocht she was a scarecrow myself the last time I saw her in auld Meldrum's field. She was gey near trippit up by an auld skirt I wouldna have washed the floor in, and she had nothin' else on but a thin bit shawl. The puir cratur' was half-dead wi' cauld.'

'She's aye cauld,' Marlene said. 'Jess'll nae light a fire for her in the sittin' room but gars her sit in the kitchen. So of course the puir auld soul doesna sit there often — and who can blame her wi' Jess sittin' there glowerin' at her like a hen at a worm? If ye ask me, that Jess is featherin' her own nest wi' the money she says she spends on coal and such-like.'

And that's what Jess was doing. Sometimes the lawyer came and kicked up a row about the bills, but Jess always managed to stave him off with her smarmy tongue. One time he nearly raised the roof when he saw how dirty and bedraggled Miss Alison was, but although she'd been caught napping this time — Jess usually managed to know when the lawyer would make an appearance, as though she had second sight — she was fit for him. 'Ay, isn't it terrible?' she cried. 'She was as clean as a new pin this morning, and that's as sure as death. But I can do nothin' with her. As soon as my back's turned she's out of that door and away to roll in the dirt somewhere. Just like a bairn! Oh, she's a terrible trauchle to me, Mr Symington, and if I hadn't promised poor Miss Sarah — God rest her soul! — that I'd look after her, I'd say that she should be sent to a Home. But she'll never go to a Home as long as I have breath in my body and the strength to trauchle on. She's the Cross I'm determined to bear for her poor sister's sake — and for her own sake, too. For they were kindness itself to me when I was a lassie, and I look on them as I'd look on my own mother. Not that I can remember my mother, for I was an orphan as you know. Come away, dear,' she said to Miss Alison, 'we'll go upstairs and you'll have a nice bath, and then you'll have a sup of toddy and we'll put you to bed. You must be tired.'

'Yes, matron,' said Miss Alison.

'Matron?' said Mr Symington.

'Ay, poor lambie,' Jess said, raising her eyes and shaking her head. 'She's taken to callin' me that lately. I cannie tell why. Except that she maybe remembers some of the stories I've told her about the matron in the Home where I was before I came here. She used to be terrible impressed with them, and she once said to me — oh, this is years ago — "I'm glad I never was in a Home like that, Jess my lassie." Her mind wanders, you know.' She shook her head again, then she took Miss Alison gently by the arm and said: 'Come away then, my lamb, and we'll have a nice bath. Say good-bye to Mr Symington.'

Things went on in this way for a long time. At nights Jess sat in the kitchen and watched T.V. while she dreamed about the day when she'd have all the McGlashen money and be able to high-tail it to London and maybe even to New York to cut a dash. And, after she'd come back from the kirk or her walks, Miss Alison would go to bed. But after three or four years Miss Alison wasn't able to get out as much. She was over eighty by this time and her constitution was nearly as weak as her brain, so she took to going to bed in the afternoon.

'And do you ken what that Jess did to her yesterday?' Marlene said one afternoon in the shop. 'I had come back earlier than usual with the messages, and I was just goin' in the back door when I saw her go rampagin' up the stair, yellin' at the pitch o' her voice. I slippit up the stair after her, so I saw it all wi' my own eyes. It's the Gospel Truth. She pulled all the bedclothes offen the puir auld body. "Get up out o' that, ye lazy limmer!" she cries. "Lyin' there like a cow in its own filth. Get up when I tell ye. Don't you dare go to bed after this until I give ye the word. Seven o'clock's your bedtime and not a minute before. Now get doon thae stairs and read your Bible until it's teatime. And not another yelp out o' ye," she says when the puir auld soul gi'es a bit howl and shivers wi' the cauld, "or I'll give ye somethin' to complain about." '

'Did ye ever!' said Mrs Rintoul.

'I tell ye what it is,' said Mrs Beedie. 'That Jess has no imagination. She was brought up in a Home and it was in a Home she should 'a' stayed. She's nothin' but a numskull. If she had a bit more brains she'd have a bit more feelings. But the trouble wi' her is that she hasn't got one ounce of imagination.'

While the wifies were gossiping, Miss Alison was kneeling on the floor of the kitchen. Her skirt was drawn up over her shoulders and her wet, sodden knickers were clinging round her bony knees. Jess stood over her, swishing the doctor's old riding-crop. 'How many times have I tellt ye about this?' she cried. 'You dirty little *orphan*! I'm going to give ye a dozen this time.'

'No, no, please matron!' cried Miss Alison. 'Please, matron, I'll be a good girl.'

But Jess just laughed and brought down the whip with relish. She laughed all the time, while the old woman screamed and tried to crawl under the table, although she was hampered by the wet knickers.

'That'll teach you,' Jess said, throwing down the whip and lighting a cigarette. 'And if you dirty your bloomers again, Alison McGlashen, I'll rub your nose in them.'

'Now, ging into the corner and sing your hymn,' she said.

Blubbering with the abandon of a small child, Miss Alison did as she was bid. Holding her bottom, she wailed:

'All things bright and beautiful,

All creatures great and small,

The Lord God made us orphans

So that matron could make us crawl.'

'Now say you're sorry,' Jess ordered.

'I'm sorry, matron,' whimpered the old woman.

Jess picked up a magazine with a lurid cover and sat down.

'Get out o' my sight,' she said.

Miss Alison hobbled to the door and stood there snivelling. 'I'm going to our other house,' she said, with one hand on the handle.

'Ye can ging and drown yersel' if ye like,' Jess said without looking up.

About half an hour later, however, Jess suddenly sprang out of the chair. The five years weren't up yet. She'd better be careful. She'd better be, and they might even reach the ten. She'd have to watch and not go over the score. What if one of these days the old limmer took her at her word? What would happen if she didn't come back? What if one of these days the policeman appeared at the door . . .

A Gone Woman

When I was a wee girl we used to go for a holiday every year to Granton to bide with Granny and Grandpa. They lived in one of the rows of cottages overlooking the harbour. There were railway lines between the cottages and the harbour, and in the early mornings my brother and I would lie in bed listening, long before anybody else was awake, to the lonely ghost-like whistles of the trains.

It was not a real bed we lay on when we were very small; it was a mattress which, through the day, was hidden away under the double bed our parents slept in. Granny used to call it 'the hurlie-bed ablow the bed', and she often said it should be on a plank-frame with little wheels, a kind of trolley, like the one she'd slept on when she was wee in her own parents' kitchen in a tenement in Dundee. Her 'hurlie-bed' had been easier to dispose of through the day. Daddy and Mammy had to drag the mattress and manoeuvre it under the valance of the double bed, and all this took quite a while and made Daddy whisper swear words.

When we got bigger, though, there were other sleeping arrangements. The cottage had only a kitchen and two bedrooms. Granny and Grandpa slept in the kitchen, in the big bed that had a red paisley-pattern bedspread and valance. Mammy and Daddy slept in the West Room. The East Room was occupied by the sailor who was Granny's lodger.

Granny and Grandpa always called him Mr Grant, but most of the folk in the cottages just called him 'Ginger', and sometimes 'Ginge'. He was a big Hielandman with a great thatch of reddish hair and sandy eyebrows that stuck out a mile. He had a crop of reddish-sandy hair on his cheekbones too, and I often wondered why he never shaved them off. I used to watch him shave, but I never dared ask why he didn't start the sweeps of his cut-throat higher up his cheeks. I wondered, too, about the long thick hair on his chest, the same colour as Granny's doormat and as bristly, that stuck out of his woollen semmit. I was cute enough not to take any notice of that either.

There was no running water in the cottages. Every morning somebody had to go to the tap at the top of the row — Granny aye called it the well — and fetch a bucketful. Several visits to the well were made each day. Of course, when they were on their own, Granny and Grandpa did not need so many buckets. When we stayed there either Mammy or Daddy fetched the water, and sometimes I went too. I liked to go because usually some of the other cottagers were filling their pails at the same time and there was always a lot of laughing and gossip. If you wanted news of anything or anybody in Granton the well was the best place to get it.

We all washed at the wash-stand in the kitchen. A large china basin and ewer with a pattern of violets all over them stood on top of the stand. They were mainly for ornament, though. It was only on special occasions that Roddy and me had our faces washed in the flowery basin; mostly they were washed in a chipped white enamel basin taken from the shelf under the stand. This bottom shelf was hidden by a paisley-patterned valance. Besides hiding the enamel basin and the water-pail, it hid a slop-pail. Granny emptied her potato water and the teapot into this, and sometimes when we were little and it was too wet or too dark for somebody to take us all the distance to the row of outside lavatories, Roddy would pee in it. I was aye feared he would do it in the water-pail instead. I never used the slop-pail myself; I aye went ben to the West Room and used the po under the bed.

Mr Grant had to use the kitchen wash-stand too. He could have used the violety basin if he'd liked, for Granny was always urging him to use it; but he wouldn't, he used the enamel basin like the rest of us. I never saw him washing in the mornings, but every night after we'd all had our tea, he would tap at the kitchen door and come in carrying his towel and shaving gear. 'Time to give my phisog its wee scrape, Mrs Trotter,' he would say to Granny.

Granny always laughed and said: 'Cleanliness is next to Godliness, Mr Grant.'

And Grandpa would add: 'Ye should grow a beard, Mr Grant, like me.'

If Mammy and Daddy were not getting ready to go up-town to Edinburgh in a cable-tram to go to the pictures or a theatre, we would all, except Granny, be sitting round the kitchen range, and we would watch Mr Grant while he shaved. Grandpa sat at the end of the sofa, nearest the fire, so that he could sweep up any ashes that fell on the hearth. When he didn't have the hearth-brush in his hand, he would be tearing an old *Evening News* into strips and making them into spills for lighting his pipe. I always managed to sit next him on either the sofa or the fender. Granny was usually clearing the table. When she'd finished she'd fold her arms and lean against the table talking to Mr Grant while he rolled up his shirt-sleeves and tucked in the top of his shirt and his semmit around his neck, preparing to shave.

I've heard Mammy say Ginger was no longer in his first flush. I suppose he was getting on for thirty when I first mind of him. He had been in the Navy in the Great War. When it was over he didn't want to gang home to Stornoway and he became a deckhand on a trawler that sailed from Granton. He got lodgings with Granny so he'd have a room to keep his belongings in and somewhere to sleep when he was ashore. He gave up the trawlers, though, about 1923 and got a nice cushy berth as second engineer on a ferry boat sailing from Leith to Kirkcaldy. He could easy have got a room in Leith, but he preferred to bide on with Granny.

'The devil you know is better than the one you don't, Mr Trotter,' he said to Grandpa. 'Not that I mean anything by that. Dearie me, it's not a very apt metaphor, is it? I hope you'll not be repeating it to your good lady. I wouldn't like to offend her.' Grandpa did, of course. He could hardly wait till Mr Grant's back was turned before he came out with it. But Granny just laughed and said: 'He kens which side his bread's buttered on. He's pleased wi' me, and I'm pleased wi' him. So we're all quite jecko.'

Mr Grant cycled every day to Leith and back. He left early in the morning; so early that he did not bother Granny by having any breakfast, he had it in a coffee house on Leith docks. None of us ever saw him until he came back about five o'clock and wheeled his bicycle into the East Room, and stood it up against the big mahogany chest of drawers. The cottage had no outhouse, and the lobby was too small to hold a bicycle.

Mr Grant had his tea in his own room while we had ours in the kitchen. It was afterwards, when he came in for his shave, that Granny and him always had their wee chat while the rest of us listened, though usually Grandpa and Mammy kept chipping in.

I was always fascinated by the way Mr Grant cleaned his razor. He made great swoops with it down his lathered cheeks, and then he wiped the lather off on his left fore-arm. By the time he'd finished there were about half a dozen sausages of shaving lather laid parallel along his arm. I was fascinated because Daddy shaved in quite a different way. Every time Daddy drew the razor down his cheeks and chin, he wiped the lather off his blade on a torn-up square of *Evening News*.

Grandpa, of course, didn't need to shave. He just gave his face what Granny called a lick and a promise with cold water, and then after a quick dry he'd spend a lot of time combing out his beard and rubbing hair tonic called 'Thatcho' into his scalp. 'Why don't you put Thatcho on your beard too, Grandpa?' I once said.

'Ask no questions and you'll be told no lies, miss.' Granny said.

Grandpa laughed and said: 'If I put it on my beard, lassie, it would grow down to ma knees and gi'e all the wee laddies a better chance than ever to shout "Beaver" after me.'

'Ye should gi'e the wee brutes a guid cloot wi' yer stick,' Granny said. 'They wouldnie daur shout anythin' after me, I's warrant.'

After he'd shaved and washed and cracked for a while Mr Grant went to his room. About half an hour afterwards, every second or third night, he would knock at the kitchen door, pop his head round it and say: 'Well, folks, I'll bid you farewell just now. Duty calls. Good-night, Mrs Trotter. Good-night, Mr Trotter. Good-night, all.'

'Where d'you think he goes?' Mammy said once.

Granny said: 'He's awa' to meet his fancy lady, of course.'

'What's a fancy lady, Granny?' I asked.

She did not answer. She frowned at Mammy and went back to her reading. Granny was a great reader. She read everything in *The People's Friend* each Friday night, and she could tell you every detail of its serials by Annie S. Swan, Agnes C. Mitchell and Rachel Swete Macnamara. She also read every Zane Grey novel she could lay her hands on, but her greatest favourites were the Tarzan books. She read and re-read them all the time. Grandpa read only the *Evening News* which one of the cottage boys delivered from the newspaper kiosk at the top of Granton pier each evening between five and six. After he'd read it Grandpa would play Snakes and Ladders or Ludo with Roddy and me.

On the nights Granny's sailor did not go out with his fancy lady, he stayed in his room. Sometimes he borrowed the *Evening News*; sometimes he borrowed one of Granny's

Zane Greys. He also spent hours making model ships. He always gave Roddy one each birthday and Christmas. They were beautifully made, and I daresay if we had them now they'd be worth a good bit of money. They were like nothing made nowadays. None of these awful plastic toys, for instance. But Roddy's bairns smashed them to smithereens long ago.

About ten o'clock there would be a light tap on the door, it would open a keek and the sailor would put his hand round it and lift the lavatory-key off its hook. He never said a word; nor did he say anything when he put the key back. If he'd been gone for more than ten minutes Granny and Grandpa would get anxious, and she was sure to say: 'I hope he's all right. I hope he's no' constipated, poor man. I wonder if I daur offer him a dose o' syrup of figs?'

Whether she ever did make this offer I don't know. All I know is that often since then, thinking about my childhood as I watched my own sons grow up in a different environment, I've thought about people like the sailor lodging in places where, although they might be comfortable enough otherwise, they suffered in those times from lack of privacy and the subsequent loss of dignity that are so essential to human happiness. Or did they suffer? And do some people still?

When we grew older Roddy and I stopped sleeping together on the mattress in the West Room. I slept on the kitchen sofa, and every night I'd watch Granny pin a thick grey woollen shawl round her middle, on top of her pink winceyette nightgown. The first time I saw it, I asked: 'What're you putting that on for, Granny?'

'Because I'm goin' to look for Franklin.'

'Who's Franklin?'

'He was a man who discovered the North Pole,' she said. 'Now, you go to sleep like a guid lassie and dinnie fash yoursel' wi' things that don't concern ye.'

138

Roddy went to sleep with the sailor. Mr Grant had a large bed, and Granny hoped Roderick wouldn't disturb him by kicking. 'If he kicks,' she said, 'we could put a bolster down the middle of the bed, Mr Grant, if ye like.'

'There'll be no need for that, Mrs Trotter,' he said. 'Roderick and me'll not fall out over a few kicks, will we, Roddy?'

Sometimes in the evenings Mr Grant would try to teach Roddy to make model ships, but Roddy was not interested. At that time Roddy was more interested in going to the pictures to see Tom Mix and Buck Jones and in driving the milkman's horse.

A lot of itinerant tradesmen and beggars, tinkers and salesmen visited the cottages. There were innumerable insurance men, tinker women selling blackberries, boot-laces and clothes-pegs, a fishwife from Newhaven with a creel on her back, an Indian with a dirty yellow turban selling socks and underwear out of a large fibre suitcase, two or three coal carts, a fish cart, a vegetable cart, a man who played a fiddle, another who sang the same three songs -- 'Mother Macree', 'Keep the Home Fires Burning' and 'The Mountains of Mourne' — each Saturday morning and then went round the doors, cap in hand. The three regular ones, though, that I remember best were Jock the milkman, Alec the baker and Tony the icecream man.

Every day in summer Tony pushed his barrow from his parents' icecream parlour and fish and chip shop in Leith to Newhaven, Trinity and Granton and then he went on to the Quarry, up the Gipsy Brae to Pennywell and Davidson's Mains. He always turned up just before dinner-time, and all the cottage kids would come running to buy cornets and sliders from the barrow that looked like a refrigerator on wheels. Tony's parents were Italian, but he'd been born in Leith and spoke with a harsh glottal-stopped Midlothian accent.

Once or twice a week Mr Grant did not sail on his boat. He pottered about in his room, or he broke sticks for Granny, or he went away on his bike. On these days he always treated Roddy and me to twopenny sliders from Tony's barrow. On the days he wasn't there we had to be content with penny cornets. The cornets were all right but they weren't as luscious as sliders and they didn't look so opulent.

Alec the baker and his brown horse came in the afternoons. His van always stopped in front of Granny's door, and all the women would converge there and gossip while they waited their turns at the open van door. I used to stand among them and eye the big wooden trays that Alec slid out and in with such dexterity, trays full of baps, doughnuts, plain cookies, Bath buns, gingerbread, vanilla cakes and other highly coloured confections. And while they were all gossiping and Alec was chipping in every now and then, telling some spicy bit of news he'd gleaned from Bacon Terrace or Goldenacre, his horse, glad of the opportunity, I suppose, would relieve itself and drop a heap of steaming golden balls.

No sooner did they hear the horse fart than the women would all laugh, and Beanie Carr, a right auld witch if ever there was one, would cackle: 'Ye'll no' need to buy any oranges this week, Mrs Trotter, ye're havin' them delivered on yer doorstep.'

Granny wasn't amused. Grandpa used to laugh, though, when he went out with a shovel and put the dung over the palings into the bit of wasteground beside the railway lines. 'If only I had an allotment,' he'd say.

'And what would you do with an allotment, ye daft auld man?' Granny would answer. 'It would be useless to ye.'

'I ken it's only a dream,' he said once. 'But it would be a grand way of gettin' vegetables for nothin'. We could maybe have got Mr Grant to give us a wee hand with it. It would've given him an interest, and digging's guid exercise.'

'Huh, he's got enough interests as long as he's in tow with that gone woman,' Granny said. Then, seeing I was listening, she said no more.

Jock the milkman came every morning about ten

140

o'clock. Jock was a very red-faced young man and he drove a skittish grey horse and trap. Roddy usually went to the end of the road leading into the cottages to wait for Jock coming. But if by any chance he happened to be in the house he'd be out of the door like a flash as soon as he heard the rattle of the milk-cans and Jock yelling to the high-stepper: 'Whoa there! Whoa there, y' brute!'

By dint of admiring the horse and stroking its nose, Roddy got to be very pally with Jock, and when he was old enough Jock used to take him for a drive every morning. Sometimes Roddy sat beside Jock on the seat at the front of the trap and was allowed to hold the whip; and sometimes he stood on the back step, ready to jump off and deliver the cans of milk to save Jock leaving the seat. Sometimes he held the horse when Jock had to make deliveries and collect cash that he couldn't delegate to a small boy. Always Roddy would gang with Jock as far as Trinity Square, and sometimes as far as Newhaven though he wasn't supposed to go that far, and then he'd come back bragging about having driven the horse along Lower Granton Road and that Jock had given him threepence to buy gobstoppers or a bar of chocolate or whatever else took his fancy.

When we were wee we were never allowed inside the East Room, not even when Granny was dusting and sweeping. When Roddy was old enough to sleep with the sailor, though, I used to go in and get him up in the morning. Roddy was aye sleeping when Mr Grant left, so the first thing he did on wakening up was to see if Mr Grant had left four pennies on the mantelpiece so we could buy an icecream slider each. Sometimes the money was there, sometimes it wasn't. If it wasn't there, Roddy would say that maybe Mr Grant had hidden it, so we would have a good rake to look for it.

Once, when I was lifting up the different ornaments and bric-a-brac on the mantelpiece, I saw a photograph I'd never seen before. It was a pretty woman with a low-cut dress and a string of Ciro pearls and her hair cut in the newfangled shingle. 'Who's that, Mammy?' I asked, for she had come in to roustle Roddy out of bed, telling him the milkman would be here before he had time to have his breakfast.

'That's Mr Grant's young lady,' she said.

A wee while later I heard Granny say to Mammy: 'Young lady my foot! She's a gone woman with a bairn that's no' got a faither. Poor man, he'll rue the day he ever took up wi' her.'

'Och, Mother, she might be all right.'

'Na, na,' Granny said. 'He'll rue the day, I's warrant. Ye cannie touch pitch without gettin' defiled. Nor do ye take on another man's leavings without livin' to regret it.'

'Och, he's been going with her a long time,' Mammy said. 'He must ken the best and the worst of her by now. Have you ever seen her?'

'Ay, he had the cheek to bring her here one Sunday and expect me to give her tea,' Granny said. 'But I put my foot down. I wasn't prepared for visitors, I tellt him. I had no fancy bread in the house, so I said he'd be better to take his lady friend up the town to a restaurant.'

'Really, Mother!'

'Well, I wasn't havin' any. Yet she had the nerve to come back on her own not long after that. She brought some photies o' her wee laddie to show me. Hopin' to win me round, I daresay. But ma heart wasn't softened. A bonnie enough bairn, mind ye, give him his due. When I was lookin' at them she brought up the subject o' the faither. "He was a sailor," she says. "He was drooned at Jutland. That's what made me take up with Ginger, him bein' at that battle too, like." I said: "I'm surprised at ye, Miss Matheson, lettin' yourself be so cheap." "Ah well," she says, "it's a cauld country and you have to do somethin' in the winter-time." "Ay," I says, "it seems to me you've been doin' it in the summer as well." '

'She took a huff then,' Granny said. ' "You don't like me, Mrs Trotter, do you?" she says. What a like thing to say to me, eh? I was fair dumbfoundered at her impidence.

142

But I never answered. I held ma wheesht, and off she went tossin' her silly wee heid. Then she turned at the corner and shouts: "Anyway, I'm goin' to marry Ginge whether you like it or not." "I'm not stoppin' you, my lady," I says. "Mr Grant kens his own bent best." '

'What's a gone woman, Granny?' I asked.

'None o' your business, miss,' she said. 'And get out o' here quick or I'll make it my business to give ye a thick ear for listenin' in when you're not wanted.'

The year I was fourteen Mammy had a letter from Granny saying Mr Grant had left. He had married his lady love and they were away to bide in Aberdeen, where he'd got a job as chief engineer on a trawler. *He wants to get back to sea again,'* she wrote. *'To the deep sea, he says, the great open spaces. A fine excuse if you ask me to get away from her ladyship.'*

That summer Mammy and I went on our own to Granton. Daddy was too busy to have a holiday, and Roddy went to Arran to camp with the Boy Scouts. He had long since lost all interest in Jock the milkman and his grey horse, and I wasn't jealous any longer of not being allowed to ride on the step of Jock's trap in case folk could see my bloomers.

Except for the loss of Mr Grant, everything was much the same. Mammy slept in the East Room, and I slept in the West. One night as we were going to bed I saw Granny was getting into hers wearing only a nightgown. I said: 'Where's the shawl you used to put on to go and look for yon man, Granny?'

'What man?'

'Franklin,' I said, remembering the name suddenly.

'I dinnie ken anybody named Franklin,' she said. 'Are you sure you're no' mixing whoever it was up wi' Mr Frank, the Store butcher? What would I be puttin' on a shawl to go and look for him for? I wouldnie give twopence for him, and I cannie imagine goin' lookin' for him if he was the last man on God's earth. Ye must ha'e dreamt it, lassie.'

I didn't dream it. I didn't dream it any more than I

143

dreamt about Jock the milkman and Alec the baker and Tony the icecream man, or Mr Grant and his gone woman. She has aye remained a figure well in the forefront of my mind, although I only saw her photograph. The last I heard, her laddie that wasn't Mr Grant's but another sailor's was a Town Councillor some place in the Highlands and doing very nicely, thank you.

Local Boy Makes Good

Davina and Kenneth were not at home when the letter came. They were on a bat that started in Soho one lunch-time and finished in a back-street pub in Pimlico four nights later. When they came back to the studio after midnight with Esther Anscombe, young Mike, George Norris, a bottle of whisky and a dozen light ales, the letter was on the mat. Davina picked it up, squinted at it, and handed it to Kenneth.

MacMahon did not even glance at it. He was bustling about, hunting for the corkscrew. After he'd found it on the floor among some broken glass, a paint rag and a torn-up canvas of Davina's, he gave it to young Mike, indicated the whisky with a nod, and held up the letter by the corner.

'Now I wonder who this could be from?' he said in his deepest, richest tones, giving each word a sonorous ring. And he turned the letter this way and that, but made no move to open it. He and Davina seldom opened letters, for usually they were bills or letters from solicitors saying that unless payment was made proceedings would be taken.

'Why don't you open it and see?' George Norris asked sarcastically. He was a big, beefy, red-faced young man just back from five years as a policeman in Kenya. He had met Davina Weir and Kenneth MacMahon for the first time that morning in a pub and had tagged along with them only because he wanted to sleep with Esther Anscombe. He had not been impressed when Esther had told him they were famous artists; he thought they looked disreputable, and their wild behaviour, their singing and dancing in crowded places, made him squirm with embarrassment. Several times he had tried to get Esther to leave them, but she had refused. If Davina and Kenneth were aware of his antagonism, they ignored it; they put up with him because he had been standing them drinks all day and had paid for the whisky.

'Maybe it's from the Duchess,' young Mike said.

'Oh ay, the Duchess never forgets me,' MacMahon said complacently, turning over the envelope again and peering at the crest on the back.

Davina, who had slumped in a broken-down easy-chair, on top of some books and an old coat, suddenly came out of her coma and, thumping the arm of the chair, shouted: 'Where's my whisky? Where the hell's my whisky?'

Mike poured some in a tumbler, almost half-filling it, and handed it to her.

MacMahon had at last read the letter. He gave it to Davina, saying: 'It's frae the Earl of Braesdale no less! His Imperial Highness wants me to open the new reservoir at Glendownie.'

'And what do you ken about water-works?' Davina cried. 'You that never touches water outside or in!'

'I wash oftener than you, my love,' MacMahon hissed, and he gave an eldritch screech. 'If I didnie keep at ye you'd never put on a clean sark.'

Davina peered at the letter, reading aloud phrases: 'It would give the Town Council and myself the greatest pleasure if you would perform the opening ceremony . . . Of course I realize you are a busy man, but as a great admirer of your work . . . deem it an honour . . .'

'Local boy makes good, eh?' George said with a snigger,

146

but catching young Mike's eye he turned it into a cough and said: 'What about a snort, old man?'

Mike poured a drop of whisky into a plastic eggcup and pushed it across the table at him. 'There're no glasses left,' he said sullenly.

'A reservoir!' Davina exclaimed. 'It would have been more like it if it'd been a pissoir.'

'Ay,' MacMahon said. 'I could have done the christening greater justice. I could have been the first customer!'

' "As Glendownie's most prominent son . . . " ' Davina muttered. 'And what about me? What about "Glendownie's most prominent daughter"? Who won the Guggenheim Prize I'd like to ken!'

'We all know you did, my love,' MacMahon said soothingly. 'Ye've never let us forget it! But ye must remember, my bonnie wee doo, that you're no' really a native of Glendownie. You were born outside the city limits in the parish of Aberlossie.'

'The city!' Davina cried. 'It shouldnie even be called a town. It hasnie got a decent street — nothing but wynds and closes! Still, I'm no' jealous. I ken my place. A woman born beyond the pale!' She peered again at the letter. 'Ay, little did your puir mother ken when she brought ye forth thirty-eight years ago what an honour she was doing to our native land.'

'Come!' MacMahon cried with dignity. 'Let us dance! Let us waggle our bums and let joy be unconfined!'

He walked solemnly to a cupboard and brought out a kilt. As he fastened it round his waist, on top of his trousers, he lost his balance slightly, but he tossed his head, advanced with exaggerated care into the middle of the room, put his hands on his hips and cried: 'Positions!'

Esther had put a record on the gramophone, and at the first strains of a Scots reel, MacMahon flung his arms above his head, snapped his fingers, and began to do a sword dance.

'Hook!' cried George.

Young Mike glared at him. 'If you can't pronounce it

right, pipe down,' he said.

'More whisky!' yelled Davina. 'I'm being neglected even in my ain hoose.'

After she'd half-emptied her glass again, she stared moodily at it and said: 'And what're we going to use for money? I notice the noble lord doesnie trouble to send us our fares. "A luncheon will be held in your honour" — but what good's a bit o' chicken and a glass o' champagne if we havenie the wherewithal to get to the table!'

'And who said you were going with me?' MacMahon hissed, leaning forward at the end of an elaborate whirl.

'Have ye never heard that there's no show without Judy?' Davina demanded. 'And you ken as well as I do that you need somebody to look after you. Where will we get the money, I say!'

'Wheesht!' cried MacMahon, snapping his fingers vigorously. 'We'll raise it somehow. We've aye managed.'

'Ah, but it's not as easy as it was ten — even five! — years ago,' Davina said. 'In the days when all we needed to do was to turn on a bit charm and the cash flowed in.'

'And flowed out again just as quick! Do ye hear me?' MacMahon yelled. 'It flowed out again just as quick!' He poured himself a good three inches of whisky and drank half of it at one swallow. 'Ay, those were the days,' he said. 'The good old days before Soho got swamped by a lot o' wee skitters running about in jeans and getting drunk on half a bitter and six cups of coffee.' He drank the rest of the whisky, threw the glass into a corner, and cried dramatically: 'Oh, 'tis a shameful place now and not fit for folk of our calibre!'

'I'll see if I can raise the money, Kenneth honey,' Esther said.

'It's good of you, Esther,' MacMahon said with dignity. 'But we must mind that you have two wee bairns whose need comes before ours. Come, another dance!'

'More whisky!' Davina shouted.

After the whisky bottle had been drained into her glass, Davina sat motionless for a long time, then suddenly she leaned forward and pointed her glass menacingly at George. 'What's that man doing here?' she cried. 'That one that shoves red-hot pokers up Mau Mau's arses. And *boasts* about it! I dinnie like him. What is he doing in my house? Get out!'

'Wheesht, my love,' said MacMahon, opening a bottle of light ale with his teeth. 'Who are you to cast a finger of scorn at the builders of empire? You that's not even fit to be asked to open a water-works!'

By the time the light ales were drunk, Davina was asleep, Esther had retired to a divan in the next room, George had been hustled out by Mike and put in a taxi, MacMahon was still twirling about like a dervish, and Mike was gazing dreamily at the Earl of Braesdale's letter that was lying on the floor, stained with beer and some red wine that MacMahon had found in the cupboard.

Esther loaned them seventy pounds from money sent by her father in South Africa. MacMahon borrowed a dark grey suit from an admirer who worked in a city office. And, after a lot of the money had been spent on a farewell party lasting three days, a crowd came to see Davina and MacMahon off at King's Cross.

MacMahon waved out of the window until the train was well beyond the platform, then he lurched back and sat on the lap of an old man who had been cowering in his corner, terrified by the frenzied screeching of MacMahon, Davina, and their friends.

'I beg your pardon, sir,' MacMahon cried, enunciating each word carefully and bowing with old-world courtesy. 'You must forgive my friends. They're a wee thing ob-strep-er-ous! But I am returning to my native land to christen a water-works, and the occasion demands it. In two days time you will be able to read all about it.'

But Glendownie's most prominent son nearly did not make it. He arrived in his home town twenty-four hours late. After the old man fled in horror to another compartment, one of three soldiers in the corridor said 'How are ye, china?' to Davina; and after she had cried: 'Oh, Kenneth, a boy from *Glasgow!*' they became lifelong friends and all went on to Aberdeen together.

Late at night old Mrs MacMahon heard a wild knocking at the door of her wee cottage, and when she went downstairs in her nightgown, her first-born fell headlong into the lobby.

'Oh, it's you, Kenneth,' she said placidly. 'Ye're in a sad shape, son. Are ye on yer own?'

'No, I've just dropped Davina at her mother's.'

'So you've not got yer marriage lines yet?'

'No, we never seem to have the time.'

'Ten years,' Mrs MacMahon mused. 'But I suppose ye're aye that busy.'

'Ay, that's it,' MacMahon said sleepily.

'Well, I just hope ye'll be fit enough to press the button or whatever it is ye're supposed to do the morn. Lord love us, laddie!' She helped him up, then she shouted up the stairs: 'Geordie! Geordie, come and help to put yer brother to his bed.'

Next morning at eleven o'clock the Glendownie Reservoir was opened with pomp and ceremony. Mr Kenneth MacMahon, the celebrated artist — 'an everlasting credit to our little town and a worthy example to all you schoolchildren gathered here today' — performed his duty with dignity and aplomb. Miss Davina Weir — 'another famous native of our town who has arrived unexpectedly for this great occasion' — nodded benignly under a small floral hat that had been loaned to her by a girl on *Vogue*: a hat she had carried in a box on the journey and that had been mislaid for three hours in a pub in Aberdeen. Friends and neighbours who had not seen him for a few years thought that 'Kenny looked a lump aulder and a wee thing peakit — but of course he maun be tired after that lang journey.'

Mrs MacMahon, who had been up since five o'clock

sponging and pressing the grey suit and taking in the neck of a white shirt of Geordie's so that it would fit his brother, was fell proud of him as she sat on the platform between the Countess of Braesdale and the Provost's wife. Only she knew how sick he'd been that morning and how his hands had kept shaking until Geordie had unearthed a half bottle of the hard stuff. And she smiled and nodded as Lady Braesdale congratulated her after Kenneth's speech — a speech that made folk laugh and put them in a good humour when he told a few tales about the time he'd been a bare-foot laddie and had guddled for trout in this very burn that had now been turned into a great reservoir. And she said: 'Oh ay, m'lady, Kenneth was aye as good with his tongue as he was at the drawing — but that was a black bare-faced lie about running barefoot! He never ran bare-foot in his life. His father and I aye saw that our weans were well-shod even though we had a hard scrape.'

Mrs MacMahon also managed to smile when Miss Davina Weir was called upon to say a few words. But the smile lost some of its affability when Davina recalled that while she was a student in Paris she had been surprised when she'd heard a Scottish voice in an art class and had turned round to find that it belonged to 'Kenneth MacMahon that I hadn't seen since we were bairns in the same class in the auld school here. I minded fine how he'd once copied my sums and when we were both wrong he'd tellt the teacher I had copied off *him*! So I just said to him: "Well, MacMahon, I hope ye'll no' copy off my easel here!" And do you ken what he said? He said: "There's no need for that, Weir my lassie. Here I am supreme! If you copy off me you cannie go far wrong!"'

Afterwards at the lunch Mrs MacMahon was not too pleased either when she saw that Davina's old mother had been squeezed into a place at the top table. She and Mrs Weir hadn't spoken to each other for going on for ten years. But she gave her a bit nod, just in case Mrs Weir didn't notice that she was sitting between the Earl of Braesdale and Sir Malcolm Arbuthnot. And then she turned her attention to the Provost, old John Macmillan that had the grocer's shop, and she laughed with everybody else when he told a long story about the time when wee Kenny MacMahon had pestered him for a job as errand-boy and how he'd given it to him at last because he'd been that quick at counting the empty bottles in the back-yard. But she turned to Lord Braesdale and said: 'I'm thinking the Provost's as glib with his tongue as our Kenneth himself — though neither of them have got what you'd call good memories. Kenneth never ran errands for John Macmillan in his life.'

A week later Geordie MacMahon and Davina Weir hoistered the celebrated artist onto the night train for London and settled him in a corner. They had consumed a lot of fare-well drinks, but nothing like as many as Kenneth. Mrs MacMahon had sponged and pressed the grey suit that morning, but even she would have been hard put to it to have recognized it now.

'Well, Davina,' Geordie said, 'are ye sure ye'll manage?'

'Of course we'll manage,' she said. 'Haven't we aye managed? The only thing that worries me is that I've lost that bloody hat!'

'There's a half bottle in Kenny's bag,' Geordie said. 'But I wouldnie let him touch it until you're well on the other side o' Newcastle.'

'I'll see to that,' she said.

'Not a drop, man, not a drop!' Kenneth roused himself and leaned out of the window to shake his brother's hand. Geordie had to disengage his fingers as the train started to move. 'It's been a wonderful family reunion, son. Wonderful! Be sure and look after the auld wife, son . . . Be sure and . . .'

His voice sank to a whisper as the train gathered speed. He withdrew his head and slumped on the seat. Davina smoothed her hair, then she rose, lifted the bag from the rack, opened it and took out the bottle. She was putting it to her mouth when MacMahon reached for it. After he had drank long and deep he handed it back with a little bow and said: 'Well, I needed that after all I've been through these past few days. Opening a reservoir's a more strenuous job than folk would think.'

'Ay, it's just a pity that we dinnie get paid for being so public-spirited,' Davina said, and she sighed as she wiped her mouth.

Princess McDougall

I

'I see we've got the Princess wi' us again this trip,' the grey-haired steward said.

'Eh? What d'ye mean, Jock?' said the young pimply-faced steward. 'Whatten princess are ye talkin' aboot?'

'Her.' Jock pointed along B Deck. 'Yon auld wife wi' the blue-rinsed hair. Her that's got a chest like a pouter pigeon. See, she's lightin' a fag. Oh, she's a real professional when it comes to lightin' a fag. Must've been doin' it since she was a bairn. Mind you, she doesnie smoke as much as she used to. But when I kent her first a fag was never outen her mouth. It just shows this cancer malarky's a lot o' balls. If it was true she'd've been a goner long syne.'

'Och, d'ye mean Mrs Wilkie?'

'Ay, that's her,' Jock said. 'I aye forget her name — though God knows I should ken it by this time, she's been wi' us that often. Her man used to call her "Princess", so I aye think aboot her like that. Oh, what a pantymime it was when he and she used to travel thegither. It was "Princess this" and "Princess that" and "Are you all right, Princess dear? You're not in a draught, are you?" I help my God, as if ye could keep out o' draughts in the middle o' the Atlantic!'

The woman they were talking about leaned on the rail, cigarette drooping in the corner of her faintly purple-lipsticked mouth, and gazed down at the Montreal docks. She was a big woman wearing a skull-fitting hat of black feathers and a mink coat. Her heavy pale face was sullen, but her light hazel-green eyes darted quickly here and there, scanning the passengers coming aboard.

'I wish I had a fiver for every time she's made this trip,' Jock said. 'She's been back and forrit frae here to Glasgow that often I've got fair dizzy keepin' up wi' her. Oh, I've kent her for years. She's a nice-like body, mind. Oh yes, she's all right. A civil nice woman. A very superior person. Even if she's gettin' a bit long in the tooth now. Mind you, she's no' everybody's cup. She has one o' those la-di-da Edinburgh voices that get yer goat sometimes. Awful high-pan, ye ken. Except that she'd never say "ken". Oh no! She aye talks awful proper. I mind fine when she made her first trip. She was a Miss McDougall then, and she was goin' to Canady to marry her man. That was a good while syne. It must've been about 1932. Mind you, she was an auldish hen then. She must've been over forty.'

'No spring chicken like,' the young steward said.

'Far from it. I was a spry young joker myself then, and I mind I thought she was near auld enough to be my mother. If she hadnie been I might've been after her, for I was a lad for the lassies and she was a fine big bang piece. But even if she'd gi'en me any encouragement — and she didnie — I knew I had to draw the line.'

Jock sighed. 'Ah well, time flies and we're all gettin' aulder. Puir Princess, she's a widdy woman now — her man died a guid few years back — and here am I wi' only another three years to go before I'll ha'e to retire whether I like it or no' . . .'

II

When Alice McDougall was a child she was so clean and

fastidious that her brothers called her the pernickety princess. As she got older she grew even more fastidious. Her fear of dirtying her hands became almost a fetish. She never stopped washing them and manicuring her nails.

The McDougalls lived in the West Cottages in Granton. At that time Granton was separated from Edinburgh by many fields and Inverleith Park. It more or less still resembled the village it had been in the days of Mary, Queen of Scots. It was feudal. Granton belonged to the Duke, and so did everything on it, including the harbour for the North Sea trawlers and the *William Muir*, the ferry boat that went backwards and forwards across the Firth of Forth several times a day to Burntisland on the Fife coast. The goods trains from Leith and Edinburgh chuff-chuffed and shunted along the railway lines in front of the McDougalls' cottage. As a very small child Alice was warned never to cross the lines without looking first to make sure that an engine wasn't anywhere near her. The only times she ever crossed the lines alone were when she went to Jimmy Greig's coffee house at the top of the middle pier to buy mutton pies or to Mrs Riddell's newspaper kiosk to get the Edinburgh *Evening News*. The other children in the cottages ran across the lines continually when they were playing among the fish-boxes or were on the pier watching the trawlers coming in. Great piles of fish-boxes, often ten or twelve feet high, lay along the side of the harbour; also great heaps of old railway-sleepers, and they made a happy hunting ground for the Granton children. But Alice seldom played there with the others; she was too afraid of dirtying herself, and she did not like the feel of the greasy fish-boxes or their strong smell.

Alice's father was a signal-man on the railway. Folk said he was a bit above himself and that he fancied his chances when he wasn't on duty. On Sundays he wore his grey homburg hat cocked at an angle, and he always spoke in a clipped accent that he thought was the same as the gentry's. George McDougall had a closely trimmed Imperial beard and he was very dapper, with small feet in highly polished shoes. He walked very erect and never moved off the pavement for anybody. But he was very polite and always raised his hat to the ladies of the Church Guild. His wife, Elspeth, was a keen worker in the Guild and never missed going to church every Sunday morning. She took her family with her, but as the years went on her sons soon found excuses for not accompanying her to the family pew, and at last there were usually only her and Alice sitting in it. Her neighbours said Mrs McDougall was like her man and 'fancied her buckie' because she was the daughter of the captain of a ferry boat that went daily from Leith to Kirkcaldy. This may have been jealousy because the brass of the letter-box, the knocker and the number 10 on the McDougall door was more often and more highly polished than the brass on most of the other doors in the cottages.

Alice was born in 1891. Her nearest brother, Willie, was seven years older. Alice had been a surprise packet. Because of this her parents wrapped her in cotton wool as much as they could. The winds weren't allowed to blow on her. When she was fourteen Alice left the Granton school, having stayed at it much longer than the girls who'd started at the same time in the infants' class, for most of them had left at the ages of eleven and twelve to go to work. Elspeth McDougall was finding life a bit of a trauchle, so Alice was not sent out to work; she stayed at home and helped her mother. Her two eldest brothers, Donald and Jim, were working on the Duke's railway, and Jock and Willie were in a small engineering firm near the Quarry, a mile and a half from home. They cycled to their work, but Donald and Jim had no need of bicycles; the goods yard was close to the cottages. When Donald, who was twenty-five, wanted to meet his girl, a housemaid in a mansion at Trinity, he got a loan of one of the bicycles, and this quite often led to rows when the younger brothers also started to do some steady wenching.

By the time Alice was seventeen she was a competent housewife. But she never got harassed and dishevelled like her mother and the other women in the cottages. She never had a hair out of place. Even when she was deep in the big tub washing her brothers' dirty shirts and dungarees she kept her sleeves down and wore the gold wristlet watch that her parents had given her for her sixteenth birthday. By this time nobody in the family ever called her 'Alice'; she was known to them all, as well as to most of the neighbours, as 'Princess'.

III

After Donald and Jock got married there wasn't so much work to do. And when Jim got engaged to Daisy Gordon it looked as though there would be less, so Alice decided to get a job since her mother was well able to look after the diminished family on her own. Alice was eighteen. She wanted to earn some money for herself. Most of the girls she knew had jobs in the rope works, the net works or the sail works, but she was not going to do such dirty work. She applied for a job as a sales lady with Hutchinsons, the big drapers on the South Bridge in Edinburgh, and although she had no experience she got it at a wage of ten shillings a week. Her hours were from half-past eight in the morning until seven o'clock at night. It meant leaving home each day about a quarter to eight and travelling by cable tram: a rocketty-racketting journey that had almost jolted her out of her corsets by the time the tram, going uphill all the way, past the Theatre Royal and the General Post Office, deposited her outside the old Tron Church in the Royal Mile.

When she'd been with Hutchinsons for three years, Alice became the head of the ladies' underwear department; but after two years of this she made up her mind to have a change. She got a better paid job in Finlay's in Princes Street as head of the children's outfits department. She stayed there during the whole of the 1914-18 war, though her brothers kept urging her to go into munitions and make more money. In 1919 she went to Robert Maule's at the

159

West End as a buyer for ladies' and children's underclothes: a job — though Princess called it a position — that meant she had to travel fairly often down to Manchester and London. She got this position through her friend Miss Cochrane, who was a buyer for ladies' coats and had been with Maule's since she was sixteen.

Miss Cochrane's name also was Alice. She lived in Granton Square, in a flat above the Bank. Her father was the head clerk of one of the Duke's offices. Alice Cochrane was three or four years older than Alice McDougall, and they'd known each other since they were bairns. But they never became chummy until Alice McDougall joined the church choir. Miss Cochrane already was the choir's leading contralto. Miss McDougall also was an alto, so naturally they clung together because most of the other Granton girls were sopranos. 'A lot of skirlers,' Miss Cochrane said.

Miss Cochrane was a big woman, and so was Miss McDougall. They were big bosomed and majestic: handsome women rather than pretty ones. They did not go in for fripperies, but they were always better dressed than any of the other young women in Granton. They had what Miss Cochrane called 'class'. In their teens they cultivated deep contralto voices and as they always spoke very politely, enunciating each word, they had to speak slowly so that they wouldn't fall back into the vernacular. The Granton folk said they were stuck up ('Though what else would ye expect wi' their faithers bein' such head bummers!' one tolerant old man said), and the young wags imitated their voices and the way they walked. They did not walk like other women. They sailed, with heads thrown back.

Once a week Miss McDougall and Miss Cochrane went together to the theatre, and sometimes they went to the Usher Hall to hear the Edinburgh Choral Union sing *Messiah* or some other cantata. They scorned musical comedies, saying they preferred something 'deeper'. They never missed seeing John Martin-Harvey in *The Only Way* or Fred Terry and Julia Neilson in *Sweet Nell of Old Drury* and other plays in their repertoire. But after seeing him as

King Lear, they never went to another performance of Sir Frank Benson's; they always went to another theatre on the weeks the Benson Company visited the Royal Lyceum.

Although they were such keen singers, they went only with reluctance to the dances the choir sometimes organized in the church hall. On these occasions they never danced; they frowned on the Military Two-Step, the Boston Two-Step, the Highland Schottische and square dances like the Lancers and the Quadrilles, and they considered the Cake Walk vulgar. They could not be prevailed upon even to waltz. But they helped to hand around the tea, sandwiches and cakes, and at spaced intervals between the dances they were always willing to sail majestically onto the platform and sing either solos or a duet. Miss Cochrane's favourite solos were 'Oh, For the Wings of a Dove' and 'The Londonderry Air', and Miss McDougall's were 'Just a Song at Twilight' and 'The Mountains of Mourne'. Their favourite duet was 'Billy Boy'. And they thought they were terribly daring when they sang:

'Where have you been all the day, Billy boy, Billy boy?
Where have you been all the day, my Billy boy?
I've been courting all the day
Of my charming Nancy Grey.
And my Nancy tickled my fancy!
Oh, my charming Nancy Grey!'

Even well into the middle of the 1920s they were still singing these songs, though most folk had got tired of them and were wanting something a bit livelier like 'Horsey, Keep Your Tail Up'.

In the summer, once a week, Miss Cochrane and Miss McDougall went to play tennis at the public courts in Inverleith Park. When they glided across Granton Square to board a cable tramcar at the terminus, with their racquets under their arms and their white shoes in linen bags, the young wags who congregated around the long wooden seat at the Smiddy Corner would shout to them in falsetto voices: 'Forty, love!' and 'Your service, partner!' And then one youth would say to another: 'Do you play tennis,

Dennis?' and the other would reply: 'No, I play hockey, cocky!'

At the tennis courts they met a number of young men of what they called a more superior class. They played doubles with bank clerks and insurance clerks. But these partnerships never developed into anything more serious. For a time Miss McDougall was rather keen on Ronald Stout, a redheaded young man with freckles, and she talked quite a lot about what Ronald thought of this and what Ronald said about that. When Willie, the last McDougall son still unmarried and at home, who was earning big money in a Leith engineering firm, asked what this paragon did, Princess said he was 'coming out to be a chartered accountant'. Willie, who always spoke in the broadest Scots as if to flout the la-di-da accents of his parents and sister, guffawed and said: 'That reminds me o' yon bar. Have ye heard it, Dad? There was a felly goin' into hospital wi' a cut hand, and at the door he met another young felly in a white overall. Are ye sure ye havenie heard this bar? Well, the felly wi' a cut hand says, "Are ye a student comin' out for a doctor?" "No," says the other yin, "I'm a painter comin' out for a pee." '

Princess was not amused.

As none of the young men they met at tennis or talked to in the intervals at the theatre ever showed any inclination to press the acquaintanceship further, the two Alices, by the time they were in their thirties, were evidently destined to be spinsters. Even older women who'd known them since they were bairns, stopped calling them 'Alice' and always addressed them as 'Miss McDougall' and 'Miss Cochrane'. Not that they were ever inclined to dress or behave like the old maids of fiction or legend. They were always in the vanguard of fashion; the first young women in Granton to sport 'glad necks' and to wear Russian boots. They were thought to be very daring when they smoked gold-tipped 'My Darling' cigarettes at the theatre, taking the little lilac coloured boxes from their dorothy bags with a flourish.

During all the years of their close friendship they always addressed each other formally. When Alice Cochrane would come into the lingerie department of Maule's to have a little gossip it was not for the benefit of the staff that she'd say: 'I'll meet you at the entrance to the Dress Circle at seven o'clock, Miss McDougall,' or 'I think it's time we went out for lunch, Miss McDougall. Will we go to McVittie's?' It was because she'd never dreamed of calling her 'Alice' or 'Princess'.

In the 1920s the two Alices, smartly dressed and consequential as befitted their positions as senior executives of Robert Maule's, began to go occasionally to lighter forms of entertainment; they needed to have some knowledge of musical comedies like *No, No Nanette, Mercenary Mary* and *Katja the Dancer* so that they could talk on slightly more personal terms with the executives of the wholesale firms they bought goods from. As they got older and their business life — trips to London and other cities — meant more to them than their home life in Granton, they went to fewer church socials and choir dances; they sang no longer in 'kinderspiels' like *Princess Chrysanthemum* and *The Princess of Poppyland,* annual near-Christmas plays in the church hall, in which all the young people of Granton either had parts or sang in the chorus, though they still continued to sing in the choir. By this time, too, they had stopped playing tennis. Once, Miss Cochrane suggested that they take up golf instead, but Princess McDougall objected. She said: 'Ectually, Miss Cochrane, I do not think it would be a frightfully good ideah. One has *so* much walking, and goaf is rether strenuous, don't you think?'

'I wouldn't say thet, Miss McDougall. But I must admit thet it is rether a perspiring game.'

Miss Cochrane was the first woman of her own generation in Granton to buy a fur coat. It was a smart three-quarter-length musquash, and it was admired on the tram cars and at church socials. Envious girls in the choir would say: 'Gi'es a shot o' your fur coat, Miss Cochrane.' And when, with a regal and patronizing air, she would allow them to slip on the coat, they would parade up and down, admiring themselves and exclaiming: 'I fair fancy myself in a coat like this. But och, the price! I couldnie afford it.'

Not to be outshone, Miss McDougall followed suit quickly by getting a full-length squirrel. She hesitated between it and a beaver, but decided in the end that the grey squirrel suited her fair complexion better.

'There'll be nae holdin' them back now,' one old woman in the West Cottages said to another while they were fetching pails of water from the communal well.

'Ay, but they havenie been able to get men yet,' the other old wife said. 'Fine feathers are no' everything, hen!'

In their twenties the two Alices were the talk of Granton because they rubbed their faces with Icilma Cream and used paper poudré to keep their noses from being shiny. When they got a little older and were seen powdering their noses with puffs kept in vanity cases people said they'd come to a bad end. 'I wonder at the minister allowin' such brazen hizzies to sing in the choir in the Lord's Own House,' old Granny Montgomery said. 'Them and their glad necks! It's scandalous. I've a guid mind to complain to the Kirk Session aboot them.'

'Ach, Granny, I wouldnie fash my arse,' Mrs Brunton said.

'I'll fash my arse if I like,' Granny said. 'You can dae what ye like wi' yours. It's a downright disgrace. They think they're sae grand wi' all their airs and graces, but they're nothin' but a couple of jezziebels.'

What Granny Montgomery would have said when the two Alices got their hair shingled will never be known; she was dead by that time. But Elspeth McDougall went her mile when Princess announced she was going to have it done. 'The Lord gave you a grand head of hair and you have no right to cut it off,' she said. 'I can't see, anyway, what you want to do it for.'

'It's the feshion, mother,' Princess said. 'And I must

keep in the feshion. I rether fency the style.'

'I wonder what Queen Mary thinks of it,' Mrs McDougall said. 'Can you imagine her having her hair shingled?'

Willie guffawed and said: 'I doot her toques would be far ower wee for her then. She's need to buy hersel' a lot o' new ones.'

'I'm sure Her Majesty will never allow Princess Mary to have hers done.'

'Och, maybe Lord Lascelles'll tell her to get it done when he gets her safely oot o' the auld woman's clutches,' Willie said. 'You go and get yer hair cut in time for the weddin', Princess, and to hell wi' everybody.'

Mrs McDougall wept when Alice came home with her shorn head. 'Oh, your braw hair!' she lamented. 'If I was you I'd never dare lift my head again.'

When she was getting on for thirty-five Alice McDougall began to grow hair on her upper lip. It was just a faint golden smear, but it wasn't long before her sister-in-law, Daisy Gordon, drew everybody's attention to it by saying: 'Jings, Princess, you're gettin' a mouser. If I was you, I'd get some o' that Veet they're aye advertising and see if you can get rid of it.' Princess received the advice with silent dignity, but she bought a tube of Veet a few days later and secretly applied it. She also took to wearing a spotted veil. So Miss Cochrane sported a veil too. They had an awful palaver lifting them and pinning them onto the crowns of their cloche hats when having tea in Fullers' in Princes Street or smoking cigarettes in the foyer of the theatre.

V

In the early summer of 1931, Robert Wilkie, who'd been taken to Canada as a small boy by his parents, a Granton man and a Newhaven girl, came to the old country to visit some cousins. Robert had been a lumberjack, and now he owned a prosperous small timber business in British Columbia. He was a big, thick-set bachelor of forty-seven, with a thatch of coarse black hair that was getting grey around his ears. He was so taciturn that his cousin Effie dubbed him 'the Silent Knight' and she kept chaffing him about getting married.

'I ken you're lookin' for a wife, Bob,' she said. 'I ken fine that's why you're here. Ye havenie come to see Davie and me. Ye're wantin' to find somebody to take hame to keep yer bed warm in yon long cauld winter nights. I expect ye're fed up wi' all the squaws in your village.'

Robert just smiled when she ribbed him, remembering the few times when he'd taken the plunge and dallied with one of the Indian girls before she had turned into a fat, greasy-faced squaw. There were only a few white women in his district, and these were all safely married — though, truthfully, he had always worked too hard to have much time to bother about women. It was only lately that he had begun to think that maybe he should have a wife to keep him company in his old age, and Effie was nearer the bull's eye than she imagined.

He got his eye on Princess McDougall at a social in the Granton Parish Church Hall. Effie kept him busy by introducing him to old people who had known his father and mother, but whenever he could Robert watched one of the women handing round plates of sandwiches and cakes: a big blonde with a superior air wearing a pink crêpe de chine blouse and a brown and white checked skirt. Although she offered him platefuls of food occasionally, his cousins made no effort to introduce her, and at last he asked Effie who she was.

'Her!' Effie sniffed. 'That's Alice McDougall. Oh, she's a big bug in Granton and fair "fencies her chence" because she's a high heid yin in Maule's in Princes Street. Davie and me went to school wi' her. Oh, she was a case when she was a lassie. Aye that genteel and feared to get her feet wet. Wasn't she, Dave?' She gave her husband a nudge with her elbow, and then gushed: 'Oh, there ye are, Mrs Forbes! I never saw you comin' in. I want you to meet my cousin Robert from Canada. You'll mind o' his mother, Nell Maitland?

And his father?'

While the tea things were being cleared away, the Minister got on the platform and made a speech. Robert could scarcely hear what he was saying above the clatter of the tea cups and saucers, but he gathered that he was asking for a vote of thanks to the ladies of the choir who had so nobly fed them. After joining in the polite applause, the Minister said: 'And now we will have the pleasure of hearing Miss Cochrane and Miss McDougall, who have kindly consented to entertain us with a duet "The Keys of Heaven".'

The Minister bowed towards the big blonde woman and a big dark woman who were mounting the steps of the platform. They made their way regally to the piano. Miss McDougall sat down on the piano stool and played a few notes of introduction, then she and Miss Cochrane, standing beside her with head thrown back and gazing at the roof instead of at the sheet of music she held stiffly in one hand, began to sing:

'Ai will give you the keys of heaven . . .
Medem, will you walk,
Medem, will you talk,
Medem, will you merry me . . .'

'I will give you the keys of my heart,' Robert Wilkie started to hum as they sang the last verse. But noticing that Effie was looking suspiciously at him, he broke off to scowl at two youths in tight double-breasted blue suits with enormous padded shoulders and wide bottomed trousers, from under which pointed patent leather shoes were peeping, who were tittering at the back of the hall. He was still glaring at them when he joined in the clapping at the end of the song.

'Thank you, ladies,' said the Minister. 'And now by way of an encore Miss Cochrane and Miss McDougall will sing you another item from their repertoire.'

Robert heard one of the youths give a theatrical groan and say: 'God help us, not bloody old Billy Boy again!' And he was preparing to rise in fury when Miss Cochrane announced:

'By special requaist, Miss McDougall and I heve decided to sing thet grend song "Tip-toe through the Tulips" from the film *The Broadway Melody*.'

Robert, bemused, tiptoed with Miss McDougall from her pillow to the shadow of a willow tree . . . then he kissed her in the garden, in the moonlight, before tiptoeing through the tulips . . . Afterwards he asked Effie brusquely to introduce them. A fortnight later they were engaged.

'He didnie take long to take the plunge,' Willie remarked when Miss McDougall broke the news. 'Oh, I tell ye, thae Canadians are quick on the draw.'

Willie himself didn't look like being in a hurry to take the plunge. He was forty-seven and had been courting Isa Moffatt for the past ten years. But Princess's decision to marry Robert Wilkie and go to Canada put the skids under him. A few years before this the old West Cottages had been condemned as unfit to live in by the Sanitary Board of Edinburgh Corporation, and as the older inhabitants died off or the younger ones moved to better houses with indoor lavatories and electric light, their cottages were boarded up. By the time half of the cottages were empty the McDougalls had made up their minds to flit before, like the rest of the tenants who remained, they were forced to emigrate to the great grey blocks of City Council flats being built on the fields of what once had been the Calderburn estate on the hill above Granton, to live there beside families from the slums of the High Street and the Canongate, who were still protesting loudly and violently at being uprooted by the Council and thrust into the new, bleak tenements. 'Bathroom or no bathroom, I could never bear to live among such keelies,' Elspeth McDougall had said, shuddering at the thought of some of the slatternly women and drunken men she'd seen coming off the new electric trams in Granton Square. And so, with his savings and considerable help from Willie and Princess, George McDougall had bought a new bungalow at Wardie, near Granton Road Station. He and his depleted family had been living there now for almost two years. Willie, who was earning big money and didn't spend much because he neither smoked nor drank and took Isa Moffatt to the ninepenny seats in a cinema only once a week, had contributed the biggest share. Princess, however, had put up some of the purchase price, and her name was on the title deeds as well as Willie's; for by the time she was thirty-eight she had given up any thought of marriage and expected to spend the last years of her life — after she'd retired from business — keeping house for her unmarried brother. But Robert Wilkie had shown her new horizons.

'You realize, of course, that my getting merried will make a big difference, Willie,' she said. 'I must have my share of the bungalow paid beck. I must heve a nest egg. I don't want to be entirely dependent on Robert. Neturally, there's no hurry about it. You can pay me beck some time when you can spare the money.'

'Canada!' Mrs McDougall wailed. 'All that distance away! What's going to happen to your father and me? We'll never set eyes on you again.'

'Nonsense, mother,' Princess said. 'You're still young, and even if Ded and you aren't able to come out to British Columbia to see us, it won't be long before we come beck for a holiday. Robert says we can easily menege in two years.'

'But we're over seventy! How much longer do you think the Lord will spare us? And you know fine I can't manage this house on my own.'

'Ded will just heve to learn to do a bit of housework. Surely he can help you? He's still quite egile.'

'You know fine, Princess, that your father's always been handless in the house. He can't even boil an egg. I wouldn't trust him to boil the kettle to mask the tea. No, no, he's better out of my way taking a daunder down to the Square and having his crack with all his old cronies at the Smiddy Seat.'

Princess shrugged. Every day her father, with his grey homburg cocked at an even more jaunty angle than any of its predecessors in his young manhood, walked down the Granton Road and sat on the bench outside the ruin of

169

what in Alice's childhood had been a busy blacksmith's shop and talked for hours to a handful of other old men who'd been their neighbours in the West Cottages. 'I can't see why he wants to spend so long with old Stumpy McGregor. I'm sure they heve been over the same ground hundreds of times already,' she said.

'Oh, it keeps him lively,' her mother said. 'Stumpy tells him about the awful-like keelies he's forced to bide beside now in the new houses, and they talk about old times. And he gets a grand view of the harbour and sees the boats coming in. No, no, I'd rather trauchle away on my own than do him out of his jaunt to his old haunts. Besides, I like to hear what's going on as well as he does. I don't like being shut away here at Wardie and never getting a glimpse of the sea that's been with me all my days. He tells me everything he sees and hears, and that's what keeps us both going.'

'Then it looks as though Willie end Isa will heve to get married and stay here with you,' Princess said. 'It's high time thet Willie was merried, anyway.'

'But Isa and me werenie thinkin' aboot gettin' spliced just yet,' Willie protested. 'And I dinnie think mother would like sharin' her hoose wi' another woman.'

'Isa won't be another woman,' his sister said. 'She'll be her daughter-in-law.'

A fortnight after their engagement Robert Wilkie went back to Canada. He had wanted Princess to arrange things quickly, marry him and go back with him, but she could not see her way to get everything settled in time. She had been so long with Maule's she felt she must give them adequate notice. 'It's not as if I were a junior member of the steff they could replace at once,' she said. 'Efter all, I do heve an important position, and I feel some responsibility towards the firm.' So Robert went back alone to arrange about their marriage in the new world. Princess sailed two months later: ten days after Willie and Isa Moffatt had a quiet wedding in Granton Parish Church and a short honeymoon in the Trossachs.

VI

It was a beautiful fall when Princess Wilkie arrived in Canada. Robert was there to meet her when the ship docked and, after a few days' sightseeing in Montreal, they were married in Quebec. On the train journey across the prairies, Princess didn't show much enthusiasm when, standing in the observation car, Robert pointed out features of the great wheat fields and cattle herds of Manitoba and Saskatchewan; she was more concerned about keeping flecks of soot and dust off the full-length beaver fur coat Robert had given her as a wedding present. It was too warm to wear it, but she'd been frightened of getting it crushed by packing it in her luggage. As the train approached the Rockies she began to show a little more liveliness, saying occasionally 'How fescinating!' at particularly lovely scenery; and even she could not help being excited as the train ran through the Rockies, and she kept exclaiming: 'Look at thet, Bob! Oh, isn't thet ebsolutely grend!'

By the time they got into British Columbia and off the train at a little branch line station Princess was getting used to the great canyons, bluffs, rivers and waterfalls, forests of towering pine and hemlock, scarlet-leafed maple and birch and lakes sparkling like sapphires in settings of dark green fir trees. And on the five-mile drive to Blunt Tomahawk Point, her new home, she did not think so much about what it was like as about whether there would be a good cup of tea waiting.

There was. Katie Mae, a slim young Indian woman with a sullen brown face, a slight cast in one eye and two plaits of blue-black hair, had prepared a grudging welcome. Katie Mae had been cleaning the house and cooking an evening meal for Robert ever since his return from Scotland, and although she had been doing it in a haphazard way to suit herself it was a lot better than any housekeeping attempts shown by a series of older Indian squaws in the past. Katie Mae, recently married to Joe Twelvetrees, a young buck who worked in the sawmill, had not wanted the job, but her husband, anxious to keep in with Big Chief Wilkie, who sometimes let him drive his Ford car, had persuaded her by treating her bottom with the buckle end of his belt. Katie Mae did not look forward to having to work for a mistress, who would be more exacting and more difficult to please than easygoing Mr Wilkie, but she was as sleekit as her sleek black hair, and she had managed to give the house a surface air of polish and tidiness.

It was a two-storey house built mainly of logs on the mountainside overlooking one of the many small lakes in the district. It was sheltered at the back by tall pines and hemlocks, but most of the trees had been cleared away between it and the lake. When Princess looked out of the windows or stood in the terraced garden that stretched down to the rough dirt road, she had a wonderful view of dark ravines and mountains covered with forests. The nearest houses were over a mile away in the village on the lakeside.

The first week she was there, Princess was too busy arranging her clothes in wardrobes and cupboards, writing letters to Edinburgh and making plans about the garden with the old Indian, who leaned on a spade or played with a rake for a few hours every day in it, to look behind the surface tidiness of the house or to say anything about Katie Mae's slapdash cooking. But after the first complacency of being a wife with a house of her own had worn off, Princess had a little talk with Katie Mae. It was years since Alice Wilkie had taken any interest in household affairs, except for keeping her own room clean and tidy, for Elspeth McDougall was still doing the cooking and as much of the housework as she could manage. Princess hadn't cooked anything but scrambled eggs, fried eggs and bacon or boiled eggs for years, but after Katie Mae placed a very burnt and shrivelled joint of beef on the table she said she'd take over the cooking. Katie Mae sulked when she was told to shift all the furniture and clean thoroughly behind it, and she would have walked out, but the memory of the bite of Joe's belt on her bare brown buttocks kept her from doing anything more than muttering angrily while she wiped away thick, black, greasy cobwebs from the backs of kitchen dresser and cupboards.

Princess did not help with the cleaning; Robert did not want her to do any work that would soil her hands. Instead, a couple of middle-aged squaws were hired to help Katie Mae for a week with a rigorous 'fall cleaning', and then one was kept on to come one day a week to help with any heavy work like scrubbing or beating rugs. To keep away from the squaws' inquisitive looks and Katie Mae's sullen murmuring, Princess strolled in the garden, played the piano or went for little walks towards the lake or up the mountainside. But when she played the piano Katie Mae and the squaws took it as a signal to down tools and gather round her, beating time to the music, giggling and making little squeals of admiration. And there was a limit to what she could do in the way of exploring the neighbourhood; she wasn't fond of walking and she couldn't drive a car. Robert said he'd teach her to drive the Ford, but she had no inclination to learn. There was a limit, too, to what she could do to entertain herself in the long hours that Robert was working in his office in the village or miles away in the forests. The few white women in Blunt Tomahawk Point, married to lumberjacks or workers in the sawmill or fishermen, were below her social level, she considered; she was affable and condescending when she met them in the village store or when she passed them in the car with Robert, but she knew it was no use visiting their homes or inviting them to hers. She had never been a reader; books didn't interest her, and she just glanced through the newspapers when they arrived in bundles by post. Sometimes she listened to the wireless, but that was usually in the evenings when she and Robert sat together by the huge log fire in the living-room that she was teaching Robert and Katie Mae to call the lounge. Sometimes, instead of putting on the wireless, Princess played the piano and sang 'Because' and 'Riding Down to Bangor' and 'Silver Threads Among the Gold' and 'Billy Boy' or whatever else Robert fancied. Princess didn't know, and he never told her, that Robert had bought the piano in Vancouver and had it brought to the house only a fortnight before she arrived.

When she got tired of taking little walks or watching the old Indian pottering in the garden, Princess sat, as long as the fine weather lasted, on the porch. She would manicure her nails or write a letter, and sometimes she would do a little sewing; but more often she would sit with her chin on her hand, gazing at the mountains and forests. It was a long time before she got used to the silence. There was such a silence that it was almost unearthly, and she was always glad to hear the occasional noise of the sawmill or the distant sound of a tree crashing or, when the wind was in that direction, the whistle of a train on the Canadian Pacific Railway. Whenever she heard such a hoot, like the faraway wail of a plaintive bird, it reminded her of the world far from Blunt Tomahawk Point and people other than Katie Mae Twelvetrees rattling her beaded bangles with temper at having to do some chore she considered unnecessary and ridiculous.

Princess was not discontented; but there were times when she was bored and she even welcomed Katie Mae coming on to the porch to complain: 'Missis, that bloody carpet-sweeper stick again. Will I go get Joe fix um?'

'There's no need for thet, Katie Mae,' she said. 'And how often heve I told you thet ladies don't use thet word? Get old Charlie Hawkeye to look at it, and if he cen't do anything just leave it till Mr Wilkie comes home for lunch.'

'Fency wanting to go all thet distance to the sawmill for such a trifle,' she said afterwards to Robert. 'But thet gel! She'd rether do anything then put her beck into the work.'

When there were no diversions like this, she would think of Princes Street on a Saturday morning with the people crowding the pavement so that they had to keep dodging each other. And the shops — Ferguson's with its window full of gaily tartaned boxes of Edinburgh rock and little dolls dressed as kilted soldiers; Thornton's with its golf

174

clubs, tennis racquets and other sporting goods; Fullers' and McVittie's and Crawford's with their iced cakes and cream buns; and Maule's and Jenners' with their windows of wax models displaying the latest fashions in dresses, suits and coats. And the Castle standing on its rock above the gardens, where the band of a Highland regiment would be playing and people would be strolling along the walks or lying on the lawns or gathered around the Floral Clock waiting for the cuckoo to come out and announce the time.

And one day when the red and gold colours of the fall were fading and there were heavy black clouds obscuring the tops of the mountains she thought of her childhood, remembering the dreadful day when she'd been taken by some older girls to play at shops among the piles of fish-boxes.

Alice, who was seven and was dressed in a brown coat with a white rabbit's skin collar and white kid boots, had been walking towards Granton Square when Jessie Meikle-john and Lizzie Montgomery had stopped her.

'Where're ye goin', hen?' asked Lizzie, who was thirteen and a bit simple, always with milky-green snotters hanging at her nose. 'Come on and play wi' us!'

'I can't,' Princess said with dignity. 'I'm going for my piano lessons with Miss Sharp at Goldenacre.'

'Pianny lessons!' Lizzie screeched. 'What're ye needin' pianny lessons for?'

'So's she can make a racket,' Jessie said. 'Have ye never heard her? Bang-bang-bangin' away at it day after day.' And she skirled: 'Do, ray, me, when I was wee, I couldnie peel a tattie! But noo I'm big, and I can dig, and I can chase a laddie!'

Alice tilted her nose in the air and walked on. But they came on either side of her and grabbed her arms. 'Oh no, ye don't,' Jessie cried. 'There's nae pianny lessons for ye the day, little Miss High and Mighty! Ye're comin' to play wi' us among the fish-boxes. So just shut yer gab and come on!'

And they dragged her, protesting, across the railway lines. Alice screamed when she saw an engine chuffing towards them, but the two bigger girls laughed with derision, stuck out their tongues at the engine-driver, and hustled her towards some other girls, who had an assortment of odds and ends like old tin cans, sea-shells and rusty nails and bolts arranged on dock leaves on top of a pile of railway-sleepers. 'We've got another customer for ye,' Lizzie shouted. 'Look, oor wee Princess has come to buy a pennyworth o' lickerish all-sorts!'

'And what else would ye like to buy, my lady?' said Mary Veitch, a red haired girl with a freckled nose, screwing a piece of newspaper into a poke and filling it with the tops of long rough grass the children called 'rats' tails'.

'Make her pay for this lot first,' Jessie said. 'Come on and cough up yer penny, yer ladyship.'

And she put her hand in Alice's pocket and took out the two pennies for her tram-fare to Goldenacre and handed one to Mary.

'She's still got another penny to spend,' Lizzie said, snuffling up the 'candles' at the end of her nose. 'What'll ye have, hen? A pennyworth o' dolly mixtures? Or would ye like a pennyworth o' soor plooms?'

'Her face is soor enough already,' Jessie said. 'Gi'e her yin o' thae penny bars o' chocolate, Mary.'

She thrust a twist of esparto grass into Alice's hand and then she skipped behind the 'counter' beside Mary. 'Now, bugger off, Princess McDougall! Away to yer pianny lessons and let other customers get into the shop.'

'But my tram-fare!' Alice wailed. 'I want my two pennies back.'

'What two pennies? What're ye talkin' aboot?'

'My pennies that you took.'

'Did I take her pennies?' Jessie asked the other girls. 'Did any o' you lot see her wi' any pennies?'

'Naw,' Lizzie said.

'Naw, she had nae pennies,' Mary said. She held up two small shells. 'That was what she paid me for the sweeties she's bought.'

'Ay, that's what she gi'ed ye,' Cissie Rankin shouted.

'She never had any real pennies.'

'She's a wee liar, that's what she is,' Lizzie said. 'Get awa' to yer pianny lessons, ye wee liar.'

'I'll tell my mother,' Alice wept.

'Clipe!' screamed Lizzie.

'Dirty wee clipe!' Jessie shouted. 'Bugger off now, ye high and mighty wee bitch, or I'll gi'e ye a cuff on the lug.'

Alice ran, with tears streaming down her cheeks, across the railway lines, pursued by the bigger girls who all were shouting 'Clipe!' and 'Dirty wee liar!' But they did not chase her far. When Alice paused for breath outside the bonded warehouse on the corner of Granton Square, she saw them going towards Jimmy Greig's coffee house to buy sweeties with her twopence. 'I'll tell my mother,' she screamed. They laughed and jeered, and Lizzie Montgomery put her thumb to her nose and waggled her fingers.

Looking now at the clouds massing above the lake, Princess remembered that she'd got her white kid boots all scuffed and covered with engine-grease when they'd dragged her across the railway lines. She'd had to walk to Golden-acre and back, and old Miss Sharp had been angry because she was late and had kept rapping her knuckles with a ruler while she was practising her scales.

VII

At the beginning of December, Robert took Princess to Vancouver for a week. 'You need a little holiday, dearest,' he said. 'The change'll do you good.'

Vancouver was about three hundred miles away. Princess was delighted with the shops and she bought several new dresses. They went to the theatre twice, and at the cinema they saw Cecil B. de Mille's latest production of *The Squaw Man* (Princess had seen his earlier one twenty years ago) with Warner Baxter who'd always been one of her favourite movie heroes, and *Seed* with two more of her favourites, Lois Wilson and dear Zasu Pitts, and a new

177

young actress, Bette Davis, whom Princess considered 'rether striking'. And they rode over the ferry to Victoria and had tea and listened to the orchestra in the great Empress Hotel.

When they got back to Blunt Tomahawk Point, Princess took two old dresses out of a wardrobe to make room for the new ones, and she gave them to Katie Mae Twelvetrees to keep her sweet. Katie Mae's face showed neither gratitude nor animation as she held the dresses in front of her. She said: 'Your bosoms, missis, bigger than mine. And your bum.'

'Of course, they'll heve to be taken in a bit,' Princess said. 'And you'll probably want them a little shorter. If you'll get the measuring tape I'll do the alterations for you.'

'No, missis, I'll sew,' the Indian girl said. 'Old grandmother she teach me good with the needle.'

A few days later, Katie Mae presented Princess with a bizarre, beautifully carved miniature totem pole that she said had been made on the reservation she came from. But Princess never saw her wearing either of the dresses. When the summer came, she saw one of them on a fat squaw in the village. It was burst at the seams and the hem was bedraggled.

By that time she and Robert had made another trip to Vancouver to see a few more films and a play. In that time, too, Princess had tried, but without success, to start a choir in the little log church at Blunt Tomahawk Point. Robert had suggested it, thinking it would give her something to do. 'It would mean that you'd have an excuse for going down to the village oftener, my princess,' he said while he was washing the supper dishes (for he wouldn't let her put her hands in greasy water) one night of heavy snow. 'It'll give you a chance to get to know some of the younger people better.'

But although the Rev. Angus McLennan and Princess canvassed a great number of people and received many promises to join the choir, the only ones who turned up at the first practice were Katie Mae, unwilling but cute enough to know which side her bread was buttered on, and Joe Twelvetrees and a hard-drinking Irish lumberjack who'd been intimidated into cooperation by Robert. This little choir sang in the church the following Sunday, but Princess had to admit that it was a failure. She hadn't been expecting Granton Parish Church standards, naturally, but even she, her bosom swelling and her eyes on the ceiling as she gave full resonance to 'Oh God of Bethel', was aware of faint titters at Katie Mae's studied mispronouncing of the words and the Irishman's slurred baritone a beat behind everybody else. She and the Rev. Angus decided, by mutual consent, not to do any more about it.

VIII

In the spring of 1933 Mr and Mrs Robert Wilkie sailed from Montreal to the Firth of Clyde. Princess found that her parents had aged far more than she'd expected. George McDougall, with a panama hat set at an angle on his bald head, still went regularly to the Smiddy Seat, but his old cronies were either dead now or not able to get to the seat, and usually he sat there alone. Unwillingly, Elspeth had turned over the running of the house to her daughter-in-law, Isa, though she still tried to keep a feeble hold of the reins. 'There's no' much change in you, though, Princess,' Willie said. 'I thought ye'd have come back wi' a Yankee twang, but ye're talkin' just as Morningside as ever — awful tosted breed, as Tom Cable yince said in a pantymime. Oh, but yon was a grand wee comic! Him and Tommy Lorne. What a gallus pair! I've laughed till I was sair at the way they used to go on. Do ye mind o' Tommy Lorne, dressed as a woman, talkin' aboot goin' on his granny's scooter and puttin' up his hands and sayin': "Oh, in the name!"'

'I always thought them very vulgar,' Princess said. 'I cen't stend pantomimes.'

On the first Sunday of their visit, after church, Miss

Cochrane sailed up to them and gushed: 'How gled I am to see you, Miss McDougall!'

'Mrs Wilkie,' Robert said with a smile.

'I just cen't get used to it,' Miss Cochrane said. 'I don't think I ever will.'

Miss Cochrane was looking older. Her cheeks were a faint mauve colour and her face was much more heavily powdered than of yore. Her chest, prominently shown by the glad neck of her pale blue jumper, was also powdered, and Princess thought it looked rather like the back of a sow. If you scratched it with a stick, the scales would come off. 'Fency you still singing in the choir, Miss Cochrane!' she said.

'Oh yes, one must do one's little bit.' Miss Cochrane gave her deep contralto laugh. 'But the poor old choir isn't what it used to be. The young people nowadays simply won't join it. They heve no music in them.'

After arranging to take Miss Cochrane to see Sybil Thorndike in a new play at the King's the following week, Princess and Robert walked up the Granton Road to the bungalow and found Mrs McDougall and Isa having an argument about the way Isa was cooking the Sunday joint. 'Isa's that handless in the house,' Elspeth said to her daughter. 'I suppose it comes of her always working in an office.'

'I think she meneges not too bedly, mother,' Princess said. 'It's a good job you heven't got my Katie Mae to deal with. My goodness, I hed such a job training her to make even eatable hem end eggs.'

'What can you expect from these heathen! I don't know how you can bear to live amongst them.'

Princess wondered the same thing when they got back to British Columbia two months later. Katie Mae had let the house go to wrack and ruin in their absence. It was evident that it had just got a hasty going over on the day before they arrived, although Robert had been paying Katie Mae to come in every day. A couple of village squaws had to be hired again to help Katie Mae do a thorough scrubbing and polishing. Princess was so exhausted by the time it was over that Robert said she needed a rest, and he took her to Vancouver for a week to recuperate. She could not help comparing the city unfavourably with Edinburgh.

In January 1934 Princess heard that her mother had died suddenly. Willie wrote that their father was also in poor health. 'So if you want to see him again I think you and Bob had better not wait too long before you pay another visit to Auld Reekie.'

Two weeks later, Princess and Robert sailed from Montreal.

IX

They stayed in Scotland for three months. Robert took her to London for a fortnight at the end of it, for he thought she needed a change and a rest from her relatives. 'You've surely seen enough of all your nephews and nieces to last you for a while, dearest,' he said. 'I know I have.'

Princess was inclined to take umbrage at this, but since Robert hardly ever complained she thought better of it. Besides, Robert's own relatives hadn't been taken into consideration; they had seen Effie and Dave only twice in the three months. On the other hand, they did seem to have spent most of their time visiting Princess's married nieces and nephews, spending whole, long evenings with them and admiring their houses and their children, as well as meeting them all at big weekly family jamborees in the bungalow at Wardie. Donald had two sons and a daughter, all married; Jock had two daughters and two sons, one married and the rest engaged; and Jim, following the example of his parents, had four sons, all in their late teens or early twenties, and a daughter, Margaret, aged eleven, who had been rather a surprise packet, like Princess herself. Margaret, Princess was glad to see, was turning into a very refined girl. Not like her mother, that coarse-tongued Daisy Gordon, who was little better than a keelie.

When they said goodbye, Princess was sure she'd never see her father again. Although he seemed to have grown even spryer and nattier during their visit, he was in his seventy-ninth year, and Princess felt he couldn't go on much beyond it.

Soon after they got back to Blunt Tomahawk Point, Robert, now past his fiftieth birthday, started to speak of selling the business and retiring. 'But you're still a comperitively young men!' Princess protested. 'It's time enough surely to think of retiring in another ten years! My Ded was sixty-five when he gave up his position on the railway.'

'I see what you're driving at,' Robert said, laughing. 'You don't want me at home every day, getting among your feet, do you, Princess?'

'Oh, I wouldn't say thet,' Princess said, though that's exactly what she was thinking. She felt she had enough to do to cope with Katie Mae, who now had two small children and brought them with her every day, when they usually cried most of the time, without having to cope with Robert into the bargain. Robert talked for several months about selling the business, but after a trip to Vancouver to see a prospective buyer he dropped the subject.

In the summer of 1935 Willie wrote that their father was ailing and going downhill, so early in August the Wilkies sailed again from Montreal. It was a pleasant voyage. Princess spent a lot of it chatting with Jock, the steward, who seemed like an old friend, about films and their favourite actress, Bette Davis.

The ship docked earlier than expected, and they arrived in Edinburgh ahead of schedule. Isa Moffatt, caught in the middle of preparing a bed for them, was red in the face with agitation.

'How's Ded?' Princess asked, prepared for the worst; she could see through the open door into her father's room that the bed was unoccupied.

'He's doon at the Smiddy Seat. I thought he'd have been back by this time.'

Half an hour later, Mr McDougall, hat cocked on the side of his head, walked in fairly briskly, swinging his ivory-handled walking stick.

'God love us, Princess!' he cried. 'You do believe in surprising folk, don't you?'

'How are you, Ded?' she asked, pressing her cheek against his.

'Oh, I mustn't grumble. My legs are kind of stiff, but I still manage to go for my constitutional. But Granton's not the same. Oh dear, no. Changed days! You would hear about poor old Stumpy McGregor? Dead and buried these four months . . . Ah well, it comes to us all. Here today and gone tomorrow. But I'm glad to say I'm not ready to go yet. Jock's youngest is getting married in three weeks, they tell me. I must bide a while longer to see if I'll get another great-grandchild. Young Malcolm's getting a very nice lassie. Nanny . . . or is it Netty? What's her name again, Isa?'

'Norma McClure.'

'Dear yes, Norma. The high-falutin' names they have nowadays! Gone are the days when they were all Jeans and Marys and Bellas. But she seems a nice, sensible-like lassie. Never forgets to bring me an ounce of tobacco when she visits us. Never forgets it's Best Golden Bar.'

Princess did not take to Norma. 'Personally, I think she's rether a common gel,' she confided to Robert. 'She looks rether fest, with thet peroxided hair and scarlet nails. Not at all a suitable person for our Melcolm to merry.'

Princess's niece Margaret, the youngest bridesmaid at the wedding, was of much the same opinion. 'Fency, Ent Elice,' she said to her stylish Canadian aunt at the reception, 'Norma ate three pies before she went to the cherch. Cen you believe it! Three pies! If I hed been her I couldn't heve eaten a thing, but she just *guzzled* them down. It made me feel quaite sick. Ectually, I heve a very delicate stomach, and I couldn't eat a pie if you paid me.'

'Well, poor Norma,' Princess said. 'She hesn't hed our advantages, Mergeret, in the menner she's been brought up. Perhaps in taime she'll learn to be a little more refained.'

'I rether doubt it, Ent Alice,' Margaret said primly. 'I think thet Melcolm won't heve all his sorrows to seek.'

Immediately after the wedding, the Wilkies sailed for Canada. Robert was anxious to get back to British Columbia to see a man who wanted to buy the business. But the man's offer wasn't big enough, and nothing came of it.

About a year later, however, Robert sold the Blunt Tomahawk Timber Company, and he and Princess prepared to move to a flat in Vancouver. She had expected that Robert would retire to Scotland, but it turned out that he still had timber interests and didn't want to leave Canada.

'In a few years maybe we'll get a wee house in Edinburgh for our old age,' he said. 'I'd rather like one at Merchiston, well away from all our relations, wouldn't you?'

'Well, I'm very fond of Grenton,' Princess said. 'Still, there are so many common people living there now, perheps we'd be better to move to the south side. Es e metter of fect, I rether think Morningside would be preferable to Merchiston.'

'We'll have a look and think about it when we go over,' Robert said.

The Vancouver flat had to be redecorated completely before they could move in, so Robert said they would have a holiday in Scotland while the decorators were busy. Princess left Blunt Tomahawk Point thankfully; she had grown tired of the mountains and forests and lakes. And she said goodbye to Katie Mae with relief and gave her all the clothes she didn't want to take with her. 'Such a silleh young woman,' she said to Isa Moffatt. 'Only twenty-three and she's expecting her fourth. She'll be an old done squaw before she can cough. I told her at the beginning thet she should go to Vancouver and see a bit of life — she could easily heve got a position as a sales lady in Woolworth's or some other store — but she wouldn't listen to me. She's just made a doormet of herself for thet men Joe Twelvetrees.'

'So ye're back again, Princess!' said Daisy Gordon, who had grown very stout. 'Your man must ha'e plenty o' money to jaunt back and forrit frae Canady like this. I just

184

wish I had a leaf out o' his bank book. Jim and me could be doin' with it.'

Old George McDougall was not quite so spry and he'd given up going to the Smiddy Seat. 'It's frequented now by some old men from the new houses at Calderburn,' he said. 'I don't see eye to eye with them, so I'd rather not have their company. They make my blood boil with all their Labour talk. It's nothing but dole this and dole that and who's on Public Assistance and making a good thing out of it. That demned dole! It'll be the ruination of the country.'

They sailed from the Clyde in early November. On the voyage Princess had several long talks with her old friend Jock about Edward VIII and Mrs Simpson and what Jock had read lately in the American papers. 'The poor king,' Princess said. 'In the hends of thet designing woman!'

X

Before they'd been in it a fortnight Princess started to complain about the new apartment. It was too cramped. She missed being able to walk straight outside and sit on the porch or in the garden. There was no view. The tiny sliver of the Pacific she could glimpse between two tall buildings didn't compensate for the loss of the lake. The people upstairs were noisy and whenever Princess played the piano they thumped on the floor, banging in time with the tune. And every time she went out the mangy old black Pomeranian in the flat beneath came rushing out at her, barking wildly and snapping at her ankles. Robert spoke to the dog's owner, Mrs Mason, a plump old matron with dyed red hair and a big rump, who said she couldn't possibly keep poor little Pinkie inside and that Mrs Wilkie needn't worry. 'Pinkie doesn't *bite*,' she said. 'She snaps — oh yes, I know she snaps — but that's just playfulness. She would never *dream* of biting. I've told her that if I ever hear of her *breaking* the skin I'll smack her bot. Hard.'

'Why don't you keep your door shut?' Robert asked.

'Door shut?' Mrs Mason said. 'I've never heard of such an impertinent suggestion. I've lived in this apartment for nineteen years and I've *always* kept my door open. Pinkie must have free access to go out and in as she wishes. She *does* have to attend to the call of *nature*, you know.'

'Why didn't you train her properly?'

'*Train* her? She isn't a *performing* dog in a circus, Mr Wilkie.'

'I never said she was,' Robert said. 'I just think she should be made to perform – as you put it – at regular intervals. Otherwise, I'm afraid my wife'll have to send you in a weekly bill for silk stockings. She's had three pairs ruined this last week with Pinkie's teeth and claws.'

'Oh, the impertinence!' Mrs Mason's face mottled with rage under its thick make-up. She stepped back and was about to slam the door in his face when she thought of a better rebuff. 'Pinkie!' she screamed. 'Pinkie! Come and rescue Mummy from this horrid man!'

Robert went upstairs after giving Pinkie's snout a hard kick with his heel. 'I guess we'd better look for another house, Princess,' he said. 'That old bitch's calling the cops already.'

They bought a bungalow in the suburbs. Robert heard about it from an acquaintance in the timber trade, Alec Mackie, who owned the bungalow next door. Mackie and his wife were natives of Aberdeen and they had been in British Columbia for twenty-five years. Alexandra Mackie, who was always called Sandy, was a perky little woman with bright eyes and quick movements like a robin. She believed she had second sight. She loved to play cards, and she loved to sing. She was a soprano. She was, she told Princess, the leading soprano in the choir at St Stephen's. 'We're Wee Free,' she said somewhat belligerently. 'What are you?'

'Well, I was brought up in the Auld Kirk,' Princess said. 'But I cen't see thet it metters much, Sendy.'

'Et thet rate,' said Mrs Mackie, whose genteel accent rivalled Princess's own, 'you'd better join our choir. We need a good contralto.'

So Princess was happy for a while. She and Robert became members of the Rev. Murdo Ritchie's church. And she joined Sandy Mackie in the choir. She and Sandy became bosom pals. They spent a lot of time together playing and singing duets, practising for church socials. Princess played and Sandy stood beside her, swaying backwards and forwards on her tiptoes, while they sang 'The March of the Cameron Men' and 'The Skye Boat Song'. These tunes soon became the stars of their repertoire and were their recognized contributions at church socials and concerts. The Rev. Mr Ritchie would announce with unction: 'And now we will have the great pleasure of listening to Mesdames Mackie and Wilkie singing that rousing old tune "The March of the Cameron Men" — a song that will stir the blood of every Scot in this audience.'

And Princess would thump the piano and Sandy would rise on her tiptoes, with her eyes shut, and they would sing in unison:

'I hear the pibroch sounding, sounding

Deep o'er mountain and glen . . .

'Tis the merch

'Tis the merch of the Cemeron men . . .'

Alec Mackie and Robert Wilkie played golf and talked about timber mergers and the price of redwood while their wives practised or went to the cinema or had tea in Vancouver's smartest restaurants. Sandy Mackie's favourite film star was Jeanette Macdonald, and they saw sweet-voiced Jeanette and Clark Gable in *San Francisco* three times. 'Such a lovely picture,' Sandy gushed. 'Jeanette is simply grend. End I do adore Jeck Holt, don't you, Elice? He's always been such a favourite of mine. I remember seeing him in such a lot of cowboy films in Eberdeen when I was a gel. But . . . Sen Frencisco's so near Vencouver! Wouldn't it be simply dreadful if we ever hed an earthquake here?'

XI

Instead of an earthquake they had the Second World War. Before it started, however, Alice and Robert Wilkie made another trip to Scotland. In the summer of 1939 Willie sent a cable to say their father was dying. Princess and Robert arrived in time to see the old man for a few hours before he died. Afterwards Princess wished she hadn't seen him. Something had gone wrong with his bladder, and he spent the last days of his life in agony, clutching Isa Moffatt's hand while she sat beside his bed, wiping the sweat off his forehead and saying: 'It's all right, Father, don't worry. Pee if you want to pee. Dinnie worry aboot the bedclothes. I'll soon get them washed.'

When it was all over she said to Princess: 'Puir auld man, it's awful that he had to die in such a way. There's something terribly undignified aboot death. He has aye looked that clean and spruce all his days. And then to have to depend on somebody, like a bairn gettin' his nappies changed in his last hours . . .'

'You know,' Princess mused, 'I never remember him being ill.'

'No, he had just a cold now and again,' Isa said. 'He hardly ever needed the doctor. Until a week or two back I can't mind o' him havin' the doctor since the time a couple of years ago when he asked me to take him to get his ears syringed. The wax in them was makin' him that deaf. I mind o' sittin' in the surgery wi' him while the doctor went about the job. "Are ye all right, Father?" I says. "Of course, I'm all right," he says. "I'm enjoying the entertainment exceedingly." '

There were a lot of old familiar Granton faces at the funeral in Warriston Cemetery. Standing between Robert and Willie, with head bowed, Princess keeked several times through her black veil at one big stout elderly woman at the back of the crowd around the grave, knowing her and yet not being able to place a name to her. It was only after the minister had said the last words and they were all turning away from the yawning hole to let the gravediggers do their job that she recognized her.

'Miss Cochrane!'

'It's so sed about your Ded, Miss McDougall,' the other Alice said, shaking hands with her and Robert. 'Mrs Wilkie I should say.'

'End how are you, Miss Cochrane?' Princess said, shocked at the change in her friend. She had got very stout and her jowls were purple-coloured. There was a bristle of grey hairs on her double chin and along her upper lip. Princess, whose own hair was now a yellowy white and who had tried all kinds of quack cures for her own moustache, wondered if Miss Cochrane ever thought of shaving. She herself did in secret.

'Fency you being in Vencouver now, Mrs Wilkie,' Miss Cochrane said. 'It must be a wonderful city. There must be some wonderful shops.'

'Stores,' Princess said. 'Yes, they're very fine, but none of them are a petch on Jenners' or Maule's, of course.'

'Binns,' Miss Cochrane said. 'Maule's was taken over by Binns several years ago. It's been called Binns for some time now. Surely you knew thet!'

'Es e metter of fect I was in Maule's — I mean Binns — yesterday buying this bleck het,' Princess said. 'But I never noticed the name was changed. But I do recollect now thet you told me about it in a letter.'

'Now thet you're living in Vencouver, Mrs Wilkie, don't you fency going beck into business again?'

'Oh no, Miss Cochrane, I'd never do thet.' Princess was frigid with shock at the suggestion. 'Bob would never epprove, would you, dear?'

'My princess will never have to work again in her life,' Robert said. 'I'm glad to say that no wife of mine ever will.'

'End how many wives heve you got, Mr Wilkie!' Miss Cochrane tittered and gave him an arch look.

'Do you never consider getting married yourself, Miss Cochrane?' Princess said as Robert went on ahead to where the funeral cars were waiting on the gravelled path and the two women picked their way carefully through the graves adorned by white marble and red sandstone headstones and artificial wreaths in glass domes.

'Et my age? Don't be deft, Miss McDougall!'

Realizing she'd been unkind, and suddenly anxious to make amends, Princess said: 'But you're not es old es all thet. A friend of my friend Sendy Meckie in Vencouver got merried a few months ago — and she's sixty-five! She's made such a good metch too! To a business colleague of Bob's end Elec Meckie's. Sendy saw it all in the cards. End then she hed a vision. Sendy hes the second sight, you know, thet she got from her old Highland grenny. She's really quaite remarkable. She seems to go into a trence end then she tells you she's seen the oddest things. I was quite prepared about poor old Ded. Sendy told me before I left Vencouver thet she saw a death in the femily.'

XII

It was a death in Sandy's own family she had seen. The Wilkies returned to Vancouver in time to attend Alec Mackie's funeral. He'd had a stroke, dying alone while Sandy was at the choir practice.

Princess was so busy rallying round her friend in the next few weeks she had little time to think about anything else; she paid scant attention to the doings of 'thet awful men Hitler' and so it was a shock when the Nazis walked into Poland in September.

'I was quaite unprepared for war,' she said. 'Bob, why didn't you warn me?'

'But surely you've been reading the papers and listening to the wireless, Princess dear?' he protested. 'And I've spoken about it often enough. I can't think how you've escaped hearing about it.'

'Well, Germany's so far away,' she said pettishly. 'I never dreamed it would come to this. Hitler seemed just full of hot air. Fency, how awful it would heve been if we'd been caught in Edinburgh! I do hope Grenton won't get bombed.'

The war was a godsend to Sandy Mackie. She plunged immediately into all kinds of voluntary war work because this, she said, helped her to forget her sad loss. And of course Princess was drawn into this war work too, since Sandy needed moral support. They attended First Aid classes; they helped at 'Help for Britain' bazaars; they collected for the Red Cross; they organized whist drives in aid of poor little Finland; and they sang in countless concerts to entertain the troops. They were in great demand. In one week alone they sang 'The Cameron Men' twenty-five times.

At one concert, after they'd heard the pibroch sounding over mountain and glen about six times, accompanied by a couple of hundred enthusiastic men of the Canadian Highlanders, a brawny young sergeant with moist eyes in the front row shouted: 'What about "The Auld Hoose"?'

Princess and Sandy looked at each other. They were breathless. Then, giving her hands a preliminary flourish over the keys, Princess said: 'Well, it's not really in our repertoire, young men, but we're always gled to do what we cen to oblige.'

And then, with a lifting of bosoms and groping for the words, they sang:

'Oh, the auld hoose, the auld hoose,
What though the rooms were wee?
Kind hearts were dwelling there
And bairnies fu' o' glee . . .'

When the concert was over and they were hoarse and panting they received the almost maudlin thanks of the young sergeant with the black moustache and the brawny legs that looked like tree trunks under his kilt. He told them that if he was lucky enough to get to Scotland he was going to visit the auld hoose among the heather in Perthshire where his granddaddy had been born. His name was Hugh Drysdale and his folk had come from near Crieff. 'If you do menage to go to Edinburgh you must go and see my brother,' Princess said, and she gave him Willie's address. She also gave him her own, for young Drysdale said he was anxious to keep in touch with two such grand Scottish ladies. 'What a chermer!' Sandy Mackie said afterwards. 'The Perthshire lessies hed better look out!'

Princess never thought she'd hear from him again, but six months later she got a card of the War Memorial in Edinburgh Castle with a message of best wishes written in a schoolboyish hand. It ended: 'Margaret took me to see this and it brought back memories of your concert, your sincere friend Hugh Drysdale.'

Princess and Sandy speculated about the identity of Margaret — 'Some fest piece from the Canongate more then likely,' Princess said — and it was only after a few months that she learned the truth when Willie wrote: 'Your old pal Alice Cochrane is going great guns with a Pole young enough to be her grandson, they tell me, and Jim's lassie Margaret has got herself engaged to a Canadian sergeant with a black mouser called Drysdale. You will maybe mind that you gave him our address. Thank you for nothing. Well, he turned up as bold as brass one day and near drove Isa and me daft with all his palavers about his father's farm in Saskatchewan so we gave him Jim's address as we thought Daisy Gordon might as well do something for the war effort, and the upshot is that young Margaret got her claws on him and has got a diamond and ruby engagement ring that cost a hundred pounds, no cheap dirt from the shilling arcade for our Margaret. She is welcome to him and his big black mouser. Don't be so free about giving away our address as we have enough to do to feed ourselves with our paltry rations without feeding big buck Canadian soldiers into the bargain. Apart from the scarcity of meat we are both not too bad, and Granton is a busy place again, having been turned into a naval base. Isa tells me to tell you that Miss Cochrane's Pole is supposed to be a Count. He must be hard up is all I can say, even though she is a friend of yours, but the Poles are running after the old women more than the young ones.'

Princess and Sandy were still marching with the Cameron men when the Japanese bombed Pearl Harbor. Robert Wilkie said they must leave Vancouver at once; like everybody else he expected waves of Japanese planes. He put the bungalow up for sale, and they moved with their furniture to a village that was even smaller than Blunt Tomahawk Point and about forty miles from it. Princess didn't like it at all, but she made up her mind to make the best of it. 'You'll heve to try end rise above it, m'dear,' said Sandy who had sold her own bungalow and was moving to stay with a nephew in Sudbury, Ontario. 'I'll feel a bit safer there,' she said. 'I very much doubt if those draidful Jeps will get thet length. Mind you, I don't know how I'll get on with Eddie and thet negging wife of his; I heven't seen them for years. Elec never liked them. But Eddie's the only relation I heve left, end, efter all, blood is thicker then water. End he knows I'll leave him everything. I'm not looking forward to staying with them, but . . .'

'You'll just heve to rise above it, Sendy,' Princess said. 'We all will.'

After six months at Roaring River Settlement, however, she realized that she couldn't. She was nearly driven to screaming pitch by the isolation. She had to do all her own housework, for there were no women in the village willing to do charring; even the old squaws had some kind of war job that brought them in more money for less effort. The nearest church was seven miles away and there was no choir. Princess organized several concerts and whist drives, but they were poorly attended. At last, fed up with greasy dishwater, dusting, sweeping, listening to news of the war in North Africa and the Far East on the wireless and, above all, fed up with the everlasting mountains, she asked Robert if it wouldn't be possible to go home to Scotland. She said: 'I feel thet we should be among our ain folk, Bob. We should be there doing something to help the war effort.'

He said it was out of the question, they'd never get passages across the Atlantic. But why not go back to Vancouver? There was no danger now of Japanese air raids.

He had sold the bungalow at a loss, but they could get somewhere else to live, and maybe both of them could join organizations for promoting victory. While they were at Roaring River Settlement Robert had gone back into the timber trade because he hated to be idle and it would help the war. It had pleased him, too, to get up at four o'clock on fine mornings to saw his own wood for the stove and fires. It had pleased him especially since he felt he had shown, by lassoing the logs coming down the river in the spring floods and dragging them into his own boom, that his hands hadn't lost their cunning and he was still as young and strong as he'd ever been. For he didn't like to remember he was fifty-eight years old. He didn't want to return to Vancouver — he disliked cities — but he was agreeable to do anything that would make his Princess happy.

So they moved back to Vancouver, to a small flat that Princess thought pokey. Robert joined a group looking after the welfare of children evacuated from Britain and occupied Europe, and Princess sang and played at dozens of concerts and helped at bazaars in aid of China, Free France, Free Poland and other good causes. Without Sandy she had to evolve a new technique. She also had to put some new items in her repertoire, even items she considered beneath her dignity to sing, and by the end of the war she was banging out 'The White Cliffs of Dover', 'Lili Marlene' and 'There'll Come Another Day'.

The audiences of soldiers, sailors and airmen of many nationalities appeared to be grateful. They certainly applauded noisily. Only once was there a note of dissension, and that was when a very drunk soldier shouted: 'Ach to hell wi' the Cameron men, granny! What aboot givin' us somethin' livelier like "I've Got Spurs that jingle-jingle-jangle"? Somethin' wi' a bit o' fuckin' life.'

Princess was disgusted to hear his dreadful Scottish accent. And absolutely mortified. She was a little mollified, however, when his apologetic commanding officer said he came from the slums of Glasgow. 'Thet explains metters,' she said icily.

As soon as the war in Europe ended Robert pulled strings to get them passages on a ship to Scotland. They sold everything except their most precious pieces of furniture; they put these into store until the time would come when they could be shipped after them. Before they sailed they visited the United States, to stay for a week with Sandy Mackie in her new home; Princess expected she'd never see Sandy again, and it was a chance to see a bit of the U.S.A., even though it was just a tiny bit. With the persistence and sense of self-preservation of the true Scot Sandy had caught another husband, a well-off American called Jerry Reisman, a retired pharmacist, and gone to live in Dayton, Ohio. She'd been there for nearly eighteen months now, and she was well established already in the choir of a Presbyterian church. While Robert and Jerry Reisman played golf — a game that Robert played badly because he was more interested really in the walnut and oak and hickory trees that lined the fairways — Princess and Sandy renewed their partnership and sang at a couple of concerts for veterans returning from Europe. Sandy was horrified when she heard about Princess's dreadful experience with the drunken soldier.

'Grenny!' she exclaimed. 'Fency calling you thet, Elice! The audecity of the low creature! But thet's all the thenks one gets for wearing oneself out body end soul for such scum. When I think of all we've done to entertain the troops words fail me. They've been fêted end entertained by everybody in Emerica. They've been given en ebsolutely grend time. End then they turn round end kick you in the teeth like thet. The base ingretitude! My word, he end his kind fairly got their horns out during the war, but maybe they won't be so cocky now thet it's over. Maybe they'll get their comeuppence!'

XIII

Mrs Sandy Reisman was wrong, of course. When the Wilkies arrived in Scotland they found a great change. The Labour Government had just come into power, and poor dear Mr Churchill, who had done so much to win the war, was having to take a back seat. Prosperity had come to the masses, and they were ungrateful to the people who'd given it to them. The Common Man knew it was his century; he was on the crest of the wave and he was celebrating his victory by flaunting about in his demob clothes and spending his gratuity recklessly since there was plenty more money where that came from. Princess was appalled to find, too, that the country was full of foreigners who had no intention of going back to their own countries even though Hitler and his kind had been defeated. Although she and Robert searched and searched they could not find a house. After staying with Willie and Isa for a month they moved to a hotel, for none of Princess's other sisters-in-law seemed inclined to give them board and lodgings. They said it was difficult to feed extra mouths with the rationing that still went on. Besides, they were chock-a-block with their own families.

Princess was taken aback at the change the war had made in her brothers' children and their families. She could hardly believe she was now the great-aunt of several young people, all utter strangers, large and vociferous and completely out of her ken; most of them barely nodded at her and Robert when they were visiting, said 'Hiya, Auntie,' and went about their own business. Two of Donald's granddaughters, girls of seventeen and eighteen, had married Polish soldiers. One, Elspeth, was going to Poland because her husband was homesick for his own country; the other intended to start a small garage in Fifeshire with her husband who was mad about cars. 'Trust them to ken where they'll make the most money,' Daisy Gordon said. 'Andrei, that Pole that Bunty's married is that sharp he'd turn the reek o' his ain fart to good account if folk were just daft

196

enough to believe him if he tellt them it was a new scent. Sweet violets!'

Daisy's own daughter, Margaret Drysdale, was preparing to leave for Canada with her husband, whose moustache seemed blacker and his legs even brawnier than Princess remembered. 'I'll be so gled to get away from Edinburgh, Ent Elice,' she said. 'It's so stultifying. What a pity you've left Ceneda. It would have been so nice if you end Uncle Bob hed still been there; we could heve visited each other, even though Sesketchewan is such a distence from B.C.'

Granton itself had not changed as much as Princess expected. The breakwater that had been the favourite Sunday afternoon walking place for hundreds of Edinburgh people ever since Princess could remember had been closed to the public at the start of the war, and the entrance to it was still boarded up; but the Middle and West piers seemed to be as busy as they'd been when she was a girl, though the styles and sizes of the ships anchored in their harbour were different. The East Cottages on Lower Granton Road still looked as they'd looked fifty years ago, their brass knockers, name-plates and letter-boxes were as brightly polished as ever, and their lace curtains seemed the same. But the West Cottages had been flattened to the ground, and some kind of factory had been built in their place. When Princess looked down from the West Road at the factory roof and remembered that once the smoke from the chimneys of forty red-roofed cottages, all teeming with life, had been there a wave of nostalgia went over her. The Smiddy Seat was still standing, but the wood had rotted and no old men were sitting on it. And Granton Parish Church still looked much the same, though it was no longer a place of worship; it had stopped being a church just before the war when a larger church had been built on the new housing estate at Calderburn on the other side of the West Road, a modern church intended to house the larger congregations anticipated by the over-optimistic members of the Presbytery. During the war the old church had been turned into an Air Raid Wardens' post; now it had been taken over by the seafaring fraternity and had become some kind of sailors' club. When Princess looked in the door she saw oars and lifebelts hanging on the walls, and several young men wearing thick white polo-necked sweaters were hunched over cups of tea in the chairs where the choir used to sit.

The Wilkies could not find a suitable house in any district of Edinburgh, so they went on a tour through the Highlands to see if they could find something there. But any place that was for sale was either too remote or too dilapidated or Princess had some other fault to find with it. When Margaret and Hugh Drysdale sailed from the Clyde the Wilkies went to see them off, and Princess put her niece into the care of her old friend Jock the steward. Before they sailed Princess said: 'Well, Mergeret, maybe your uncle end I will be able to take a trip beck to Ceneda end visit you sometime.'

'Thet would be lovely, Ent Elice,' Margaret said.

'I'll look forward to it,' Princess said. And truly she thought that perhaps she and Robert might pay a visit to Canada in a few years' time before they were too old to travel.

But they went back to Canada far earlier than she'd ever imagined. After they'd been in Scotland for six months and there was no sign of finding what they wanted Robert said they'd have to go back to B.C. if they were going to survive. Though their native country was beautiful it was no place for them; they'd soon be ruined by this Labour government who'd take the coats off their backs if they could. So they sailed once again from the Clyde, and their pieces of furniture that had never got farther than a depository in Glasgow sailed with them. Princess and her friend Jock moaned to each other throughout the voyage about the changes the war had made in Scotland.

The Wilkies bought a house in a Vancouver suburb, and Robert had to pay far more for it than he intended. It was larger than they wanted, so they had to buy a lot of new furniture, and what with this and new curtains and carpets and having the place redecorated before Princess considered it would be habitable it cost Robert a great deal of money. While waiting for the redecoration to be finished, they went to Dayton to stay with the Reismans for two weeks, then they went on to New York because Princess had always wanted to see it. They stayed for a week at the Waldorf-Astoria and went to a different show every night.

They had been only ten days in their new house when Robert got up one morning, gave a little stagger, said 'Oh, my God!' and collapsed. He died half an hour later.

Princess telephoned to Hugh Drysdale on his Saskat-chewan farm, and he flew to Vancouver that day. Margaret didn't come with him; she was just about to have their first baby. Hugh did all the business with the undertaker and the grave-diggers and the minister. It was a very simple funeral service, and a number of old men, strangers to Princess, attended it and shook hands with her and Hugh, most of them saying they'd known Robert years ago.

A couple of hours after the funeral, before he caught his plane home, Hugh asked Princess what her plans were. 'I thought I might come end stay with Mergeret and you for a little while till I make up my mind,' she said. 'It's all been so sudden . . .'

'I'm afraid you can't, Auntie,' he said. 'It's out of the question just now with Margaret being in pod and ready to burst out in such a big way at any moment.'

'But I thought I might help with the baby . . .'

'My mother and the nurse will do the needful,' he said. 'Sorry and all that. We'll be delighted to have you visit us some other time, of course, Auntie. Later on, when the baby's up a bit and Margaret's herself again.'

So Princess was left alone in the empty house that was far too big for her. And then Robert's lawyer gave her another shock. Robert had left everything to her, but it turned out that there wasn't as much as both he and she had expected. The lawyer, a youngish blond Jew with a bustling bum and a vocabulary of pedantic expressions that obviously he used to bamboozle people, told her that

Robert had been unwise to spend so much on travel; he had been living well beyond his income ever since he retired; he'd been drawing on capital all the time, and in efforts to make up the capital again he had made several investments that had lost money. The lawyer advised her to sell the house at once and take a small apartment. She would not be able to live any longer in the style to which Robert had accustomed her. 'In fact, Mrs Wilkie,' he said, 'if you were a lady of less mature years I would recommend for your consideration that you undertook to perform some occupation of a part-time nature that would reward you in a pecuniary fashion.'

'I heve no intention of going beck into business,' she said. 'Mr Wilkie would never heve epproved.'

XIV

In the next few months, while the lawyer tried to sell the house, Princess took part in the activities of the Ladies' Guild of the church she and Robert had joined. She sang and played at several concerts; she had a stall at a rummage sale; she sold flags on the streets for two or three good causes; and she helped at sales of work, buying and selling. But she could not do this on the grand scale any longer. She was having to watch every penny she spent. And her life was curtailed in another direction too. Although she was friendly with a number of nice churchgoing ladies and they had little tea parties together, she didn't make any close friends like Sandy or Miss Cochrane. Often she felt as she'd felt in those first years at Blunt Tomahawk Point — except that there she'd always had Robert.

When, at last, the house was sold for a much smaller sum than Robert had given for it, she sold all the furniture except the few precious possessions they had kept before and taken to Scotland and back. Then, instead of taking the small apartment the lawyer suggested, she told him she was going back to Scotland. Since Robert's death she had been thinking about her share of the family bungalow at Wardie. During all the years she'd been in Canada she had never forgotten that she'd put down a certain amount of the purchase price. She had never troubled about it, even after her father died — though she had kept it conveniently at the back of her memory — but now she saw no reason why she shouldn't ask Willie to pay back her money. With interest, of course. It would help her to get a small flat in Edinburgh: somewhere near Princes Street, she thought. Perhaps a couple of rooms in Queen Street or Cumberland Street, one of the top flats overlooking the Firth of Forth. She pictured herself spending the rest of her life there, comfortably, visiting her relatives occasionally, or giving little supper parties for them, having morning coffee in Crawford's in Princes Street, having tea at Fullers' or McVittie's with Miss Cochrane and going with her to the theatre once a week. It would be just like old times.

But before she left Canada she would visit Margaret and Hugh in Saskatchewan and see their baby: her great-nephew Hamish, who was nearly six months old. Since Hamish's birth she and Margaret had talked a few times on the telephone, conversations that had been limited, naturally, because of the expense of long distance, and they'd corresponded spasmodically. Margaret always kept saying how nice it would be if she'd come and stay with them for a few weeks -- though she must remember, of course, that they were 'in the wilds'. The nearest town was ten miles away, 'end thet would herdly suit you, would it, Ent Elice!' Princess didn't think it would. Still, she was willing to give it a trial since it would be for only a few weeks.

When she called Margaret to tell her what she'd decided, her niece's tone was more than chilly. 'I'm afraid it's quaite impossible et the moment, Ent Elice,' she said. 'Neturally, we'd love to heve you, but — well, Hugh's mother is staying with us for an indefinite period. End then there's the nenny for Hamish. She hes the only other room. End then Hugh is so terribly terribly busy. End I don't feel up to scretch et all. I've been in a very bed state of health ever since baby was born, end I don't feel capable of heving visitors — even you. Don't you think you should wait until you come beck from Scotlend?'

'But I'm going to Scotlend for good, Mergeret.'

'Oh, Ent Elice, don't be silleh! You know you'll never settle down in Edinburgh. End Uncle Bob is buried in Vancouver. You know your heart will always be there.'

So Princess went across the Atlantic without seeing her new great-nephew. She complained bitterly to her friend Jock: 'Fency not letting me see the little led. Mergeret knows perfectly well I'll never be beck in Ceneda.'

'Och, I wouldnie say that, Mrs Wilkie,' the steward said. 'Of course ye'll be back. I'd miss seein' you on the trips. Ye're a guid auld customer! The shipping line'll go bankrupt withoot ye!'

Princess sniffed. It was not often Jock spoke out of turn, but she considered his so-called humour in bad taste.

'Anyway,' Jock said quickly, seeing her expression, 'your niece will likely be takin' the wee boy to see his grandparents before long, so ye'll see him then.'

'I expect so,' she said.

'It was very very sad aboot Mr Wilkie,' Jock said, anxious to change the subject. 'He was a fine man. A grand man, and ye'll miss him. We'll never see his like again.'

And for the rest of the voyage he soft-soaped her about Robert and her unexpected widowhood. She basked in his sympathy like a blackbird in the sun, spreading her wings to take in every particle of sunlight.

She expected to bask in her bereavement when she got to Edinburgh, but after their first cluckings of commiseration her relatives soon showed that they were more interested in their own families and their doings than they were in her. Before she'd been there a week Willie said: 'I'd like a word wi' ye, Alice. It's a good opportunity when Isa's away to the hairdresser's. I was just wonderin' how long ye intend to bide here. Mind! I don't want ye to take offence. Dinnie leap up like that like a cock at a grosset! We're very

202

pleased to have ye bidin' with us here, but . . . I would just like to ken whether it's to be for a couple o' weeks or a month? So that we'll all be prepared for it. I don't want ye to think that yer room is preferred to yer company, but well — Isa and me's used to bein' on our own, and although ye're no' a stranger we're aware o' ye all the time.'

She said: 'I would heve you remember, Willie McDougall, thet part of this bungalow belongs to me.'

'Och, ye're haverin'.'

'I em not havering,' she said. 'You know perfectly well thet I gave two hundred end fifty pounds towards the purchase price of this house. My name is on the title deeds es pert-owner.'

'I dinnie care whether your name's on the title deeds or no'. This house belongs to me. Dad left it to me when he died.'

'It wasn't his to leave,' Princess said. 'He owned only part of it. He couldn't leave my share to you, for I gave him no authority to do so.'

'Now, look here, Princess,' Willie said. 'Enough o' the argy-bargyin'. You ken fine that when you went awa' to Canady sixteen years ago you gave up ony share you had in this hoose. You gave it to Mother and Dad.'

'I did nothing of the kind.'

'Mind you,' Willie said in a conciliatory way, 'you may not have thought ye did it, but ye did. It was your share o' helpin' Mother and Dad in their auld age, as ye might say. After all, ye married a rich man.'

'Robert was by no means as rich as you think.'

'Well, a weel-doin' man then, if ye want to put it that way. When ye went to Canady he was goin' to take care o' ye, so naturally you left what share ye had in this hoose to the auld folk because ye werenie goin' to be here to give them so much money every week to help them spin out their pensions. Like the rest o' us did. It was some kind o' compensation, as ye might say.'

'No, I would not say, Willie McDougall. Compensation my eye! I never heard of such nonsense. I paid two hundred end fifty pounds towards the building of this bungalow, and I want it beck with interest.'

'Interest?'

'Neturelly. Efter all, it's just like a loan. Let's see now. Sixteen years et — shell we say five per cent?'

'No, we'll not say,' Willie said angrily. 'I never heard the like. Tryin' to rob yer ain kith and kin!'

'There's no robbery about it. It's just pairfectly good business. Efter all, I em a businesswoman.'

'Ay, ye are that, ma bonnie wee hen! Or should I say ma bonnie auld hen? Humph! And no' sae bonnie either wi' yer dyed hair and all yer falderols.'

'There's no need to be insulting,' Princess said. 'I know when I'm not wanted. I'll leave here tomorrow end go to a hotel. But before I go I want my two hundred end fifty pounds, plus sixteen years interest et five per cent.'

'Well, ye can whistle for it,' Willie said. 'I havenie got it. Where do ye think I'd have all that money? Me that'll be retirin' on the auld age pension in three years.'

'Don't give me thet flennel, Willie McDougall,' she said. 'You've been en engineer earning big money all your life. You must heve made a pecket during the war.'

'I tell you, me and Isa havenie got twa pennies to rub together. As soon as I stop work we'll just have the pension between us and the grave. I've never been able to save a cent what wi' havin' to keep Mother and Dad all thae years.'

'But you've just said thet the others . . .'

'Ach, that was a slip o' the tongue. None o' them ever contributed a penny towards the auld folks' keep. Not a solitary sausage!'

'And the chorus is "believe it if you like",' Princess said.

'I dinnie care what the chorus is,' he said. 'I'm tellin' you the God's honest truth. I havenie a penny to bless myself with. So ye can ronny away about yer twa hundred and fifty till you're black in the face.'

'Two hundred end fifty plus sixteen years' interest,' she said.

'You cannie take the breeks of a Hielandman, Princess,

whatever else ye may be able to do wi' that palavery tongue o' yours.'

'I shell leave this house et once,' she said, sailing with swelling bosom towards the door. 'You'll be hearing from my solicitor, Willie McDougall.'

XV

Princess didn't mind staying in a hotel for a few days, but she saw no reason why she should go on paying high hotel prices when she had such a monstrous regiment of relatives in Edinburgh. None of them seemed keen to have her, however, even though she explained that it would be for only one or two weeks until she found a small flat of her own.

'Oh ay, I've heard this tale before,' Donald's wife said. 'It may be a year and it may be forever! Do you know that small flats are very difficult to come by? You may be lucky to get one, of course, but again you may not. No, Alice, no, I'm sorry, the answer is no.'

Daisy Gordon was equally adamant. She said: 'No, Princess, I'm not goin' to beat about the bush. I'll tell you straight. I couldnie be doin' with your ladylike ways. Now that we've got rid o' all the family I like the hoose to myself so that I can have a guid fart if I feel like it.'

Miss Cochrane was no help either. She was still a buyer in Binns, though she was preparing to retire in another couple of years. She had left Granton in 1936, when her parents died, and she had a two-roomed flat near the Dean Bridge. Princess suggested that she put her up for a few weeks while she looked around, but Miss Cochrane didn't think it would be a good idea. 'It might ruin our friendship, Miss McDougall,' she said grandly. 'We might not be competible.'

At last, Princess's cousin Jean and her husband Harry gave her a room in their bungalow at Davidson's Mains. 'We'll give it a try, Alice,' Harry said. 'Mind you, we're plain folk and you'll just have to put up with us. I'm very blunt and I believe in callin' a spade a spade. So if ye cannie put up with our ways don't be blate in steppin' forward and complainin'.'

She stayed with them for three weeks. By that time she wasn't on speaking terms with them. She told Miss Cochrane they weren't good company.

'Herry just sits and reads the paper every night efter he comes beck from work. He never speaks — except when he's being "blunt", end thet's usually because he wants to complain about something. Es for Jean — she's either washing dishes or falling esleep with her mouth wide open. I never heard such snores. End then her false teeth keep falling out. It was really very upsetting. I got quaite nauseated. End they wouldn't play cards, end Herry objected when I wanted to listen to progremmes of choral singing on the wireless. He ectually hed the audecity to switch it off one night when the Glesgow Orpheus Choir were in the middle of the *Messiah*. I switched it on again. End do you know what he said to me?'

Princess's bosom heaved with indignation. 'He said, "We're for none of that bloody religious rubbish in this house. Religion is the opium of the masses, and I won't stand for it."'

'Fency, Miss McDougall! What an uncouth creature!'

A week afterwards, when Princess had moved into a bed-sitting room in Hamilton Place so that she'd be reasonably near Miss Cochrane, she saw her cousin Jean coming towards her in Princes Street. Jean saw her at the same time — they were about six yards from each other — and she gave Princess an icy nod and, turning abruptly, went into Forsyth's.

Princess stayed in the room in Hamilton Place for a fortnight, and then she moved to another bedsitter; she couldn't bear the noise of the children playing in a nearby school-yard. But she wasn't satisfied with the new bedsitter either; an old woman in the next room kept knocking on the wall to enlist her help whenever she dropped a stitch in her knitting or couldn't find her spectacles. Princess had her name down with every house agent in Edinburgh, but as the weeks passed there was no sign of getting the kind of small, smart apartment she had visualized. She found too that she wasn't always welcome when she called on the relatives who were still speaking to her; either they said they were preparing to go out, or they wanted to listen to something on the wireless, or they had some other excuse for cutting her visit as short as possible.

As far as Miss Cochrane was concerned, Princess soon discovered that her old friend had no intention of returning to their former footing. Miss Cochrane now had a gentleman friend: Mr Grant, a bachelor of sixty with a fat red face, a bulbous nose full of large pores, an almost feminine giggle and a variety of bright silk ties. He was the manager of a men's outfitters, and his staff of willowy youths kept changing. He was an avid cinemagoer, and he and Miss Cochrane usually saw three films a week. Princess accompanied them to the cinema several times, but she didn't care for Mr Grant's choice of films; he never asked if the ladies had any special preference, he simply led them to the cinema that was showing a cowboy or a war film or one that had a predominantly male cast. She couldn't put up with his giggles and remarks during the programme. He kept saying things like, 'My, that's a fine big hefty fellow!' or 'What a nice looking boy! I wish I had him in my shop. He'd fairly draw the customers in.'

After a time Princess could stand Johnny Grant no longer, and when she remarked to Miss Cochrane that he really was a bit of a nancy, they came near to quarrelling.

'He's a very nice chep,' Miss Cochrane said, 'end I simply cen't understend what you heve against him, Mrs Wilkie. He reminds me so much of my Polish gentleman friend during the war. He always was so polite end so emusing too. Stefan was much younger, of course, but he was like Johnny — such a perfect gentleman. He's so understending too. He takes such en interest in my clothes end all thet. End he never says anything coarse.'

Another thing Princess couldn't stand was the Edinburgh weather. She had forgotten how cold her native city could be. And it seemed infinitely colder in that dreadful winter of 1947, when there was a coal shortage and great electricity cuts. She shivered in front of the feeble electric heater in her bed-sitting room and longed for the warmth of Canadian log fires and stoves.

At last she decided to go back to Canada. She booked her passage, paid a round of farewell visits, and sailed from the Clyde once again with her old friend Jock. She took her precious pieces of furniture with her. She had been in Edinburgh barely six months.

XVI

Back in Vancouver, Princess got a shock when she saw Robert's lawyer. 'I'm afraid you will have to economize a great deal, Mrs Wilkie,' he said. 'The capital has depreciated considerably with all the inroads you have made into it, and there have been a lot of other setbacks. I fear you'll have to live very simply. Far be it from me to suggest what you should do, but I would very much like to propose that you attempt to find a position as companion to a lady of greater affluence than your own.'

Princess gave up the idea of renting or buying a small apartment; she moved from her hotel into a boarding-house. Then, with time hanging heavy on her hands and her former acquaintances proving slow with invitations when she telephoned them, she got a job as a part-time assistant in a dress shop. But this didn't last long since she and the owner, a lady with a ginny voice and peroxided hair, didn't see eye to eye about the kind of dresses they should stock.

She applied for several other jobs of the same nature, but the prospective employers all regretted that they wanted a younger woman. Being forced to economize, she tried to cut down her smoking, and she went only once to the cinema each week. She sold two of her fur coats, but she kept her mink; she felt that with it she still would be able to face the world with proper dignity. And she sold her precious pieces of furniture, including her beloved piano, for it was costing a small fortune to keep them in store.

She arranged to visit Margaret and Hugh in the fall and stay with them for a couple of months; but a fortnight before she was booked to fly to Saskatchewan Margaret wrote that she must postpone her visit and did not say for how long she'd have to postpone it. Margaret was expecting another child. When Princess called her from the communal telephone in the hall of the boarding-house Margaret was coldly apologetic. 'I'm sorry, Ent Elice, but you'll heve to wait until the spring after the baby arrives. Ectually you would be a much greater help then, for Hamish is getting such a hendful, end Nennie isn't able to cope with him on her own.'

Once a week Princess went to the cemetery. It was odd, she often thought, while arranging the flowers on Robert's grave, that he was lying there only a few feet beneath her. And she wished that the clock could be set back and they were safely together again in their comfortable house at Blunt Tomahawk Point. If only they'd stayed there and not gallivanted backwards and forwards so much to Scotland, she'd be a lot better off now. What good had all these trips done her? Her relatives hadn't appreciated her visits at all. When she thought of all she'd done for her brothers and their wives and children, of the many and costly presents she'd given them, of the way Robert had taken parties of them to expensive dinners in the Caledonian and North British hotels ... 'Really, I never met such base ingretitude,' she whispered once into the roses she was arranging in the vase in front of the headstone. 'Fency thet Willie end thet awful Isa treating me like thet ...'

Disappointed at not being able to visit Margaret, she called Sandy Reisman and asked if she might go to Dayton for a few weeks. 'Elice, my dear!' Sandy said dramatically. 'We'd love to heve you, of course. But ... my dear, we're just on the point of setting out for Bermuda. Jerry's thinking about buying a house there. Won't it be thrilling?

Perheps, efter it's all settled end we've moved there, you might like to come for a wee holiday . . .'

In the spring of 1948, after another talk with Robert's lawyer, she took a job as a sales lady in the children's outfits department of a large store. She did not particularly care for children, and she did not particularly like the job, but it gave her a certain amount of dollars each week.

The children's department was on the ground floor, and the counter where Princess worked was near the window. When business was quiet and she was tired of rearranging the stock or pretending to dust she would stand and look out at the traffic. One morning she watched a huge scarlet Cadillac draw up at the entrance. It was full of children. Princess closed her eyes for a moment, praying they would be going upstairs to the toy department. When she opened them again she saw, to her horror, Katie Mae Twelvetrees sweeping through the swing doors, leading the gang of children towards her.

Katie Mae had got fat and her face had coarsened, but there was no getting away from it that it was her. She had a mink coat slung over her shoulders, and her garish blue silk dress accentuated the fact that she was at least six months' pregnant.

She looked Princess up and down, gave a long low whistle and said: 'You come down in the world, missis. You jump now when Katie Mae crack the whip, eh?'

She laughed derisively and said to the children: 'See this old squaw, you kids? She the high and mighty Missis Wilkie your mammy used to work for. Changed days, eh, missis? Joe Twelvetrees a big man now in the timber trade. We got plenty money. You show us the best kids' clothes you got, missis. And get crackin'!'

Next day Princess handed in her notice. A month later she sailed for Scotland.

XVII

'I hear that My Lady is back from Canady,' Daisy Gordon said to the McDougall's cousin Jean. 'She just took one look at the clock and bolted back hame. I suppose they didnie fête her enough and make a big fuss o' her. Well, if she thinks the red carpet's goin' to be put down for her here she's got another thought comin'.'

Jean said: 'She doesnie need to visit me, anyway. Me and Harry had enough o' her high and mighty ways the last time. She'll no' get into my house. Never again!'

Miss Cochrane was still keeping company with Johnny Grant, and she soon showed that she had no time for Alice Wilkie. 'Perheps you might come to tea three weeks on Sunday, Miss McDougall,' she said when Princess telephoned her. 'I heve a very full progremme until then.'

Princess got a bed-sitting room at Goldenacre; she wanted to be as near Granton as she could, though now she knew hardly any of the people there and it had become just another suburb of Edinburgh. The room had a lot of drawbacks, but lodgings were hard to find and she had to put up with it. She had given up the idea of a small flat as she couldn't afford it. She visited Daisy Gordon and Jim, who were getting ready to have a holiday in Canada to see Margaret's children, and she visited Jock and Donald and their wives, but she did not go near Willie and Isa. She had done nothing about her threat to put a solicitor on Willie's track about the two hundred and fifty pounds and now eighteen years' interest. She thought about it sometimes, but she could never make the effort to do anything.

She asked Miss Cochrane if there was any chance of getting a job in Binns as a sales lady, but Miss Cochrane said: 'Well, frenkly, Miss Mc — er — Mrs Wilkie, there isn't a hope. If you don't mind me saying so, you are just on the retiring age and our directors would never consider you.'

She managed, at last, to get a job in a cheap dress-shop near Tollcross. The hours were long; the wages were poor. But it helped to make ends meet, and it kept her occupied.

She joined a church at Goldenacre and the organist was only too delighted to have her singing in the choir.

After she'd been in Edinburgh a few months she sold her mink coat. She bought a heavy tweed coat with a beaver collar and hoped it would be warm enough in the cold winters. She scarcely ever saw any of her nephews and nieces and their children. They hadn't taken much notice of her when she was their rich aunt from Canada; they took even less now that she was an assistant in a second-rate shop.

Once, after she'd spent a lonely evening in a cinema, she was going back to her lodgings when Willie and Isa got on the same tram. They walked past her, looking straight ahead and sat down a few seats away from hers. They stared out of the window all the way up Inverleith Row, without speaking to each other and Princess stared out of the window at her side. She got off the tram at Goldenacre and never looked in their direction.

Two years after her return to Edinburgh Alice Wilkie felt very peculiar one night when she came back to her bed-sitting room, after she'd been alone to the gallery of the Royal Lyceum Theatre to see a modern play she didn't like. She'd had nothing to eat since lunchtime, and that had been only sandwiches. She lit her gasfire, made herself a cup of cocoa, and sat down to sip it. She was sure she'd got pneumonia or something with this awful Edinburgh cold. Waves of nausea were coming over here, and she was reaching for the biscuit tin, thinking it might help to eat something, when she felt a violent pain in her side. She screamed and fell over sideways.

She was dead when her landlady found her next morning. The landlady telephoned the police.

When a nervous young policeman came to Daisy Gordon's door, he took off his helmet, wiped his brow with a very white handkerchief, and said: 'I'm afraid I've got some bad news for you, Mrs McDougall. Your sister-in-law, Mrs Wilkie, was found dead an hour ago. The body's been taken to the mortuary.'

'There's nothing I can do,' Daisy said. 'She's got nothing

to do with us. She hasn't visited us for nearly a year. We weren't on speaking terms. You'd better go to some of her other relations.'

She gave him the addresses and shut the door.

He went to Willie's. Willie, retired and in his garden with a pair of shears clipping the hedge, said: 'Poor Princess, so she's awa' with it. Poor soul, kickin' the bucket like that.'

The policeman told him what Daisy had said. 'That's all right, ma laddie,' Willie said. 'I'll come with ye to the mortuary, and I'll see to everything. I dinnie mind the expense o' the funeral whatever the rest o' them may think.'

XVIII

'I wonder if yon princess'll ever come wi' us on another trip?' the young steward said.

'It's a funny thing you should say that,' the old steward said. 'I was just thinkin' last night that it was high time she was on her travels again. It's two years since she made the trip. She must be gey fed up wi' Edinburgh and her relations by this time.'

He put a tray piled with dirty dishes into the serving hatch. 'What made ye think about her, Larry? Ye only saw her once.'

'I dinnie ken,' Larry said. 'She just flashed across my mind last night. I was standin' near the corner of B Deck, leanin' on the rail, when I saw somebody that looked awfie like her standin' near the bow.'

'It was a favourite place o' hers,' Jock said. 'She aye liked to stand there because she said it put her in mind o' her grandfather that was the captain o' a wee ferry boat that used to go frae Leith to Kirkcaldy. She aye said she was pretendin' to be him, like. Funny, eh?'

'Ay, funny right enough,' Larry said. 'I could 'a' sworn it was her. It was a woman in yon same kind o' fur coat — I couldnie see her face, mind — and then — well, it's real funny. She was there one minute and she was gone the next. Vanished, like.'

'Ach, ye're haverin', laddie. Ye'll be tellin' me next you've seen a ghost. Any road, it's about time for her to make another trip.'